COLD AS ICE

"You're not as cold as you make people believe you are," Carla says.

"I've never been much of a talker."

"I don't know why. You have a lot to say."

"Only to you." He holds her tight. "I don't know how that happened."

"I'm glad you feel that way," she says.

"Carla, I feel a lot with you. My life hasn't been the same since I moved to Vancouver. I want you in it." Devin lifts her chin and brings her lips to his. "I want you; I want us. I don't want to live life passing me by and not do anything about it. I want to start right now. You and me, together," he says, firming his hand around her back. "You mean too much to me to let you go."

"Don't ever let me go," she whispers.

"I won't. You're mine." Devin kisses her and holds the back of her head to secure the passion he feels for the woman he's always wanted. . . .

Books by Charlene Groome

HIS GAME, HER RULES

COLD AS ICE

Published by Kensington Publishing Corporation

COLD AS ICE

CHARLENE GROOME

KENSINGTON BOOKS
KENSINGTON PUBLISHING CORP.
http://www.kensingtonbooks.com

KENSINGTON BOOKS are published by

Kensington Publishing Corp.
119 West 40th Street
New York, NY 10018

All Kensington titles, imprints, and distributed lines are available at special quantity discounts for bulk purchases for sales promotion, premiums, fundraising, educational, or institutional use.

Special book excerpts or customized printings can also be created to fit specific needs. For details, write or phone the office of the Kensington Special Sales Manager: Attn. Special Sales Department. Kensington Publishing Corp., 119 West 40th Street, New York, NY 10018. Phone: 1-800-221-2647.

Kensington Books and the K logo Reg. U.S. Pat. & TM Off.

First Electronic Edition: December 2014
eISBN-13: 978-1-60183-346-4
eISBN-10: 1-60183-346-6

First Print Edition: December 2014
ISBN-13: 978-1-60183-347-1
ISBN-10: 1-60183-347-4

Published in the United States of America

ACKNOWLEDGMENTS

I am so grateful for the opportunity to be able to do what fulfills me the most and that is to write romance. It's even better when I can write stories about hockey players falling in love with women they least expect.

As always, I'd like to thank my wonderful literary agent, Dawn Dowdle of Blue Ridge Literary Agency.

I am most appreciative for the support and guidance I receive from my team at Kensington Books. My extraordinary editor, John Scognamiglio, whose advice and suggestions make me a better writer. My copy editor Randy Ladenheim-Gil; production editor Ross Plotkin; and the design team for making an eye-catching cover. Thank you!

I also want to thank Emily Lawrence, who is always so willing to be my first reader and to give me a little direction when I need it.

Writing and raising a young family are challenging times, so to have the support of family and friends that understand my schedule is beneficial to my career. My husband, Jared; my kids: Kathryn, Samantha and Carsten for fulfilling my life with their love and support; as well as to my mom, dad, Ben and Renie.

Furthermore, thank you to my supportive friends Miranda, Alana, Shauneen, and Jamie. Your friendship means the world to me. xo

Prologue

Carla Sinclair skims through her notes as the buzzer rings, indicating the end of the second period. The Dome is a loud and exciting place to be for Warriors fans. Eighteen thousand people erupt, cheering them on. Tonight they're playing against Carolina, a team that isn't doing so well, which makes Vancouver's winning streak even longer.

Devin Miller, the Carolina defenseman, who was on the ice for two of the four goals scored against his team, screened his goalie when Vancouver scored the first goal, and the second time he didn't cover his man, which left the net wide open.

Tragic. He's the best defenseman in the league.

Carla shakes her head. *Some defenseman!*

The Carolina players head off the ice and strut down the hallway, drawing the banter closer. She throws her notebook into her bag, drops it to the ground and grabs her microphone from Randy, the cameraman. She arranged to meet with Devin in the corridor, where other interviews will be taking place.

Carla stands straighter, lifts the microphone under her chin and wipes her other hand down the length of her pencil skirt. She waits and watches for Devin to walk around the corner. Her mind races with potential questions.

Carla sucks in a breath when a red-and-white jersey comes around the corner. He comes into view without a helmet or gloves on, no hockey stick in hand. A giant in skates—six foot two and two hundred pounds of muscle, Devin is even taller than she imagined. As he approaches, she realizes her five-foot-six-inch height—thanks to heels—only reaches his chest.

"Hi." Carla flashes him her TV smile. Her stomach flutters and she warms all over. Why is she suddenly nervous? She's used to speaking to male athletes, especially those as attractive as Devin. "You can have this." She hands him a face towel displaying Channel Five's logo.

He dabs his face, proceeding to run the towel over his short black hair and down the back of his neck.

For a moment, she pictures him drying off after a shower as the water droplets slide over his tightly sculpted muscles. *What would his hard body feel like against hers?* "You, uh, can wear it." She blinks to return to reality and remembers to close her mouth.

His face is clean shaven and, from what she can see, his teeth are all intact.

"Y-you can wear it around your neck while we interview."

"Thanks." He gives her a sturdy glance that weakens her knees.

She turns to face Gary, the cameraman. "Ready?"

He gives her a nod and she begins by bringing the microphone into position and starts with a quick introduction.

"The last two goals were unexpected." She pauses, looking up to meet Devin's cinnamon eyes. "Can you run us through what happened with the first goal?"

Devin wipes his face again with the end of the towel and puts a hand on his padded hip. "One of those things." He looks down. "I saw Keller with the puck. He faked a shot. . . . I tried to block it, but I was too far out and he managed to score on the other side." He sniffs, wiping the bridge of his nose. "The net was open."

"And the second goal?"

He shakes his head and takes a few seconds to answer. "Yeah, well, one of those things . . . the puck was loose, and we couldn't get control of it." He wipes his face again, holding the towel at his collarbone.

"I want to talk to you about your contract. You'll be an unrestricted free agent." She pauses to think of her question without the distraction of his wet lips. "With the end of the season approaching, are you planning on staying with Carolina or is a trade something you're interested in?"

He looks at the rubber floor and shakes his head. "I don't know." He chuckles, wiping the sweat from the corner of his mouth.

She waits for him to expand on his answer. Those lips of his are widening as he laughs again. He rubs an eyebrow and looks at her patiently. Carla is sucked into his gaze again. She has to get him talking. There's one more minute left to kill before signing off. Carla wiggles her moist fingertips on the microphone, trying to air them. Her face heats. She gulps. Three seconds of silence wasted. Devin is looking at her now, urging her with a stretch of his eyebrow. Her pulse intensifies as she scrambles to think of something to say. Anything. She doesn't want to look like a fool in front of Devin, or her audience, but she fears the damage is already done.

"Well?" She keeps the microphone up to his face.

"I don't know."

She inhales, giving herself a chance to ramble out something, anything, so she's not standing in front of him like the worst sports reporter he's ever come across, but Devin is the big deal right now and probably knows it. She swallows to moisten her throat. "Have you been approached by any teams?" She wants to break the story first.

Devin wipes his face with the end of the towel, revealing an eagle tattoo on his forearm. "I can't talk about it."

"I'm sure you can tell us if a trade is possible."

"I'll talk about the game, but not my contract."

She can't let him get away without hinting about his future. She has to know. Wants to know about the best defenseman in the NHL. "I heard a rumor you might be traded to Vancouver. Is there any truth to that?"

He shakes his head. "You're unbelievable, Carla." He laughs. "What more can I say? I told you, I'm not talking."

"I'm sure you can tell me something." She stares into his dreamy eyes.

"No." He licks his bottom lip. "Are we done?" He steps away. "You're pretty good, Carla. You're pretty good." He hangs his head as he walks back toward the locker room.

Carla puckers her lips and drops the microphone to her side. *I looked like an idiot.*

Devin disappears around the corner.

He's never gonna want me to interview him again. She pouts and blows out a breath while looking at her cameraman in dismay.

Chapter 1

Devin sits alone at the bar, cupping his pint of beer as he watches an NHL game on the big screen above. He takes the last swig.

"Another beer?" the bartender asks while pouring an ale from the tap in front of him.

"Sure. One more. Thanks. Two is all I'm having," he says, taking out his wallet. He lays his money down, more than enough to cover a tip, and slides his empty glass in exchange for the new one. The bartender drops the glass down in front of him.

"Where're your buddies?" the bartender asks, referring to his team-mates.

"I don't know. I was planning on being a tourist tonight, drive around, check out the city . . . but I wasn't sure where to go and I ended up here." Devin gives a half smile.

"Good choice," he says, holding steady as he pours whiskey into a shot glass.

Buckley's Bar and Grill is uptown, with brick walls and track lighting. Music is always playing and a continuous ray of loud conversations are what keeps the place lively.

It's taken Devin a couple of days to settle in to his new city. For the first time since his teammate Mark Buckley invited him and some of the guys out for a beer, Devin's making an appearance by himself.

"What's good to see around here?" Devin asks.

"You'll need a guide to show you around," the bartender says, placing a vibrant blue concoction down on a tray. He wipes his hands on his white apron and gets started on another drink.

Devin takes a sip of his beer, tapping his lips together. He understood why his dad loved his beer so much; the settling taste filled him with satisfaction, knowing he could have a drink and forget about things. Although he never got out of control, never having more than three or four drinks. He feared ending up like his dad, where alcohol played a role in his life. Devin focused on hockey and being as great as he could at the sport he loved the most.

"Depends what you're in to. There's stand-up comedy shows, a playhouse if you like live theater . . . Granville Island. Concerts . . ."

The bartender walks to the opposite end to take a couple's order. Roaring laughter is coming from a booth at the end of the bar. It gets Devin's attention. He smiles, expecting to see college girls having a good time, but he takes a second look and to his surprise, he notices Carla Sinclair sitting at the booth across from two women. It's that reporter who interviewed him last year. His heartbeat quickens and his chest tightens, like he's just completed a set of push-ups. Her wave of blond hair lay past her shoulders and he watches as she talks with her hands, telling a funny story, he's sure. Devin turns away and takes a gulp of beer. *Should I talk to her? What does she care? She just wants to interview me, but she's so damn hot.* He glances her way again, hoping to catch her eye. Carla's long legs are angled so that her shiny black heels are tipped sideways. She loosens her shoe, revealing a bare foot, and then puts it back into place, repeating the motion in rhythm with her excitement.

"What's that blonde over there in the booth drinking?" Devin asks with a raised chin and using his eyes as a pointer. "I want to buy her a drink."

"Whoa! You know who that is?" the bartender asks. His eyebrows lift at the same time as his jerky grin.

"Yeah." Devin takes out his wallet and puts down another bill. "That should cover it."

"Do you know her?" The bartender places a drink down and starts mixing another.

"We've met before."

"Not giving up, then?" he asks, his lip curling.

"What do you mean?" Devin asks, knowing well what he's hinting at. Carla must be a big deal in this city. What guy wouldn't want to get with her? She's pretty, knows sports and can obviously relax and have a good time. She probably has a huge Twitter following too.

The bartender concentrates on pouring shots into a glass. "Has she turned you down?" He chuckles.

"I haven't tried," Devin says with an honest gaze, watching the smirk on the guy's face get bigger. "I'm not trying to score a date with her, although I wouldn't turn her down."

The bartender pours vodka into a cocktail shaker. "She's divorced."

"Is that right?"

"You didn't know? She was married to some television producer. They were featured in the newspaper, got lots of publicity. It's been a few years now." He pours the drink into a cocktail glass. "She's kept a low profile lately. Don't hear much about her."

"Is she dating anyone?"

The bartender laughs. "No idea, but she's pretty to look at. Makes the evening sports report a lot more interesting." He garnishes the glass with an olive. Then talks to the waitress about the drink, and she carries it over to the booth. "From what I've heard, she's not easy to get along with. One of those I-can-do-it-myself kind. A real professional, though." He takes a white towel and wipes down the bar. "Not many women are as tough as Carla, at least that's how she comes across."

"Tough?"

"Sure. She's a small thing, but she must be tough, working with guys."

"Oh." Devin laughs. "Not the kind of tough I was thinking."

"I wouldn't let looks fool you. I heard she works her ass off; that's how she got the job."

"How do you know so much?"

"Ah." He shrugs. "Everyone knows that."

"I see. Word gets around."

Carla takes a drink of her semi-sweet martini and holds her glass to her mouth, ready to take another sip. "Would you go back to the playhouse and watch another show?"

"I don't know," Michelle says. "The acting was so bad! It wasn't like the movie at all."

"Well, at least it wasn't boring," Gabby chimes in. "I'll give them that. It could have been worse."

"It could have been," Michelle says. "But at least the actors weren't trying to be perfect."

"They were making fun of themselves when they screwed up a line. Like when that girl took pills to settle herself down on the plane, had a drink and closed her eyes, and the other passenger whispered, 'Aren't you supposed to be obnoxious and dance around?' Now that was funny," Carla says with a giggle and points her finger. Perhaps two martinis was too much for her. She licks her lips.

"That was the best part!" Michelle screeches. "Don't you think?"

"Maybe next time we'll hit the movie theater," Carla suggests. She sips her drink, letting her fingers slide down the smooth stem. It was going down too good. Thankfully, she didn't have to work the next day, giving herself permission to sleep in.

"This was good for a change. It was more fun. Didn't that actor guy look like Timothy?" Gabby asks.

"My Timothy—I mean, my ex, Timothy?" Carla asks, putting down her drink, fixated on her best friend.

"Yeah. Don't you think? His body language? He stood with his hand in his front pocket—"

"Timothy does that?" Carla asks, perplexed.

"He has a stance, you know? Relaxed. And the way he talks? Totally like Timothy."

Gabby's green eyes and mouth are wide open.

"For sure!" Michelle says, slapping her hands on the table, exposing her painted pink nails.

"I guess a little," Carla admits.

"I can't believe you two still work together after your divorce," Michelle says.

Carla shrugs. "He's harmless. He keeps to himself."

"And it doesn't bother you that you know about his personal life? Who he dates?"

"He hasn't dated—"

"That you know of!" Gabby says. "You know he has."

"What does it matter?" Carla says. "We don't associate with each other, anyway."

"I guess if you don't talk to him, much," Gabby says.

"We talk. Mostly about work." Carla twirls her glass, her eyes dropping down to her drink. "We're adults. It's not like we don't get along."

"What's wrong?" Gabby asks softly, extending her hand across the table, trying to reach her friend's arm. "Should I not have mentioned Timothy? I thought it was okay to say . . . you've been your old self again, and well—"

"No, I'm fine. It's not that." She lifts one shoulder. "I was thinking about what my mom said the other night. I haven't forgotten or talked to her about it."

"Now what happened?" Gabby asks, her bangs falling forward, enough to cover her glittery eye shadow. "Last time she insulted you by telling you about her single neighbor guy."

"Curtis?" Carla asks.

"I think that was him. She told him you were single, that's all I remember."

"Yes. And he's old!" Carla says, making a face.

"She needs to mind her own business," Gabby tells her.

"I went over to her house for dinner and she said I work too much and if I didn't settle down soon, I'd be a lost cause."

"Your mom said that?" Gabby asks, picking up her glass. "What does she want from you?"

Carla flicks up her hand. "She knows what she's saying. She doesn't care."

"That's not fair!" Michelle says. "She's your mother! Of course she cares!"

"She thinks by putting pressure on me that it's like reverse psychology, I'm going to find some random guy to have a baby with." Carla rolls her eyes. "As if it's not hard enough being divorced and now single at thirty-one. How many women do you know who are divorced?" Her girlfriends stare blankly across the table.

"Besides me!"

"There's a fifty percent divorce rate," Michelle says. "It happens. Don't beat yourself up over it."

"It wasn't supposed to happen!" Carla bellows. "I was supposed to be married to Timothy, have his babies and live happily ever after." She blows out a breath and buries her head in her hands. "My mom's right; maybe I blew my chance."

Gabby lowers her face. "No! Don't listen to her!"

Carla pouts.

"I didn't know you were still upset about it," Gabby says, toning down her voice. "Sweetie, I had no idea. Aw, I'm sorry."

"I'm okay, really." Carla rubs her forehead and wipes her eyes. "It's not about Timothy. I mean, I loved him."

"You married him, of course you did!" Michelle says, patting Carla's arm.

"I always wanted to have a husband and kids, and now that I'm thirty-one and single again, my chances are slim." Carla sniffles. She will not cry. She can't cry, not about Timothy. Not about their costly wedding. Not about the cat he had to have and she bought for him as a birthday present. Timothy's not crying over her. So why is she so upset about being single and starting over?

"You're still young!" Gabby says, flashing her a glossy pink smile. "You have plenty of time to find someone again to start a family with. That's if it's what you want."

Carla nods from side to side. "I'm not looking and I'm certainly not looking to be knocked up just to please my mom." Carla bites her bottom lip and twirls her glass between her fingers, although she wouldn't be upset if it happened.

"You shouldn't."

"I won't!" Carla snaps.

"What are you going to do?"

"About what?" Carla twirls her glass.

"Meeting someone," Gabby says, sipping her drink. "It's time!"

"You think?"

"Yes! Of course! You're not going to marry the first guy you date. Come on! You need to start building relationships with guys. Get out and meet someone!"

Gabby slams down her hand. "I've got it! You should make up a story and tell your mom you're dating a guy from another country and that he wants to get married and have a baby really bad."

Carla puckers her lips thinking about the idea. "That," she says with the point of a finger, "could go either way. My mom might be a detective and find out everything there is to know about this fake guy, or she just might love the idea."

"Are you kidding? What mom would think that's okay?" Michelle asks, tucking a long, dark brown strand of hair behind her ear. "She'll want to meet this guy, won't she? And where did you meet this future husband?"

Carla lifts an eyebrow.

"He's a reporter from overseas, visiting . . ." Gabby says.

"That won't work," Carla says with a little shake of her head. "My mom has the potential to be a crazy lady. I don't know what's gotten into her lately, but because my sister is married—happily married, I might add—and has a baby, my mom is putting pressure on me to settle down again. She doesn't realize how annoying it is. It's all I hear from her. *Are you dating anyone?"* Carla mimics her mom. *"Why haven't you found anyone? What's wrong with asking someone out from work?"* Carla tightens her lips before continuing. "It's like she's forgotten that Timothy and I met at work, and look where we ended up!"

"Maybe she needs something to do," Michelle says and sips her drink. "She's thinking too much about your personal life and not enough about her own."

"She does that a lot," Carla admits.

"What about your brother? Any pressure on him?" Gabby asks. "He's still single."

"Gavin can do no wrong." Her eyes bounce from one friend to the other. "Besides, he's been with Mia for something like two years." She takes a sip and swallows hard. Her eyes squint from the sweetness of her drink. "As far as I know, he's doing fine. He doesn't say much. What about you? Still with what's his name? Cracker?"

Michelle hangs her head. "Graeme. And yes, it's going well, thank you." She lifts an eyebrow and smiles. "He's a good guy. I'm happy. He's taking me to a junior hockey game Saturday night."

"Since when do you like sports?" Carla asks.

"I'm only going because he's been talking about it since our first date. His nephew plays for the team. He wants to introduce me."

Carla lets out a barely there whistle. "Sounds serious if he wants you to meet the rest of his family."

Michelle's eyes sparkle. "So far his family has been accepting and very kind."

"Why wouldn't they? You're thoughtful, educated."

"This drink was just bought for you," the waitress says, sliding a martini over on a coaster toward Carla.

"For me?" Carla asks. "From whom?"

"That hockey player . . . Miller," the waitress says. She thumbs over her shoulder.

"Did it come straight from the bartender?" Carla asks, skeptical. The last thing she wants is a drink laced with some drug.

"Uh-huh."

"Did he say why he bought this for me?" Carla asks.

"Nope. He's at the bar. Ask him," she says and walks away.

All three women turn their heads to the bar and stare.

"Where is he?" Michelle asks. "It's hard to tell from this angle."

"Is it the guy wearing the military boots or the one with the ponytail?" Gabby asks, trying to keep a straight face.

Carla lets out a huge breath and wiggles out of her seat, securing her shiny black heels on her feet. She ignores her friends' questions and takes a step out of the booth, marching toward the bar, where she spots Devin watching the big screen overhead. She swallows hard as she stares at him. The closer she gets, the slower her feet move. His large shoulders are hunched over, his hands cradling a glass like he wants to be alone. She notices the cut on his cheekbone and wonders if the pain is as bad as it looks.

She inhales a big breath, holding it and counting to three before taking the last step before saying hello. Carla opens her mouth to speak and when he turns his head toward her, she is taken back by his tanned complexion and dark brown eyes that make her insides melt. He straightens his back and his shoulders roll into good posture, revealing his muscular upper body. There's another cut above his eyebrow that alarms her. Even still, his face is a handsome one.

"So, Miller," she says, making a popping sound with her lips. "You could have admitted to me that you weren't staying in Carolina."

"I didn't know."

"You had to have known."

"It was too early to tell." Devin pushes his coaster away from him. "How did you know?" His eyes narrow in on her.

"You had to make a move. My guess was you were done with Carolina and wanted a new team to play with that had better chances."

Devin shakes his head. "You called it."

"So, what do you want?" Carla asks, one hand on her hip. Devin gives her a half smile, looking at her with his weighty brown eyes. The thickness of his eyebrows and short black hair have Carla taking in his every facial feature.

He hasn't stopped looking at her. Is her makeup okay? Is her shirt too revealing? It always feels good wearing something loose or low-cut, something she wouldn't or couldn't wear to work.

"Nothing," he says. "Thought you'd want a drink. Who are you with?"

"Why? Are you interested in one of them?"

"Nope. I'm interested in you."

She throws her head back and her heel falls behind her other foot for balance. "Seriously?" Carla puckers her honey-dipped lips and puts a hand on the bar, facing him.

"I am!" he says, turning his hand over before grabbing his glass. "You don't believe me."

"I'm not sure that I do," she says, eyeing him.

"Have a seat!" he says, with a wave of his hand at the empty seat.

She looks beside her at the empty bar stool. "I can't. I'm with my friends," she says. "I'd invite you over, but I'd want to interview you." She steps away from the bar. Does he remember the last time they spoke? Didn't he think she was an idiot? "I've had a couple of drinks, so it would be unprofessional."

"I'm sure we can find something to talk about other than hockey."

She blinks her eyes. "Tempted, but hockey's on my mind," she says. Work was always on her mind. If she could interview Devin and break a story—a story that's desperately needed in sports right now because the reporting has been so dry—it would excite her and her audience. "Plus, I'd want it taped."

His expression goes from smirk to serious. "I can talk hockey anytime. It's never stale."

"Let me know when you're available." She flips her hair back off her shoulder.

"Give me a place and time. I'll be there."

"Come on, Miller, you're not that easy. I've been trying to get an interview with you since you arrived here forty-eight hours ago. You never returned my calls."

"I don't remember giving you my number," he says, feeling the wet glass with his fingertips.

"You haven't," she snaps, folding her arms against her chest. "Your PR lady said she would pass along the message. Did you get it?"

His eyes close slightly, his look mysterious, like the first time they met at the Dome.

"Maybe I did," he says. "I don't remember now."

"I'm a reporter, not a crazy fan," she says. "You don't have to worry; I won't give out your number."

"I like crazy fans," he says, arching the side of his lip.

How kissable those lips must be.

"I can only imagine," she says, blinking, thinking about two different things. She had to stop thinking about Devin's lips, and how they would feel against her skin. He probably had a girlfriend or girlfriends.

He wouldn't be interested in her anyway, and she is definitely not interested in him. No way would she be caught gallivanting around with a guy who is on the road half the year with God only knows how many women nipping at his feet.

"Imagine what?" He tilts his chin.

"That you have an entourage following you everywhere you go? I don't doubt it."

"Every team has them," he says.

"Sure they do."

"It's a bit crazy at times here, too, after a game . . ."

"So, Devin, what do you want from me?"

He glances down at his almost-empty beer. "If you want an interview, I want a night out with you. Show me the city."

She burst out laughing. "You have teammates for that," she says, staring at his prickly chin. "Ask one of the guys."

"I plan to stay here for a while. I need to know about the city I'm playing in."

"Do you do this in every city you play in? Get a chaperone to show you around?"

"No, this is the first." He looks up at her and their eyes meet. For a second, Carla can barely breathe, mesmerized by his seductive eyes, so dark they make her heartbeat carry on with double rhythm.

She swallows hard. "For some reason I don't believe that."

"Believe it! Do you have a hard time making friends?"

"No."

"Then it shouldn't be a problem if we get to know each other."

She stares at him, contemplating. "That can't happen."

"Why not?"

"Because . . ." She's stumped. "Because it can't."

"You don't think I'm good enough for the team, do you?"

"I didn't say that!"

"You implied." He looks at his glass and then at her. "I know how you feel about me."

"I don't know what I said." She tries to recall her last newscast.

"It's not what you said, it's what you want."

"Is that right?" She taps her toe. *Is he always this cocky?* "And what do I want?"

"You have questions about me being here, I can see that. Hell, you mentioned it on your last broadcast."

"I did? Look, the Warriors need a new forward line," she mumbles. "And we were fine before the trade."

"I'll let you interview me and you can judge for yourself."

Carla laughs. "That doesn't change a thing."

"It will." His back arches, leaning into the bar, and he takes a sip of his beer. His head turns in her direction. "I want to see my new city. I'm gonna be here for a while."

"Six years?"

"We should get to know each other better. Don't you think?" He takes another sip. "I'm sure I'm going to see a lot of you at the games. We might as well be friends."

Carla smirks. "Is this your way to get on my good side?" Her grin tightens.

"Do you have a bad side?" His eyes brush over her face as though reading her. "Never mind, don't answer that." He cups his beer. "When do you want to do this interview?"

"Sounds like you want it more than I do." She throws a hand on her hip. "When are you available?"

"Next practice."

"You won't stand me up, will you?"

He brings a hand to his chest. "I'm insulted!"

"I'm sure you are," she says with a wink.

He smiles at her. His teeth are white and straight, like she remembers. She wonders how many are real, knowing he's probably knocked out a few over the years. "See you at practice!" she says and returns to the booth. Her girlfriends are watching her, blinking their eyes with wide grins. If they only knew what Devin was really like, maybe they wouldn't be drooling over him.

"When are you seeing him?" Gabby asks, her mouth slightly open.

"I'm not!" Carla slides into the booth and takes a sip of her paid-for martini.

"Why? He's cute!" Gabby exclaims.

"How did you get to know him?" Michelle asks.

"I didn't. He wants me to take him out and show him our city. Can you believe that? What nerve. He must be a jerk if he thinks so highly of himself. He thinks I want him. Please!" She shakes her head. He probably thinks every girl wants him.

Michelle and Gabby stare at their friend with perplexed expressions on their faces. "You said no?" Gabby shrieks.

Carla lifts a shoulder. "Why should I? He just wants me to rave about him on the air. It's not because he wants to get to know me," she says, believing that his comment about being friends is just a front. "There's nothing more to it."

"Why does he care what you think?" Michelle asks.

"I don't know. Last year, I predicted he'd be traded to Vancouver. I caught him off guard during an interview and I guess he hasn't forgotten. I might have also said that the team didn't need the trade."

"Meaning him," Gabby says, resting her chin on her fist.

"That's not nice!" Michelle retorts.

"It's the truth!"

"So, you can't say that. You can hurt a guy's ego," Gabby says. "You know that!"

"And this is coming from a woman who gave away her boyfriend's favorite T-shirts because she didn't like the look of them?"

"They were V-neck! And he has chest hair!"

Carla rolls her eyes. "I saw how hurt he was."

Gabby waves a hand as though done with the conversation. "It didn't last anyway."

"Jeez, I wonder why."

"He had it coming," Gabby says. "I told him I hated them on him, but he didn't care. Anyway, this Devin guy is eye candy, if you ask me."

"So attitude has nothing to do with it?" Carla asks.

"To a certain extent it does." Gabby tucks a caramel strand behind her ear. "Devin isn't your ordinary guy. He's something to look at. If he wants to take you out, go for it! Hah! What would your mother say to that?"

"I wouldn't tell her I was dating him, not that I plan to. I can only imagine what kind of guy he is off the ice if on the ice he's all tense and aggressive. I've seen how he reacts when a call isn't made in his favor."

"Well, there's only one way to find out and that's to find out for yourself," Michelle says.

"Nothing's going to change my mind about Devin," Carla says with a grin, grabbing hold of her martini and sucking it down. "He may be the hottest guy I've ever met," she says, directing her words with her fingers, "but he's certainly not a good guy. An interview will prove it." She looks over at the bar to get another view of Devin, but he's already gone. A twinge of disappointment hits her. She wants to dislike him, but he gives her a reason to talk about the Warriors. The team needs a push to make better decisions, and if no one is watching the team and on their case, they could make more mistakes if they're not careful. More reason for her to interview Devin and make him accountable for his game.

Chapter 2

Channel Five News is a busy, productive television station. A lot has been going on in the city of Vancouver: A small plane crashed, missing greenhouses and taking out livestock; a targeted shooting at a major intersection; an Easter bunny that was thought to be at the mall for photos robbed a jewelry store.

For Carla Sinclair, the sports department is also a triumph of hockey trades and basketball predictions. She has been at work researching stories since midmorning. After the noon news hour, she is on the phone with agents, trying to secure interviews to update her information for the six o'clock news.

Carla hangs up the phone with a hard twist of her wrist. She leans back in her chair. "Got our top story," she says to her coworker, sitting at the desk beside her.

"And what's that?" the young twentysomething says out of the side of his mouth, staring at his computer screen like he doesn't want to miss whatever it is that's captured his attention.

"It's official, Devin Miller's no-trade clause was broken. Guess he wanted out of Carolina."

"I heard the rumor," Ryan says.

"It's not a rumor. It's big news, considering the Warriors are paying him forty-six million on a six-year contract. Ridiculous!" she mutters as she types on her computer. "Can you believe the Warriors will pay Miller an insane amount of money, yet they let their forward line suffer?"

Ryan swings his chair around. "I wouldn't say they're suffering."

"They didn't make the play-offs last year. They're suffering!" Carla snaps, looking over at her junior reporter. "This trade better make a difference or I'm sure the public will be making a stink about the team."

"I think Ted Walker is more afraid of what the media says. He can convince the fans whatever they need. This city is devoted! They'll stand behind the Warriors even if they're in last place." Ryan turns himself back to face his computer.

"I still think the team needs new forwards to sharpen their offense, not another defenseman. They also need more setup and action in front of the opposing team's net," she says, watching Ryan grin slightly and then glance at his computer.

"The bottom line is," she continues, "they need more goals in a game. They've plateaued! And why did Walker agree to sign Miller?"

"Come on! Miller's a decent player," Ryan says. "Just 'cause the guy didn't perform well in Carolina; he rocked it in Florida and Ottawa."

"Which makes me wonder why they traded him," Carla hums.

"He needed a change." Ryan shrugs.

Carla blows out a breath. "Did he want a trade or did his agent?"

"Money talks, money talks," Ryan says smoothly, clicking away on his keyboard. He stops and tilts his head. "Why do you care so much about this guy? Do you know him or somethin'?"

"No!" she snaps. "I don't know him! I just think the team makes stupid decisions." She sits back in her chair. Carla wouldn't want Ryan or anyone at work to know she chatted with Devin last night. Ryan is still looking at her. "What?"

"Nothing," he says, shaking his head and smirking.

"What is it? Do I have something on my face?" she asks, rubbing her cheek and chin. Panic sets in. Could she have blueberry on her face from a muffin she ate earlier?

"No, no." He shakes his head. "Are you still single?"

Her face feels warm. The word *still* sounded like the word *years* to her. It wasn't easy finding a date that accepted her headstrong personality and career-focused devotion. Her last two relationships were short-lived, if you can call two weeks a relationship. There hasn't been anyone who has kept her on her feet and had her missing him when they were apart.

"A bunch of us are hitting the club after work. There'll be some single guys if you're interested."

"Do I look desperate?" she asks with an awkward smile.

"No, no, not at all," Ryan says, pursing his lips and shaking his head. "Just thought you might like options. You know, a younger guy—"

"I'm not old!"

"I didn't say you were."

"Your friends are like, what, twenty-three?" Carla guesses.

"Twenty-five."

"No, thanks. Not interested. Besides, I don't want to meet someone at a club."

"How else will you meet someone? You're always working."

"For your information, I just so happen to like working."

"Nothing wrong with it. Just thought I'd mention it since you're always here."

Carla sees that her phone is blinking. "Got a call! Maybe it's Ted Walker. I've been waiting for him to get back to me."

"I just spoke to him," Ryan tells her, keeping his eyes on his computer screen.

Carla shoots him a look. "When?" Her hand is on the receiver.

"He called me this morning. I had a question about Mark Buckley. There was an assumption that he would be out the next five games with a groin injury."

"What did Walker say?"

"Buckley will be back playing tomorrow. He's fine."

"Carla Sinclair!" she answers, resting the phone between her shoulder and ear as she reaches for her notebook and pen.

"Hi, Care Bear," the voice soothes.

"Hi, Mom," Carla says, releasing her pen to her notebook and hovering over her desk, holding her head. "You should always call my cell."

"I'm saving you minutes."

"Doesn't matter. What's going on?"

"There's a dance up at the community hall. Catered dinner, auction. Do you want to go?"

"No."

"Your dad doesn't want to go either," she whines.

"Ask Aunt Marie. She'll go with you."

"I thought you could meet someone."

"Mom! It's going to be all fifty- and sixty-year-olds."

"Have you given much thought to Curtis?"

"Your neighbor?"

"He's a nice man," she defends. "Trims his hedges so well."

"He's a landscaper. And about your age! Mom, I don't need your help finding a man, thanks," she hisses. "Why can't people leave me alone? I like my life!"

"You need someone, honey. You haven't brought anyone home to introduce me to lately."

"There's a reason for that," Carla says, glancing up at the clock on the wall. "You scare guys off. You talk about weddings and babies. Not something guys want to hear the first time they go out with someone."

Ryan is chuckling to himself. Carla throws a balled-up paper in his direction to make him stop.

"You'll know where they stand if you get the big questions out of the way."

"What's with everyone? Why can't I be single and happy?" She glances at Ryan, as though directing the question at him too.

"That's not happiness, that's loneliness."

Carla looks up at the wall clock. "Mom, I have to go. I've gotta get back to work."

"Are you coming by for a visit soon? Haven't seen you in a week."

Carla blows out a breath.

"I'm making dinner for Sadie and Gavin tomorrow night. Do you want to come over?"

"Yeah, sure."

Carla hangs up, sweeps her hair back from her face and stands up, straightening her skirt. It's time to take her place at the desk to report her sports findings for the day. Carla walks to her seat and attaches her lapel microphone during a commercial.

"Cookie?" David Gillies, the news anchor, offers, waving the box in front of her.

"No, thanks," she says, appalled that he'd ask, considering they're on air in thirty seconds.

"Shortbread. Melts in your mouth."

She chuckles and adjusts the height of her seat so that her hands are folded together as she waits for David to introduce her.

"Good evening," Carla begins. "Good news, the Warriors should be able to make the play-offs now, thanks to a huge deal for defenseman Devin Miller." She pauses. "Acquired from Carolina, Miller missed five weeks in January due to a knee injury and then suffered a concussion from a hit from Patrick Morris. Does the team need another guy added to the injury list? Is he worth the money? Here's what Ted Walker had to say. . . ."

Carla watches the clip play, her fingers lightly holding on to the paper script in front of her.

When the clip ends, she arches an eyebrow in response to the praise Ted gave his new player. "There you go! According to Walker, Miller is worth it. Let's see what he can do for us during the play-offs, hopefully a lot more than what he was doing in Carolina," she scoffs. "And if he doesn't, we have someone to blame, don't we?"

Carla reads the next story. Her report is finished and the news hour ends. She takes off her microphone and wraps it over her chair.

"We're heading for dinner," David says. "You're welcome to join us."

"Thanks, but I'll pass tonight," she says.

"Have you left the building at all today?" he asks, taking off his blazer. At fifty, David is a handsome man, with light brown eyes that are as calm as a marshy pond. The trace of gray along his temples adds to his mature look and seasoned reporting.

"I haven't needed to," she says, stepping off the platform.

"You haven't left the building all this week. What happened to your afternoon walks and escaping for a latte?"

"I took the week off," she admits.

"A brisk walk is what you need to clear your mind."

"Maybe." She heads to her desk, shaking her long hair behind her to create airflow behind her neck. The hot overhead lights keep her warm, even with the cool fans blowing.

Carla pulls her chair out from her desk and sees Timothy peeking over his computer. "Is it just me or are those lights getting hotter?" She rubs a strand of hair off her forehead.

"We can turn up the air," he says.

"Anyone else complain?"

Timothy shakes his head. "Just you."

"Is that right?"

"I heard what you said about Miller. You might get an interview, after all," he says.

She sits down in her chair. "I doubt it."

"He's going to want to defend himself."

"I didn't say anything on the record. It's Ted Walker that's hard to reach. He doesn't like speaking if he doesn't have to," Carla says, opening up a new file on her computer. "It was hard enough getting a quick comment on Devin Miller's contract."

"Don't take it personally."

"I don't."

The newsroom becomes a distraction of phones ringing, reporters talking and some eating, which makes it hard to concentrate.

"He'll get back to me," she says, shrugging it off. "I'm not a priority."

"Well, you should be. The Warriors have always spoken to us. Look, if you're having trouble—"

"I never said I was."

"I was going to suggest Ryan. He's well liked and he's interviewed Ted before."

"So have I. But Ted doesn't want to talk because he knows what I want to ask him."

"Maybe you should say something nice about his team and then he'll talk," Timothy suggests.

"I report the facts."

"And your judgment," he says with a snicker. "I'm just saying, next time praise him when he does something good. You might be surprised."

Carla sits up straighter and leans her chin into the palm of her hand, staring at a blank screen. It's getting harder to get in touch with the important people; they don't seem to want to talk, and she doesn't seem to have the patience these days either. Carla blows out a breath.

"What's going on?" Timothy asks, tapping his pen on his thumb.

Carla can't look at her ex-husband. He knows her well and she knows he can ask the right questions to make her open up, even if she doesn't want to. That's what she loved about him, and what pulled her close to him was his ability to listen. She was at ease with Timothy; but then he was laid-back and easy to get along with.

"Nothing," she says, her bottom lip curving up into a pout. She couldn't look at him. Carla runs her hand across her forehead; wisps of her hair thread through her fingers. She stops, letting her cheek rest on her hand.

"Is it your mom again?"

The question is an honest one. "She's gotten a bit better," Carla admits. "Now that Sadie is a mom, she's focused on the new addition."

"So the pressure is off for a while?"

"Yeah, until Brinley is six months old and looking for a friend to play with."

"That's how it works," he says.

"Your mom and dad always left us alone," Carla says.

"That's because my sister had two children as soon as she signed her marriage license."

Carla lets out a relieved chuckle. "I forgot about that."

"Don't let your mom get to you."

"Yeah," she answers, tapping her index finger on her desk. "I try not to." Carla looks at the clock again. It's time to go, yet no one is waiting for her at home nor does she have any plans. Her days seem to roll into together. It's been like this for two years. Maybe her mom is right; if she doesn't start looking or at least try to get a date, her options in finding someone will be jeopardized. Her mom had a way of dissecting her life and Carla, as strong as she was, fell for it every time.

"She's trying to get control of you, make you believe that you failed when you have a life she wishes she had."

"I don't think so. I have nothing she wants."

"Sure you do. She was always tied down with your dad and the kids."

"That's what she wanted." Carla shakes her head. Was her ex trying to make her feel better?

"She also wanted to be able to travel."

"She can still do that," Carla says, shrugging it off.

Timothy stops flicking the pen. "Your dad's a homebody. You have freedom, she doesn't."

Carla can't disagree, but the idea of having a family of her own burns within her like a candle she can't blow out.

"Don't let Ryan overstep you," he says.

She looks Timothy's way. Ryan has been giving her a hard time since she got her promotion. "Why, what have you heard?"

"He wants your job."

"I heard they all want my job. Have you heard something I don't know?"

There was always the fear of losing a job. Not because of bad reporting; it has mostly to do with "structure" and a new face, to compete with the other stations. It's always fresh, always new, and the

set or reporters were always changing every few years or so to keep
the audience entertained.

"I'm not getting fired, am I?" Carla asks timidly, sliding her chair
over to have a closer conversation. Sometimes when someone was
getting fired, that person was the last to know. It seemed unfair, but
that's how it went working in television. The person with the job loss
was the one who was stunned, like getting hit from behind.

"There's talk about restructuring, but I don't think it has to do with
your department; more on the production side of things."

"Really?" Carla can feel the tightness in her throat. "You would
know," she says, relaxing her shoulders. "It would be silly to get rid
of me. I've been here for six years."

"Time doesn't mean anything," he says, and she knows Timothy is
right.

"Did you see the job posting for the Sports National?" he asks.

"No, I haven't been looking," she tells him, turning around, but all
she can see is his mound of brown hair and the slight crease of his
forehead, probably from staring at his writing on his computer. He's a
good news writer, quick and precise. He would be hard to replace,
considering he is labeled a veteran and great at what he does.

"It's up your alley," Timothy says. "National, working with guys,
probably would suit you just fine."

"I'm comfortable." She shrugs. "That's what happens when you
work and enjoy the same things as males. You blend in."

"You want to be known as the best female sports reporter, here's
your chance."

"Thanks for thinking of me. I'll check it out."

"Well, it's dinnertime," Timothy says, getting out of his chair. His
body is lanky and lean. He hasn't changed in all the years she's known
him. He never did put on pounds after marriage like his grandmother
said he would, even though he's a big eater.

Carla used to tease him about how much food he ate without
putting on any weight. He looks the same now as he did six years ago,
when they first met. She'd just been hired at Channel Five and he'd
offered to show her around, which led to having dinner. They saw each
other every day at work. Most of the time their shifts would end at the
same time and they would have dinner together. Timothy was always

there for her, and Carla liked having someone who wanted to be with her night and day. He was easy to be around, never demanding, always laid-back and offering advice when needed. There were times when Timothy suggested that she should slow down her presentation and take deep breaths between stories during a newscast. He helped her to focus. Carla trusted him and could tell him anything; he was her backbone when she needed it. Then, when the sports director position became available, no one was thinking about hiring a female. It was Timothy who had vouched for her and supported her. She loved that he knew his stuff and stuck up for her when she needed someone on her side.

They dated, but that seemed like a waste of time. They so loved being together and working together that they'd tied the knot exactly twelve months after they met. They bought an apartment and carpooled to work. They were inseparable. Timothy knew Carla wanted a baby; he didn't show any interest in being a dad, yet that was all Carla could think about. She made every effort to plan their lovemaking around the best time to conceive, but after no success and the thrill of being pregnant and then the disappointment of the two miscarriages they'd had, they drifted apart. They were unable to agree on anything. Carla couldn't stand being around Timothy, angry at him for not wanting a baby, not wanting to try. Didn't he want to make her happy? Weren't they supposed to band together to fulfill each other emotionally? Timothy gave off an apprehensive vibe that only added to Carla's disappointment. She didn't want to be around him. Every time she was with him, her feelings got hurt, which led to arguments, which led to the separation. She couldn't stay married to him. Timothy didn't take the separation lightly, claiming he loved her, but she realized she wasn't in love with him anymore. Once separated, they both talked about one of them leaving their jobs, but it wasn't fair that either had to leave when they were both doing well in their careers. They liked where they worked and had put so much into their jobs.

The separation was hard, seeing each other at work and going home for dinner without the other had its downsides, but Carla was determined to have a baby with or without Timothy. Going through the divorce, she'd had spurts of hope that Timothy would change his mind about a baby, or that she would magically fall in love with him

again and be happy childless. But she knew it wouldn't happen. They
were too far gone from what had begun as lovers and ended as two
strangers. Carla had to live with the choice she had made, a decision
she still thought about from time to time. She still wondered if there
was something she could have done to prevent the breakup.

"You'll be gone before I get back, I hope." His eyes narrow on hers.
"Your shift is over. Go home. You need to eat." Timothy grabs his
jacket from his chair.

Carla glances at him and waves, then turns her attention to her
computer, looking for the job posting. Her desk phone rings and lights
up. She grabs the receiver. "Carla Sinclair!"

"I saw your broadcast tonight on Devin Miller."

She exhales, rubs her forehead. Maybe she shouldn't have said the
Warriors had no use for him. She squints her eyes and leans forward
against her desk.

"How can I help you?" she says, composed, waiting for an outburst
of unkindness. Warrior fans were like vultures when their team wasn't
performing well. They didn't want to hear the truth.

"Do you want an interview with him?" the guy asks.

"Sure," she says, sitting up straighter, having no clue as to who this
person is. For all she knows, it could be a prank call.

"I can tell you where to reach him."

"Where's that?" she asks, not wanting to hear this guy go on and
on with a made-up story.

"If I tell you, you have to promise me I get to meet with him."

Carla rolls her eyes and lets out a breath. This guy is wasting her
time. "Are you a fan?"

"Yes. His biggest fan."

She laughs. "That's the first."

She rubs her head some more and decides to get off the phone.
She really should be getting home. She's been at work for ten hours.
It's time to have dinner and go to bed and do this circus all over again
tomorrow.

"The team has a Web site with their media relations contact info
on it," she tells him. "Why don't you call them? They'll be able to help
you," she says, moving the phone away from her ear slightly. Maybe
this guy will have better luck.

"I've tried that many times. They're not helpful."

At least it wasn't just her who had a problem with them.

"I don't think I'll be much help," she says honestly. "They haven't felt like talking lately."

"I'm sure you'll have better results."

"I don't make promises," she says. "What are you asking for? You want to have something signed?"

"No. I want to speak to him."

Carla rolls her eyes. "There are better players on the team who would love to talk and probably are willing to chat with a fan."

"It's Devin I want to talk to."

"I don't take special requests."

"Can you make an exception? I'll give you an address where you can find him."

Carla laughs. "He just was traded here. I don't think he has a house yet."

"He bought a place in West Van."

"Okay." Carla laughs again. Good guess; most of the team live there or close to it. It was the upscale place to live. "So, I'll just show up at his house and expect an interview?" she asks, chuckling. This is one reason she didn't get into investigative reporting. She doesn't like the confrontation of getting into people's personal lives. Thankfully, she excelled in sports, had the coordination to throw a ball and shoot a puck, as well as the confidence to be face-to-face with celebrities.

"I can give you a phone number," he tells her.

"You have Devin's address and phone number?" she asks, doubting very much that this guy is for real. "Why don't you just call him yourself?"

"I have, but he won't speak to me."

"Because you're a fan?"

"He chooses not to talk to me. We haven't spoken in years."

"Wait a minute, are you stalking him?" Carla asks. Perhaps this could be a news story: Crazy fan from Carolina didn't want Devin to leave.

"He ignores my calls."

She sucks in a breath. He's a stalker! Her heart races and she swallows hard. "You should give up, then. He obviously wants his privacy." Carla doesn't blame Devin for his actions. It must be tough, weeding out the obsessive fans from the everyday people.

"Because I have something to say to him in person."

A chill runs down her spine. This could be serious. "And you want me to break the ice for you? Either call him or show up?"

"He'll listen to you. You're a pretty girl. You'll get his attention. I've seen you interview him. He knows who you are."

She tucks a handful of hair behind her ear and rubs her hand along her skirt. "I'm sure Devin would like to hear from his biggest fan," she says, playing along.

"Not anymore he doesn't."

"And why is that?"

"I'm Keith Miller. Devin's dad."

Devin is getting ready for his first road trip as a Warriors player, heading east the next morning before returning home for a stretch of games to wrap up the regular season, before play-offs. He is quite relieved he was traded; at least he would have a chance at his team winning the Stanley Cup. Last year had been a flop in Carolina and again this year; they weren't even close. At thirty, he'd called a variety of cities home; Raleigh was his longest at four years. He hoped now that he was in Vancouver—the fourth place he'd called home since playing for the NHL—he would remain here for six years, and stay on when his contract expired.

He had caught the evening news as he packed his bag, throwing in socks and extra T-shirts just in case he needed them. He didn't do laundry on the road; he waited until he came home, so packing extra was a necessity.

Since moving to Vancouver five days earlier, he hasn't missed Channel Five's evening news. Not because he was caught up in what was happening in the city but because the sports anchor, Carla Sinclair, was the hottest reporter he'd ever seen, and the most sassy as well. How did she know he was going to take a trade? Whether she remembers or not, it doesn't matter. Does she realize how entertaining she can be?

Devin stands at the side of his bed, throwing clothes into his suitcase as he watches the flat-screen TV on his bedroom wall. As soon as Carla has the spotlight, Devin plunks himself down and stares at her full, coral lips and vibrant blue eyes. She is staring at him as she talks about his move and why it's ridiculous that he's an overpaid defenseman. Devin's back becomes strained as he leans forward, taking it all in. Speechless. "What does it matter to her what I make?" he mutters, still glued to the screen.

"It would be nice to make the play-offs and credit the trade, but really? Is one trade going to do the trick?" Carla says, looking at the news anchor sitting beside her, as if wanting him to weigh in on her opinion. "Time will tell," she says, before talking about the NHL standings.

Devin blows out a breath and gets up. *Is that how the city feels about me being here?* He scratches his head. He was warned by several old teammates that this city was one of the toughest in accepting new players, and that he would be under a magnifying glass until he could prove himself worthy.

I need to get something straight; I'm an asset to the team or I wouldn't be here. Devin picks up his iPhone to search for Channel Five's number. He types an e-mail directed to the Sports Department. After writing a sentence, he stops and clears the message, knowing it could take a few days before the message was received, and decides to call the newsroom and ask for Carla. He'll leave her a message on her voice mail and tell her what he thinks of her. No need to leave his number. He can get it off his chest, and maybe she'll think twice about making comments about him in the future.

"Channel Five newsroom!"

"Can I please speak with Carla Sinclair?"

"I'll transfer your call. One moment."

Devin puts his hand on his hip and paces, wondering what kind of message he will leave.

The beeping hold stops and the phone is ringing. Prepared to tell her she should keep her opinions to herself, that no one cares what she thinks.

Carla answers the phone nonchalantly, as though he caught her in deep thought.

"It's Devin Miller," he says, tongue-tied, and then pauses. "We met—"

"Devin, hi. I didn't expect you to call me." She pauses. "I've been waiting for your agent to get back to me so I can interview you. You didn't give me your number when I saw you at Buckley's."

"I'm not calling for an interview. I'm calling to defend myself."

"So you're a defenseman on and off the ice," she says. "I had a phone call a few minutes ago from a man who said you were hard to reach, but just my luck, you're on the phone."

"Listen, what you said about me isn't what the public needs to know."

"I'm reporting the facts."

"You don't need to share."

"Yes, I do. It's what matters in this city."

"Let the fans make the decision. Let them be the judge of whether I'm worthy enough to play here. Your comments are planting seeds in people's heads before they have a chance to judge me for themselves. Besides, I am what the Warriors need or I wouldn't be here."

"Not for forty-six million dollars. Sorry. We need goals scored."

"And saved. That's what I'm best at."

"That's a goalie's job."

"I'm not calling to argue with you, but I'm telling you that I would appreciate it if you didn't talk about me unless it's about the game I play."

"Sorry. I didn't think I'd hurt your feelings."

"You haven't," Devin says, leaning against the doorway, looking out onto the mountain of boxes in the living room. "I'm telling you because I don't like people talking trash about me."

"I'd never talk trash, Devin." She says his name directly, keeping his attention. "My job is to report on sports. I'm fair. I'd never say something that's untrue," she says. "Now that I have you on the phone, I need to book an interview with you."

"So you can beat me up?" he asks and then laughs. She has some nerve.

"I want to talk to you."

"We're talking."

"For the record. I want it taped," Carla says.

Devin's chest tightens. "I don't know if I can trust you," he says.

"You can trust me. It's you I'm unsure about."

"What do you mean by that?"

"If you're calling me to tell me you disagree with the truth, what are you hiding?"

"Nothing!"

"I want to know what you're going to do to prove you're worth the money." Her voice was all innocence.

"Ouch! Do you do this to all the players?"

"Only to the ones who think they're too good for the team."

"You think I'm good?" he asks, his lips tightened into a grin. He couldn't help himself. He was beginning to enjoy the banter.

Her silence captures his attention.

"Guess you'll have to prove it. Show us what Walker sees in you and convince me."

"Thanks. Didn't know you were paying my salary."

"When it comes to the job, money talks. The more money you earn, the more fans care about who you are."

"I guess I'll be well liked then."

He wanted a city to call home permanently, and closer to Seattle, where his mom and stepdad lived. He was going to give it his all and make a difference during the play-offs. He needed it just as much as the team did.

"You're not too conceited."

"Hey, money talks," he says, unable to hold back. He likes playing along with her. She's easily irritated and tenses up. He could tell by her tone. He could imagine her little oval face going red with frustration. He's entertained.

"You know, we're good," she says. "My mistake. I don't need an interview."

"Yes, you do."

"No. I think I got what I need."

"I'm afraid to ask what that is," he says with a chuckle.

"Attitude. And if I have questions, I'll go through Walker."

"Look, sorry. You can interview me," he says, surrendering. "I'm heading on the road, but when I get back we can set something up."

"You're not leading me on, are you?"

He chuckles. "You'll know when I'm leading you on. I'll give you my phone number."

Chapter 3

Carla scrolls the postings on a media job board, checking her back from time to time to make sure there isn't anyone peering over her shoulder. She comes across one for Sports National in Toronto. Could she move away from her friends and family? Maybe a change of scenery is what she needs to meet someone and settle down again.

"Carla! Looks like a secret admirer," Pamela says, cooing.

Carla turns around. "For me?" She reaches out to take the fruit bouquet from Pamela's hands.

"You don't see many of these; they cost more than flowers. Must be a real catch. Who's it from?"

"I have no idea." Carla sets down the painted ceramic vase on her desk, unwraps the cellophane and plucks the card out from between the pointy strawberries on long white plastic toothpicks. She skims the words. Her face grows warm. Her stomach flips. She has to reread his name. "Devin Miller."

"The hockey player?" Pamela shrieks.

Carla bites her bottom lip and places the card down. "I'm just as surprised as you are."

"Tell me something juicy!" She claps her hands together.

Carla shakes her head. "Believe me, there's nothing to tell."

"Then what does he want?"

Carla's eyes widen. "Nothing. He's just hurt that I called him out on air. My opinion, of course," she says, eyeing the fruit arrangement and picking off a row of grapes, popping one after the other into her mouth. She sits back in a daze as she gets ready to place a grape in her mouth. She chews and swallows, then says, "He didn't like that I shared his high salary with everyone. He thinks he's worth it, but he's not." Carla looks at Pamela, who is standing in front of her, wearing a long skirt and blouse. She is nodding and pausing at Carla's story. "At least it's not what the Warriors need right now," Carla carries on. "But then, who am I? I don't get paid the big bucks to make those types of decisions. They were desperate to fill the skates of a veteran player and Miller wanted out of Carolina. They haven't been doing well this season. It's just too bad we didn't get a new center man, though. We could use more power on the offense." Carla shakes her head and slides a strawberry off the pick, staring up at Pamela's brown eyes.

"They should trade a whole forward line instead of focusing on defense. There's nothing wrong with what they have or had," Carla rambles on, chewing on a berry.

"Okay, well, I have to go," Pamela says.

Carla exhales and swings her seat around with a push of her toes. The job posting is visible on her screen. With a rise in panic, she clicks off and opens the Warriors' home page. She slips off another strawberry from the pick and bites into it. She sucks the juice as her eyes gloss the screen. There is nothing new, so she makes her rounds on the Internet to other media sites to see what stories are making headlines.

"There was a fight that broke out over an international table tennis game," a voice says from behind her, snapping Carla out of her concentrated state.

She turns her attention to the young sports reporter. "Okay," she says, raising an eyebrow.

"I've never heard of it before," Ryan says.

"Neither have I. The sport needs more attention. It's boring as watching paint dry."

"I don't have anyone to talk to yet," he says. "I'm waiting on a call. Should hear back this afternoon."

"That's fine," she says, clicking her keyboard.

"I've got a call out to Ted Walker and Steve Morrow."

She stops, tilts her head. "They're on the road."

"Steve is. I don't expect him to return my call, but it's worth a try."

"He might. What's the story?"

"Well, the trade deadline is this Wednesday, has to be more trades.

I heard Brandon Keller might go to Pittsburgh in exchange for a two-man deal."

"They won't do that."

"No?"

"No, Keller is worth more; they'll get someone like Lawrence Grattan and a first-round draft pick."

Ryan walks away, and Carla stops typing and looks at the card from Devin. She picks up the card and rereads it. Is he worried she'll call him out again? What does he want from her? If Keith Miller is who he says he is, then why doesn't Devin want to talk to him? Could it be a guy with the same last name, claiming to be his dad? What's the story?

Carla takes her cell phone in hand and punches in the number Devin gave her. She types a message, "Good luck tonight. We'll see how sweet you are," and hits SEND.

"Carla!" a voice yells.

She puts down her phone and turns in her chair.

Ryan runs over. "Ted returned my call!"

"That was fast."

"I've got an interview with him!"

Her eyes bulge. "How did he reach you?" she asks, and then punches her lips together, shakes her head and blinks. "I mean, did he call the newsroom?" she asks hopefully.

"He called asking for me," Ryan says.

"So he's agreed to an interview," Carla says, disappointed that she didn't get a personal call. Ever since she got the job at Channel Five six years ago, it's been an uphill battle to get recognized as a knowledgeable sports reporter, and now as the sports director, it seems even harder.

"He said he could manage a few questions."

"Yeah, that's what I would expect from him," she says, eyeing his jeans and polo shirt. For a twenty-five-year-old, Ryan is going places. His charming smile is enough to capture an audience, and even though the guy isn't brilliant, his looks are. "Is it a press conference?"

"He said he invited me and Channel Nine."

"It will be a press conference," Carla says directly. "More than one media outlet is a press conference. I'd expect a full room, considering Ted hasn't made an appearance in weeks. When is it?"

"Today. At three."

Carla checks the clock on the wall. "In an hour. There's something big. Make sure you ask about Devin Miller. I want to know why they're paying him a big salary and not strengthening the forward line instead."

"Okay, boss," Ryan says and rushes off, calling for his cameraman.

For the next hour and a half, Carla checks her phone. There is no reply from Devin or Ryan. She's desperate to know what Ted is announcing, and if it's anything important.

Carla does her best to put together her information for the six o'clock news. Whatever Ryan gets from the press conference, it will have to be added at the last minute. Her adrenaline always rose when stories broke and the last story got shortened or bumped. It made her job exciting, and to be able to work under pressure was a gift. She worked with some reporters who had panic attacks every time they were on the clock, but not her; she was excited. It fueled her.

She checks her phone again as she hears the buzz. A glance at the sender, and she hesitates to answer. Carla wants to finish up with one more thing before concentrating on something else. When her phone buzzes after a message has been left, she puts her phone to her ear.

"Hi, Care Bear. I made lots for dinner. See you when you get here!"

Her phone buzzes again, indicating a text. This one's from Ryan. Her heart beats faster. She swallows hard, anticipating the news.

Ted says Devin is worth every cent.

"What?" Carla asks out loud. "You're kidding me!"

Did he say anything about their forward line? she types, and then sets her phone down in front of her, waiting for his reply.

Her phone buzzes. *Said they are working on it. Looks like Brandon Keller will go to Pittsburgh for Lawrence Grattan and their first-round draft pick.*

"What's going on with the team?" she mutters to herself.

How did you know Grattan was in the deal?

He's the cherry on top. Why wouldn't they want him? He's worth more than the Warriors can afford now that they're paying Miller. I'm sure of it. I'll see you when you get here. Carla sets down her phone and gets working on her story, ready to fill in the blanks as soon as Ryan gets back so she can view the clip and report on it for the evening news.

Carla begins typing as she hears her name being called. She freezes in midsentence, expecting a quick question, but instead it's Pamela standing at her desk, holding on to something pink in her hands and grinning so wide that her cheeks are round like plums.

"Hi, Pamela," Carla says. "What's going on?" It's not often that Pamela needs something from a reporter besides relaying a message.

"I have this scarf that I've never worn and I just thought . . . well, I want you to have it." She hands it over.

"Thank you. That's kind," Carla says, taking the accessory from Pamela's hands. "Are you sure you don't want it?"

"I've had it in my closet forever and I never wear it."

"Do you want something for it?" Carla looks at her, wondering why she's shown an interest in her.

"No! No! I'm just glad you can use it," Pamela says, jumpy.

"I'll wear it tomorrow," Carla says with a quick nod and folds it over, setting it beside her computer.

"Great," Pamela says, disappearing from the newsroom.

Finally, Ryan comes cruising in, chirpy and proud. "Got it!"

"What is it?" Carla asks.

Ryan stops in front of her and bobs his head, pointing his thumb back. "Do you want to have a look? Kyle is cutting it down. The feed's too long."

"I don't have time. What else did he say?"

"They traded Vince Merelli to LA."

Carla falls forward. "What? He's top line!"

"Well, you knew he wanted out, he told us he'd take a trade if an opportunity arose. It's a good trade for Merelli. He's playing with Keaton Williams, his old teammate from Boston."

Carla shakes her head. She loves the Warriors. Not only is she a fan but they are her hometown heroes as well. She grew up watching the game with her dad, who is a devoted fan, a sports enthusiast, and will watch pretty much anything that involves teams and an object to score.

"I have to finish up," Carla tells him and spins around to type one last sentence.

The six o'clock news is two-thirds over and Carla madly types the last of her script and hits PRINT.

"Are you ready?" Timothy asks, his voice cause for alarm.

She jumps up and scurries over to the printer. "I'm going!" She grabs her papers and steps on to the platform.

"Thirty seconds!" the floor director yells.

She takes a seat, fastens her microphone to her blazer, flips her hair off her shoulders and relaxes in her chair as she hears the countdown. From a distance, she spots Pamela talking to Timothy. They both laugh, yet he is focused on watching the anchors. Carla looks down at the papers in front of her and prepares herself for her opening in five seconds.

She exhales at two seconds.

"Good evening," Carla says with a very slight nod. "Another big trade for the Warriors today. Not what was expected, considering Vince Merelli was our top line. He said before he would take a trade if the right team wanted him. . . ."

She finishes her read, and after a last-minute comment about the weather, David Gillies ends the news with a "Thanks for watching. Good night."

Carla stands up, throws her papers into the recycling bin and grabs her purse underneath her desk.

"Good night," a voice says.

She sees Timothy at her desk.

"Dinner plans?" he asks.

"My mom's house. My weekly appearance."

"Still doing that?"

Carla shrugs. "Beats eating alone."

"Does she still make cabbage rolls?"

Carla nods. They were Timothy's ongoing request but he would eat anything her mom cooked and praised her after every meal, as though Carla didn't cook for him. Timothy got along with her family, even when arguments broke out at occasional dinners between Carla and her mom. They were arguments about minor things: traveling before having children, buying a house in the suburbs or the newest health scare. Timothy would be the referee and never took sides, and that would cause disagreements on the drive home. Carla felt like he always agreed with her mom, but he said it wasn't worth getting involved.

"She makes the best," he says.

"I'll tell her to make you some. She still tries to send me home with leftovers."

"The last time I ordered them in a restaurant they weren't the same."

"She'll be happy to hear that."

"Say hi to them for me." He walks past.

"Will do. 'Night!"

A half-hour drive to her parents' house, and she is starving. Even though her mom could be suffocating at times, Carla can't decline a dinner invitation. Her mom could turn anything boring into something appealing; no wonder Timothy looked forward to Sunday-night dinners. It's hard to believe Carla wasn't an overweight child growing up, although she didn't appreciate good food until her college years, when fast food seemed to be the norm.

"I'll heat up your dinner," her mom says, running into the kitchen.

Carla takes a seat on the couch beside her dad.

"We were watching you tonight," her brother Gavin says, sitting across from her wearing his Vancouver police uniform. He has short, light brown hair and hazel eyes like their father and fair skin like their mother, yet the siblings all have similarities to one another. They all have the same thin nose and fair eyebrows. "Hard to believe we got Grattan."

"Why?"

"He's good! If he can score as many points as Merelli, we'll be okay."

"David Gillies is a handsome man, isn't he?" Mom says, handing Carla a plate of food.

"Thanks, Mom. Yeah, he's handsome."

"He's married?" she asks.

"Yes, he is. You've asked me that before."

"Mom has a crush on him," Gavin says.

"No, I don't!" Mom says, blushing. "I think he's handsome, that's all."

Dad chuckles.

"Speaking of a crush," Gavin says, "my buddies at work ask about you."

"They do?" Carla asks.

"You should set her up with someone," Mom says.

"No way! Carla's not going out with any of them."

"Maybe I should have my dates go through you first." Carla snickers.

Gavin narrows his eyebrows. Carla wonders if this is the same look he gives when he pulls people over for speeding and asks if they know how fast they were going.

"Anytime," he says. "Can't let my sister—my celeb sis—date losers. I'll check them out first."

"Thanks, Gav," Carla says. "Where's Sadie?"

"Changing Brinley," Mom says.

Carla eats her meal while watching the Warriors hockey game on TV.

Her eyes follow the players, trying to spot Devin. She sees his number nineteen on his jersey. He skates up the ice with the puck and passes it to another player before making a line change.

"Now that we've made some trades, we can start scoring goals," Dad says. He takes his team personally. "It would be nice to beat Boston in the play-offs."

"If we make the play-offs," Carla says. "We have to win more games."

"We lost Merelli," Gavin says.

"We'll see how the Warriors do."

"You didn't like the trade?" he asks.

"They should have kept him. Nothing wrong with him."

"It was a stupid move, if you ask me," Dad says, wearing his Warriors' T-shirt.

"I leave the room for ten minutes and you're still talking hockey," Sadie says, carrying her five-month-old outward so everyone can see her daughter's precious smile. They both have round faces and blond hair.

"Hi, Brin!" Carla says, leaning forward to grab her niece's foot. The baby coos. What she would give to have a little girl of her own. "How's my favorite baby?" More coos come Carla's way, which makes her heart grow bigger. Everything else fades away for the moment because this baby is the center of attention and knows it.

Brinley waves her arms in response.

"You'll have to have one soon," Mom says, her light blond and gray wisps of hair falling out of her loose bun, shaping her face. "Brinley needs a cousin to play with, don't you?" she asks, taking her granddaughter's hand in hers and making baby sounds.

"I hope to be married first, Mom."

"You've got lots of time," Sadie says, shaking her head. "No time for yourself once you have one."

"Isn't it worth it?" Carla asks, staring at her niece and envisioning what her own daughter might look like.

"Of course! I miss me time, though. Not to mention the sleep. Look at the bags under my eyes."

"You'll get it back."

"I keep telling myself. Probably in ten years," Sadie says, running her hand over her blond ponytail.

Mom laughs. "And once they're grown up, you forget what me time is. Isn't that right, Pete?"

Dad nods, his eyes glued to the television, muttering, "Come on!" He slaps his knee and lets out an "ah."

"You've always liked your sleep," Carla says. "Remember when we went camping at the lake and Dad told us whoever got up early with him could go fishing? Gavin and I tried waking you and you hid under your pillow and refused."

"I wasn't getting up to sit in a boat for hours when I could sleep instead."

"That was when I caught my first fish," Gavin says, extending his neck.

Dad points to the fireplace mantel. "Still got the picture."

"It was fun," Carla says.

"For you two," Sadie says, bouncing her daughter.

"You've always been that way," Gavin says.

"It's a good thing you're not. I don't know how you work your night shifts," Sadie says. "That would kill me." She rolls her eyes.

"Doesn't bother me," Gavin says.

Carla sits back, resting her plate on her lap. "Where's Brian tonight?"

"Working. He had some things to finish up at the office."

Gavin and Dad yell at the TV. The Warriors score, grabbing Carla's attention. "Yeah!" she says.

"Assisted by Miller," Dad says. "He's not working out too badly. Hey, did you see that table-tennis match and how beaten-up that guy got?"

"They got kicked out of the tournament and the league," Carla says.

"Serves them right," Mom says. "What's gotten into sports? If there's fighting, it draws an audience."

Sadie holds her hands out to take her daughter.

"To be the best, one wants to prove himself," Carla says, handing over Brinley, and pays attention to the television, where a fight has broken out.

"See? See?" her mom says, rising to her feet and throwing her arms up in the air. She grabs Carla's dinner plate.

"It's part of the game." Dad yells, "Get him, Miller! He deserves it!"

Carla can't take her eyes away from the screen. Miller gets punched in the head and is taken down by his opponent. She swallows hard and sinks into the couch, watching Miller laying on the ice; he is slow to get up. Her heart is in her throat.

"You need to start dating more, Carla. You need to find someone."

She watches Devin being escorted to the bench by a referee. "I've tried."

"Gavin? Are you sure there isn't someone you can set Carla up with?"

"I'm not desperate," she says.

"You work too much," Mom says.

"I enjoy work. Look where it's gotten me."

"Divorced and childless."

It's like the air has been sucked out of the room. The only sound is the commentators on the TV.

Carla holds her lips tight. A burn of tears are behind her eyes, and any second she might let the tap go. She won't cry in front of her family, she tells herself. She has to be strong. It's what got her through her divorce with Timothy. When everyone was telling her they were sorry and she'll find happiness again one day, she wanted to ask *when?* Not everyone gets a second chance at falling in love. Although being with Timothy was love, not in love, like a desirable lifeline that one can't live without.

In the beginning, Carla had been attracted to Timothy and liked being around him. He understood her job and she liked that she could trust him. She didn't have to worry about Timothy talking behind her back; he cheered her on and wanted to see her accomplish her career goals. That was enough for her to stick with him and believe that his smarts and professionalism was what was missing in her life. By the second year of marriage and one miscarriage, she hadn't craved being with him every day. She'd started to blame work. Carla thought that as soon as they had a baby, it would bring them closer. They were trying. There were months of disappointment. Timothy said he didn't have a desire to be a parent like she did. Carla started to have doubts about the marriage and questioned her true feelings about Timothy. She pressured him about having a baby. Even after the second miscarriage, he hadn't shown much emotion except for her loss. She wondered if he was secretly celebrating, and that made her hold a grudge. Timothy told her it would happen when the time was right, but it couldn't happen fast enough. Carla made doctor appointments to have herself checked out to see what the problem was, but Timothy discouraged her and said they didn't have a problem; it just wasn't their time. She blames herself for the breakup and for hurting Timothy, but she also blames herself for not aggressively finding a solution.

"Why do you do this, Mom? Why do you make me feel like I've screwed up and won't have a family?"

"If you were married to Tim—"

"Well, I'm not! And I was talking about success. I wouldn't have an anchor position if I didn't put in the time and energy."

"Isn't finding someone more important?"

"What do you want me to do? Stand on a street corner with a sign that spells out SINGLE?"

"There must be someone at work."

"Yeah, my ex-husband, who, by the way, says hello."

"I'm sure one of your friends can set you up with someone. You know, the older you get, the harder it is to find someone."

"It already is."

"And the older you get, the harder it is to conceive. Look at our neighbors across the street, Florence and Jeff. They're forty-five and just had their set of twins. They'd been trying for seven years."

Carla stares blankly at her manicured fingernails, clicking them together to loosen the invisible grime. She can't look at her mom.

"When the time's right . . ." her dad says.

"It wasn't my fault that I couldn't have a child, and you know what? I'm glad I didn't have one with Timothy because I would be a single mother right now."

"You'd have made it work."

Carla puts her hands together, looks at the television screen and then at her mom. "I couldn't. I love my job. I'm not giving that up. I've worked really hard to get where I am. My job is who I am. This is where I'm meant to be," she says, feeling a nudge of disappointment. "You can't have everything."

Dad looks over. "Are you happy?"

"Very happy," Carla says in a monotone.

He holds up a hand. "Well, that's what matters," he says, looking over at her and then refocusing on the TV.

"When will you accept me for being who I am?" Carla asks. "Why not be content that you have healthy kids who are happy themselves?"

"I do!" her mom defends herself.

"Can't you be happy for me? Can't you understand that if Timothy and I could have, we would have stayed together? We tried having children. It didn't work for us. You're lucky; you didn't go through the pain of conceiving the way I did for three years. Some women aren't as lucky." The burn in Carla's eyes makes her blink. Her head gives a sharp turn as she walks toward the door. "You're going to have to get over Timothy."

Carla slips on her flats and leaves before anyone can stop her.

Chapter 4

Carla applies for the Sports National job on her home computer, curious whether she'd get the job with her experience. It would be a good opportunity, working for a station that has the same interests as she. Timothy might be right; she would do well working in a male-dominant environment where sports was the focus. Maybe leaving Vancouver would be a good change for her. It would give her a fresh start; she could leave her past behind.

Before heading into work, she drove to a long-awaited doctor appointment to see a gynecologist about her chances of conceiving. She had gone to the doctor when she miscarried the first time, and he had told her that those things happened and to relax; it was nothing she had done, which put her at ease. The second time she miscarried, Timothy told her it wasn't necessary to see a doctor; she would be told the same thing as before. Carla remembers telling Timothy there could be a problem, but an argument ensued and he talked her out of seeing a specialist every time she mentioned the word *baby*. She couldn't shake the idea of not being a mom when she was married, and now the fear of not having children was eating her up more than ever. She was a little bit older and still single, anxious that she wouldn't get the chance. Maybe her mom was right; she could be a single mom. Lots of women did it. Not by choice, but sometimes it happened. It wasn't the perfect scenario. What Carla would give to fall in love, to be in love with a man who cherished her and their relationship.

Carla sits on the examining table. What's the doctor going to tell her? Maybe she can't have kids at all. She should have discussed this issue when she was married to Timothy to find out what was happening; not knowing gives her little hope of a positive outcome.

There's a knock at the door and it opens.

A female doctor wearing khakis and low-profile running shoes smiles as she walks in. "Carla? Hi, I'm Dr. Fossett," she says, stepping forward to offer a handshake. She puts down Carla's medical folder. "You're here to discuss infertility?" the doctor asks, skimming the information.

Carla nods. "I want to know if I have a problem with getting pregnant."

"Are you trying?"

"No." Carla sucks in her lips. "Well, not right now. I was married and had two miscarriages. I don't know if it's me, but I need to know. I want kids."

"But you're not with anyone at this time?" The doctor's eyes concentrate on her patient's, as though trying to grasp the concern.

"I'm not. No, I don't know if I ever will. . . ."

"When was your divorce?"

"Two years ago."

"You're what? Thirty?"

"Thirty-one."

The doctor gives her a gentle grin. "You have time."

"But women's eggs start to decrease in their thirties, making it harder to conceive. I want to know what my chances are."

"True. But it doesn't mean that you can't, or won't, be able to. I mean, it may take a longer time, that's all." The doctor tucks a strand of her shoulder-length brown hair behind one ear.

"But I've had miscarriages."

"It happens." The doctor grips the clipboard at her chest. "Are your periods normal?"

"Yes."

"Have you had any tests done to see if there were any problems?"

"No." Carla swallows.

"At this point, it's hard to say if there is a problem." The doctor puts down the clipboard at the raised counter, keeping her hand on the papers. "Once you start trying, we can look into it." The doctor smiles. "Women who are focused on having a baby tend to be unsuccessful because of the pressures they put on themselves. There could be environmental factors, not necessarily an infertility issue. At this point, my suggestion is relax, look after yourself, get yourself baby healthy, as I like to call it—multivitamins, plenty of rest—and things will work themselves out."

Carla can feel her chest grow heavy. Wasn't the doctor going to do any tests? Doesn't she care that she has been unsuccessful getting pregnant before?

"What about artificial insemination?" Carla spits out.

The doctor holds her laugh and says, "You don't want to go down that road unless it's the last resort. You need to try naturally first."

"When I was married, we had a healthy sex life. . . . I just don't understand."

"Men also experience infertility. That's why I'm saying it's best to wait to see if it happens naturally. We need to start at square one."

"Look, I don't know if I'll ever marry again. Honestly, I don't see that happening for me. And if it does, I'll be too old to have a baby, never mind being an old mom. I don't want that. I'm thinking about this now, something I should have done with my ex-husband."

"And be a single parent?" The doctor shakes her head. "It's a hard job. Motherhood is tough, and when you don't have support from your partner, it's even tougher."

"I want to be a mom so bad. I feel like I've missed my chance, you know?" Her eyes sting as the realization surfaces. If only she and Timothy had tried harder, wanted it more. If she'd exhausted her efforts, she wouldn't be here.

The first time she got pregnant she was ecstatic. They'd tried for three months and finally it happened. The hardest part was keeping it a secret for the recommended twelve weeks. Carla felt so good and was exercising regularly and eating well. It came as a surprise to her when she started spotting at work. Panic struck and she knew something was wrong. She had only been pregnant for eight weeks; she was still getting used to the idea of motherhood. She went to her doctor, who told her that there was nothing he could do, and to rest. The news devastated her. She couldn't eat or sleep and was stressed. She lost the baby. Timothy reassured her that they would try again. Six months later, they were pregnant again. Carla was determined to keep this baby. She took sick days to rest and took multivitamins and ate lots of dark green vegetables—did everything in her power to prevent another miscarriage. She couldn't smile any wider and laugh any louder. This was what she was missing in her life. A baby. It would be everything she needed to make her feel complete. Carla wouldn't know if that was true because at twelve weeks she was once again faced with disappointment. She was crushed at losing another pregnancy.

She had just told her family and friends the news because she was going to burst with excitement if she didn't, unable to keep the secret any longer. Her mom screaming about the first grandchild and the new bed she would buy for future sleepovers and the savings plan she wanted to start. Gabby insisting on being called auntie.

The tears fell harder and faster, making it more difficult than the first miscarriage. She couldn't possibly go through it again. Carla tried to stop focusing on having a baby and concentrated on work, but her mind would always go back to motherhood and what might have been. Nothing had ever stopped her before, but this was out of her control and she hated it.

"Are you dating anyone?" the doctor asks.

"No."

"May I suggest you put the idea of a baby aside and start dating? If being a mom is what you really want, you need to think about your baby and what he needs. Two parents are ideal for a healthy child, although it's not always the case," she says, grinning, revealing a dimple in her cheek. "At least trying is the solution."

"What happens if I can't conceive? I'm afraid the older I get, the harder it will be, and honestly, those two miscarriages were the most devastating times of my life."

"Of course they were."

"I don't ever want to experience that again, and if I can prevent it and learn if there's something wrong with me, then I can . . ." Carla pauses. Then what? Will she market herself as a woman who wants a baby and not a man? Will she be desperate for a man and not look for love the right way?

Tears fill her eyes. She wipes her finger across her eyelid and sniffles. "I've always wanted a family," she says.

Dr. Fossett hands her a Kleenex. "I have no doubt that you won't be a mom. You know, women tend to blame themselves for a miscarriage, when in fact, there is nothing wrong. It happens." She puts a hand in the air. "It's not to say it won't happen again. You're young. Healthy. You have a few years to think about this. Don't worry," she says. "Give it some time."

"When will I know if I can't have kids?"

"You won't until you start trying. If you're in a relationship and you both decide that having a baby is what you want, and if nothing is happening, then please come back to see me. We'll look at the problem, if there is one. For now, relax, have fun, date and give it time. Okay?"

Carla gets back to work, forcing herself to forget about having a baby, but it seems worse now that she's not taking the next step and getting tested to see what problems, if any, were preventing her from carrying a baby to term. She doesn't want to date just anyone; the father of her baby has to be someone who wants a child as much as she does. He also has to be a man who loves her. Where is she going to find him? There's nobody at work she's interested in, and she's not sure if she wants to have a romantic relationship with someone she works with again.

Carla stares at her computer screen.

"What are you thinking about?" Timothy asks, approaching her with a magazine.

"Nothing," she says, tightening her lips.

"Did you see this?" He points to the cover. "Lawrence Grattan is a hotshot poker player. He's also a new dad. Unfortunately, his daughter was born premature."

Carla gasps and places her hand to her mouth.

"He'd be a good one to interview for the Warriors Heroes Campaign. Although his family is still in Pittsburgh, I think."

"I'll be at the campaign."

"Great. I'm done reading this, if you want it."

"Sure." Carla places the magazine on a pile of papers by her computer. She looks up to see Timothy still standing there with a blank stare on his face, as though he's deep in thought. Carla knows that look of dread, like something is bugging him. She's afraid to ask him what but knows he's going to tell her because when he has something on his mind, he says it, even if it's not the right time or thing to say.

She leans back in her chair waiting, tapping her pen on her desk as though signaling him to hurry up. Why does he think she has so much time on her hands?

"I was cleaning out the spare room and found this in the back of the closet on the floor," Timothy says, reaching into his pocket and pulling out a small silver object.

Carla's eyes widen. "I don't remember the last time I saw that." She studies the heart charm.

"I don't think you want it."

"Yes, I do," she says and lowers her head, rubbing her lips together. "Why wouldn't I?"

Timothy shrugs. "Because it was from me. Good thing I asked."

"I like it. Besides, it was a gift," she reminds him. "It fell off my bracelet. I wondered where it went." She looks up at him with softened eyes. "Thanks."

"Sure." He takes a step away from her, stops and then asks, "It doesn't mean anything to you, does it?"

She thinks about his question. It meant something to her at the time, when they were married. But now?

"A little, yes," she answers. "But I always liked it."

Timothy nods and grins.

Carla's phone lights up, catching her attention. "I better get this," she says, reaching for the receiver as Timothy walks off.

"Carla Sinclair!"

"I'm calling on behalf of youth soccer. We have a tournament this Saturday. It would be great if you could come out. The teams have worked really hard. . . ."

Carla writes down the information. Another call comes in about a girls' softball team. When she has twenty minutes to escape, she heads downstairs to the cafeteria to grab a latte. The afternoon lull has staff drifting in for a caffeinated beverage before the first show at five.

Carla hands the cashier some change and proceeds to the next counter for a lid.

"I'm interviewing Lawrence Grattan," Ryan says proudly, reaching for a straw for his blended coffee. He peels the paper off and flicks it into the garbage.

Carla turns to him, her mouth slightly agape.

"How? Have you asked?" Ryan leans into her so that his shirtsleeve brushes against her blouse. He took the words out of her mouth.

Why does he constantly challenge me?

"I was fishing for a story, reading up on articles, when I came across one about Grattan."

"Let me guess," Carla says, walking away from the counter, Ryan in stride with her. "It was a magazine article?"

"Yeah! Yeah! Did you read it?"

"Not yet. It's on my desk."

"So, what do you think?" he asks.

"About interviewing him?"

"Yeah."

"I guess," Carla says with a shrug. "He's going to be at the Warriors Heroes Campaign and I was going to interview him there."

"About that campaign—am I supposed to be there?" Ryan asks.

"I guess, if you're interviewing Grattan. Might as well set it up then."

"Good idea. That's great. Yes, I can do that then," Ryan says with a leap in his step. "I'm off with Gary to get a few clips of a boys' basketball game. Apparently there's a kid on the team who's getting international attention."

"Have fun," she says, bringing her latte to her mouth.

Devin plunks himself down on his bed. Ten days on the road makes him appreciate his own place. Even though there's nobody to come home to, he relaxes, having three days off to refresh before playing five home games. The play-offs start next month and there's a good chance his team will make it. What he would give to actually win the Stanley Cup, to wear the winning title on his finger. Some women dreamed of weddings; hockey players dreamed of winning the cup. It was that simple.

Devin picks up his phone on the second ring, always a thrust in his voice when he says hello.

"Hi, Devin," the female voice purrs. "It's Brittany. Remember me?"

"Sure." How could he forget? He met her through another player's wife. Brittany had long red hair and a pierced nose. She was anything but ordinary. One night at Buckley's they'd shared nachos, and she'd invited him back to her place. He'd accepted. Ever since their brief encounter, she's been calling, wanting more. He hadn't been with someone so fierce and fast under the covers for a long time; it left him wondering if she was even enjoying herself enough to call again. But she had.

"Are you up for company?" she asks. "We could meet somewhere, or I could come over if you're not up to going out."

He never invited girls over to his place. He liked to keep that much of a distance between him and women. He liked his privacy.

"I just got home from being on the road," Devin says.

"I know. That's why I'm calling." Her voice was sweet and innocent. "You don't play for a few days."

There was no hiding in this city.

"I can meet you at The Landing at nine-thirty," he suggests and hangs up the phone.

Devin can't remember the last time he asked a girl out. Maybe in ninth grade, when he asked Mary, a girl he'd had a crush on all year and finally had the courage to ask her to the dance. She'd turned him down.

He winces at the memory.

Devin turns on the TV while reading his text messages and comes across one he doesn't recognize. Usually he hits DELETE, but he notices in the subject line the words *sweeter* and *good luck*, so he reads it thoroughly. Before looking up the mysterious number, he thinks it sounds like it's from Carla, but Devin didn't remember giving her his number. He didn't give out his number to just anyone; he'd learned that when he played junior and girls would be calling him at all hours. At first it was flattering, having disposable phone numbers, but then it became annoying, distracting him from his game. He'd desperately wanted and needed to prove himself to get noticed by agents; hooking up with girls had become secondary.

Devin watches Carla talk about what's coming up on sports before going to commercial. Her fair skin brings out her sharp blue eyes. They suck him in every time. He can't take his eyes off the screen. When she wore a blouse or a low-cut shirt on air, Devin took in her whole physique and could only imagine how perky her breasts were and how his hands would fit on her hips. She looks better in person, he muses, watching the screen change over to a Windex commercial.

Maybe he should call her, but then what would he say? He squeezes his phone in his hands, staring at it as though it would decide for him. Should he ask her if she's going to interview him? He promised she could interview him when he got back from his road trip. She followed the team, so there was no hiding from her, and no excuses that would warrant him an extension.

Should he call? Shouldn't he?

If she wants me, she can call me.

If only she wanted him, then maybe he would pick up the phone. He doubted she did. A woman like Carla had to be taken. Not that it mattered; he wouldn't get involved with her anyway. She's a reporter and probably talks a lot. The last thing he needs is to talk about his privacy.

Besides, the interview would only serve the purpose of enlightening Carla. What would be in it for him? She could interview him at a game if she wanted to. What questions would she have for him anyway? He clutches his jaw at the question a reporter in Florida had asked. What was it like growing up playing hockey with your mom at every game? He answered, remembering how she made him feel. "That question is for my mom. I don't answer personal questions. I play hockey." His answer made the newspaper and Devin was considered rude. Devin thinks of his dad. How does a guy leave his family? Alcohol problem or not, no one deserves to be deserted; he left without a return date or contact information to keep in touch. It's like dying and being left with a ghost. Where is his dad these days?

Devin throws his phone aside and makes a sandwich for dinner. He sits at his island counter, taking a bite and thumbing through his mail. Utility bill, a real-estate flyer, junk ads and another letter. He picks up the white envelope and places it in a kitchen drawer, along with all the others. It was addressed to his mom and forwarded to him. He has no desire to read it. Maybe one day but not today. He was better off without his dad. He's come this far without him, why would he need him at thirty years old? Devin rubs his eye, forgetting that he has a cut on his cheekbone. His hand feels the raised scar. He'd taken a good hit, but it was worth it. It was the best he'd played in weeks. Maybe opportunity or the luck of the draw. Whatever it is, he plans to play hard in the hope of staying on as a fan favorite, including Carla's.

Devin puts his plate in the dishwasher and settles in his living room, picking through the boxes left by the moving company that he hadn't opened yet. There isn't much to them; after all, he hasn't had a permanent home in which to hang pictures and buy accent furniture.

Now that he knows he's here for six years, he decides that opening every box is a good way to make this new city feel like home. He opens the box labeled OLD STUFF. Devin peels the packing tape off the top and puts his hand inside to fish for the first object. It's wrapped in tissue paper. Must be breakable. He rips the paper off to find a glass lantern and holds it up to the light. A little dusty, and the tea light is melted inside. Probably hasn't been used since he played in Ottawa. He had a small condo there with a deck. Some nights he would light the candle and relax in a chair, taking in the city.

Devin puts the lantern down and pulls out a blue box. His heart picks up pace as he opens the lid. He had forgotten about this box. It used to sit on a bookshelf in his room when he was a boy. It holds memories only a parent would treasure. A mold of his footprint when he was a month old, a clipping of fine hair and a silver rattle. Stuff he doesn't need. He holds the rattle in his hand, imagining tiny fingers shaking it. A baby. How great would that experience be if he ever had the opportunity to be a dad? To see what his child would look like and grow up in a home that had two parents. Secure. Loved. Happy.

Devin closes the box and carries it into the spare room. It's more of a storage space, a place he wasn't sure what to do with. When he bought the house, he thought the five-bedroom bungalow was the right size, considering it had a game room with a bar and a Jacuzzi. Maybe the house was too big for a single guy who is constantly on the road. Thankfully, he has a housecleaner who comes every week, and a gardener to keep up his maple trees and wild flowers. It's the perfect house for a family.

He shuts off the TV and decides to take a shower and get ready to meet Brittany at The Landing. He takes out a pair of jeans and a shirt. He could call her and cancel, say he's just too tired from being on the road, that he needs to catch up on his sleep. Is there a future with Brittany? He likes her, but not enough to want to see her every weekend.

His phone rings as he takes off his shirt. The shower is running hot, steaming up the bathroom. He picks up his phone to see the number. It's a local one, but he can't place it. Whoever is calling can wait. He undoes his belt buckle and loosens his jeans so they drop to the floor. His phone beeps, indicating a message. He wonders if it's one of his teammates, but then, he doesn't talk to any of them on the phone that much.

He listens to the message. It's Carla. His chest tightens as he hears her voice. Sweet yet to the point. "If you're available for an interview, I'll be in the office tomorrow afternoon," she says, leaving her number.

"Damn!" Devin says, putting down his phone. "I have practice tomorrow afternoon." One of these days they'll talk. He wants to talk. It's as close as he's going to get to her. He's sure of it. So sure that he tries to forget about her as he gets ready for his date, but the petite blonde keeps entering his mind. The only way to forget is to think about Brittany and what was in store for tonight.

His phone rings again and Devin jumps to answer it. "Hello?"

"Uh, hi, Devin?"

"Yeah!"

"It's Carla. Sorry to bother you. I just called and realized that tomorrow afternoon won't work for me. . . . I was seeing if you were available for an interview. . . . I know it's last minute. . . . Is there a day that works best for you?"

"Next week is fine. The afternoon is usually good, except tomorrow, I have a game."

"Right! I knew that. Okay, we can look at the day after—" She stops in midsentence and the line goes quiet.

"Carla?"

"Yes?"

"I thought I lost the call."

"I'm looking at my day planner."

"You can call me back with a time," he says.

"Sure. Sorry. I probably caught you at a bad time. You're probably out, it being Friday."

"It's fine. Really. Um, we could do it Monday. You work Monday?"

"Uh-huh."

"Are you working right now?"

"Yes."

"Do you always work late on Friday nights?"

"It's not too late," she says.

"It's nine o'clock," he says. "Can't imagine much goes on in sports at this time, unless it's a hockey game."

"It's nine o'clock!" She gasps. "Sorry, I didn't realize the time. I wouldn't have called you so late."

Devin laughs.

"I had a bunch of stuff to do and lost track of time. We can finish this up on Monday, then."

"We could do this now," he says.

"Now? No way! Not over the phone. I need a cameraman and I don't have one. Look, I shouldn't have called so late. My apologies. Can I meet you at the rink on Monday before practice?"

"Yeah."

"Okay, great. That's perfect."

"Carla?"

"Yes?"

"How late were you planning on working? Is there anything going on in sports right now?"

"Well, not really. I had other things to do."

"Like what?"

"It's not just about reporting. . . . I had research to do and other stuff. . . ."

"Research?"

"There's stuff to look up and stories to find."

"Right."

"You don't believe me."

"I do! I just think you choose to work instead of getting out."

"I like my job."

"I don't doubt that." He laughs. "Do you want to grab a drink?"

She is slow to respond. "When?"

"Now."

"I don't know." She sighs.

"I can meet you close to where you are."

"Do you even know where the TV station is?"

"I have GPS."

"I better not. I'll see you at practice on Monday, then."

"I thought if we met up for a quick drink, then you could get to know me better."

"Why would I want to do that?"

The line is quiet.

"Sorry, I didn't mean it the way it sounded," she says.

"You know who I am, but you don't know me," he tells her.

"I have a good idea," she says.

"That's the thing," Devin says, running his hand over his head. "You say things on the air like you know me."

"I do?"

"You tell people how much I make like it's a bad thing."

"It's public knowledge," she says and pauses. "It's a bad thing if a player doesn't perform well."

"Are you saying I'm not performing well?"

"Let's agree that you're doing better here than I thought you would."

"Are you always this critical?"

"I'm doing my job."

"You're still critical."

"I call it the way I see it."

"Next time, can you say something positive?"

"Like what?"

"Look, I'm trying to win fans, not lose them."

"If you want my advice, show up to every corporate event and talk to me. I'll interview you. It's the only way people will get to know you."

"Do you want to get to know me?"

The line is quiet for a few seconds. Carla hums before she answers. "I do. I want to know what kind of player the Warriors acquired."

Doesn't she want to get to know me personally?

"Set something up," he says.

"I will."

"Okay! Call me."

Devin hangs up, wondering if he'll hear from Carla or not.

Chapter 5

Carla settles into her desk and turns on her computer as Timothy saunters over.

They make eye contact and he stops to talk. "Good weekend?"

She takes out her cell phone and places it on her desk, along with a pack of mints. "It was okay. How about you?" She looks up to meet his golden brown eyes. They used to draw her in and make her feel full, completed, loved, and now those eyes are full of memories. A flashback of Timothy agreeing they should separate. It was after the second miscarriage. Carla had been devastated. Timothy hadn't comforted her the way she expected him to. After all, it was both their loss, yet he seemed to hold it together just fine, whereas Carla had to muster every ounce of energy to report the sports. She focused on work to get through the drama.

They put baby making aside so that Carla could have some time to heal. A month turned into two, two turned into four and four turned into six. During that time, in their second year of marriage, they drifted farther apart, unable to see each other's need to have a baby. The desire burned inside of Carla, fueling anger toward Timothy for not wanting it as much as she did. At seven months she was willing to try again, but their marriage wasn't the same. The closeness they once shared had shifted from loving to resentful. Carla tried to love him, but he too had become distant, probably because she always had baby on her mind. She tried putting the idea of motherhood aside to concentrate on her marriage. Timothy took her on a two-week Hawaiian vacation, sparking a quick cure, but once they were home, back on track with their lives, baby was again on Carla's mind. She didn't vocalize it as much as she had, holding in her excitement with every purchase of a pregnancy test.

Going into their third year of marriage and no baby, Carla wondered if it was ever going to happen. They began to argue more, and despite the bitterness she was feeling, she couldn't talk to Timothy the way she used to. They barely spoke and were like strangers living under the same roof. One night, Carla came home from work hungry for dinner. Timothy had grabbed a bite to eat when he was out and hadn't brought anything home for her. Out of frustration, she yelled at him, accusing him of being inconsiderate and a lousy husband, which led to her telling him she wanted out of their marriage. Timothy agreed and Carla told him she would be gone in the morning. It felt like the right thing to say and do, considering their third year of marriage was a complete lack of communication. Carla called her sister in tears, and Sadie welcomed her to stay with her until she found a place.

It wasn't a surprise to Sadie. She knew about the ups and downs of her marriage, and it didn't come as a surprise, although to her mom and dad it had. They were torn. Timothy was a part of her family, and to them it was a shock. A year of separation became the norm, and Carla asked Timothy for a divorce. He didn't hesitate, telling her it was for the best. He didn't fight for her the way she'd expected, making her more bitter and therefore satisfied about ending their relationship.

Tears had filled his eyes and hers as well, knowing at that moment that they would never be the same. He tried calculating time apart. *If we give it six months, maybe we'll be back to how it was.* "We need time," he had said. But time had made things worse. The more time spent apart, the more of a realization that they didn't need each other the way they'd hoped. Acquaintances were all they were.

"Good. Good. Um, you know our bedroom furniture?"

She blinks, looks at him sharply. "You mean *your* bedroom furniture?" she asks, folding her arms at her desk as she looks up at her ex-husband. "I got the couch and table, remember?"

"Yeah." He shoves his hands in his front jeans pockets. "Do you want the night tables and dresser? I want to ask you before I get rid of it."

"I hated that set!" she snarls. "It's ugly."

"You agreed to buy it," he says. He's always so calm and composed. It's a wonder he didn't explode when she asked to keep the apartment.

She ended up moving into a town house anyway. "Couldn't have been that bad. You slept with it for three years."

"I had no choice; you kept telling me it was a great deal and we needed a set because nothing matched."

He nods his head and smirks. "It's not that bad. Still looks like new."

"It's bad." She rolls her eyes. "Trust me. The dresser looks like it belonged to my grandmother." She opens her notebook. "Actually, her stuff is nicer."

"I guess that's a no, then. All right."

Carla takes out a mint from the metal tin on her desk and pops it into her mouth. "Why are you getting rid of it?"

He throws his hands up. "I don't know. No reason."

"No reason?" She stares at him.

"I'm getting a new set." He walks off.

"See? It is bad." She laughs to herself and opens her notebook, making notes of upcoming stories to follow and reminders of what interviews to do.

"Boss!"

Carla looks up at Ryan, sporting dress pants and a button-down shirt. "The Warriors are practicing this morning. I'll interview Devin Miller, if you want."

"No, that's okay. I'll be there," Carla tells him. "I'm leaving in a few minutes."

"You're going to practice? I thought you only hit the games."

"I go to their practices. Just not regularly."

"Oh, okay. I have another interview to do not far from there; are you sure?"

Carla nods. "Yeah. Thanks."

"Just thought you had other things to do and that it would free up your day."

"I'm fine," Carla snaps. Her phone rings. Ryan walks away shaking his head.

She takes a call from someone wanting her to come out to a high-school lacrosse game, and after carefully explaining that they only cover amateurs if an individual is picked up to go pro, Carla spots Pamela staring at her own painted pink nails, brushing them with her fingers, as if deciding whether they need cutting.

Carla hangs up the phone. "Pamela! Hi!"

"A bunch of us are going for lunch, if you care to join us. It would be great if you could. . . . We'll be across the street, so you can meet us there after the news. . . ." Pamela's hair is pinned back with strands of blond hair circling her face. Her long-sleeved blouse and full-length skirt make her look tall and much older than her midthirties.

"Sure," Carla answers. Maybe getting to know Pamela is a good idea. She seems to want to be friends, although she's not sure why. "I'll try to make it. I'm running out to a Warriors practice right now."

"That's wonderful," Pamela says. "I'll save you a seat."

Carla nods. "Okay." She watches Pamela pivot and walk off with a bounce in her step and gets up from her desk, grabs her light jacket and heads outdoors to meet Randy, already sitting in the station van, waiting for her.

They drive to the Dome for the Warriors practice.

"Is it just Devin Miller you're interviewing?" Gary asks.

"Yeah, and maybe Lawrence Grattan, if he's willing. He's supposed to fly back to Pittsburgh to his family for a few days."

"His daughter is sick."

"Apparently doing better."

"It's the worst when you're a parent, seeing your kid sick," he says.

"I wouldn't know, but I can imagine."

Gary changes lanes and returns his hand to his forehead, looking ahead. "My son had pneumonia and was in the hospital. That was scary enough."

"I bet."

"He was our child who always got hurt. His mother worried sick about him." He pauses. "He once fell off a playground structure and broke his arm. He got stitches once, playing street hockey." Gary shakes his head. "Kids."

Carla flips open her notebook, scanning her questions for Devin.

"Are you interviewing before or after practice?"

"After. It gives me the opportunity to note who's playing and what happened at practice."

Gary stares ahead.

"I'm interested in speaking to Devin."

"Is there something between the two of you?" He looks over.

"No." She wisps her bangs from her face. "I'm curious about why the Warriors signed him when what they really need is a scoring line."

"What do you expect to hear from Devin?"

She glances down at her questions and taps her finger on the page. "I want to know how he's fitting in—"

"He seems to be doing just fine. The Warriors have been on a winning streak since Devin joined the team. Don't you think?"

"I want him to talk."

"And there's nothing between the two of you?" Gary looks over, his eyes narrow on hers in a quick glance before he returns his eyes to the road.

"Nothing ever has happened. Nothing will," she says confidently. "I'm not interested, if that's what you're asking."

"Okay, okay," he says, raising a hand. "I'm looking out for you. It just seems like the two of you have something going. You talk about him a lot on the air."

"What's wrong with that? He's a hot topic."

"For you, maybe."

Carla's mouth is agape. "Doesn't anyone want to know about him and how he's doing on the team he wasn't planning on playing for?"

"That's what I'm saying. All hockey players make a lot of money."

"Yeah, but Devin has the top salary for all defensemen in the NHL. He should be scoring goals too."

"He does. His job is defending, and since he's been here, he's been doing his job."

Carla brings her lips together. Maybe she's making a big deal of nothing, but why should she let Devin get away with not being accountable for his paycheck?

"I know what you're trying to do," Gary says.

"You do?"

"You like him—"

"I do not!" she gasps.

"You're making a big deal about him for nothing. I'm wondering why you're not interviewing Mark Buckley, who's recovering from an injury."

"I think it's important that our audience has the facts about Devin, that's all," she says. "I'll interview others." She looks out her window.

"Like who?"

"I'm interviewing players at the Warriors Heroes Campaign this week."

"All I'm saying is you have to have fresh information. By now everyone in the city knows who Devin is and how much he makes. You need another angle."

Carla's face falls. She looks at her notes. Who else can she interview? And is it that obvious she wants to talk exclusively to Devin?

"Sorry. I shouldn't tell you how to do your job. You do a great job. I'm worried about you."

"Why?"

"There's talk about job shuffling."

"They wouldn't get rid of me."

"I don't think so. I want you to do your best. Wouldn't want you to lose your job."

"What have you heard?"

"Nothing, really. Not about anyone in particular."

Carla lets out a breath. "I hope not."

"You're safe."

"I'm not safe," she mumbles.

"No one is."

Carla looks away. If only she could ask Devin about his personal life without offending him.

Practice is close to finishing when they arrive at the Dome. Gary captures the players listening to Coach Steve Morrow's instructions and a breakout in play. Carla spots Devin's number-nineteen jersey on the opposite end of the ice. She's standing at the plexiglass watching, observing who's at practice and if there's anything that's changed. She focuses on Mark Buckley, skating in good response to his injury, and notes Lawrence Grattan fully immersed in making a play as he skates up to the boards.

Carla spots Devin skating down the ice, turning backward to defend his goalie. She stares at Devin as he cuts sharply to the boards. He looks up to make eye contact as he skates past.

Carla drops her hands to her sides, her notebook hanging by her fingers, hoping he'll skate back toward her to say hi, to acknowledge that she's there. *Why does he care?* she thinks. And why should she care if he knows her? Does he really want to get to know her, or is it all part of his scheme to build fan appreciation?

Practice is over. The players skate off.

"Let's go!" she tells Gary. "I'll grab Devin."

As they walk over to the bench, Carla searches for Devin but doesn't see him. Her eyes narrow, checking each player as they come off the ice.

"Where is he?" Gary asks.

"I . . . I don't know," she says, staring. "I didn't see him leave."

"Hey, Carla!" the assistant coach says. "Who are you here for?"

"Miller," she says directly. "Can you please tell him I want to speak to him? Devin is expecting me."

"He probably forgot."

"I don't think so," she says, looking over her shoulder at Gary. "In the meantime, let's see if we can have a word with Buckley."

"Lead the way," Gary calls out.

"Mark!" Carla says, rushing toward him. "A couple of questions for you."

He takes off his helmet and wipes his face with his hand.

"Your injury set you back six games. How do you feel today?" Carla asks, raising the microphone to his face.

"Good. I'm ready for tomorrow night's game."

"The Warriors lost against the Flames last time the teams met. Any strategies for tomorrow?"

"We have to get the puck to the net. Simple. Make smarter plays. . . ."

"What about defense?"

"Yeah." He shrugs. "The Flames dominated last game, tied us up in front of our net. We can't let them get past us. Defense will be on them."

"Thanks, Mark," Carla says, signs off and drops the microphone. "Let's go see where Devin is." Gary follows her in the direction of the locker room.

"Carla! Hi!" a voice says, approaching her with an extended hand. "It's good to finally meet you. I'm Keri, director of community events. We've spoken on the phone."

Carla smiles. "Yes. Hi! Haven't we met before?"

"Maybe at an event," she says.

"Will you be at the Warriors Heroes Campaign?"

"Yes! Of course!"

"Great! We'll see you then."

Carla looks past Keri to see which players are walking out of the dressing room.

"Can I get anyone for you?" Keri asks.

"I'm looking for Devin Miller. He said I could meet with him after practice."

"I saw him leave."

"You did? Are you sure?"

Keri nods. "Yeah, he's gone. You might be able to catch him."

Carla and Gary head down the long hallway, trying to spot a well-dressed man walking toward the exit.

"Carla!"

She hears Gary's voice but doesn't stop.

"Carla!"

She slows down and then stops, looks around and then at Gary.

He gets close to her. "He's not that important," Gary reassures her.

She opens her mouth to speak. Does she want to ask Devin about his dad? Would she ask if she had the opportunity? He's been playing here for two weeks now. What more can she ask him? It comes down to personal questions, and she doubts he's going to want to share. Carla drops her shoulders. "You're right."

"There's always next time," he says.

At the campaign? She'll have to forget about Devin until there's a real issue to be made. How can she possibly ask Devin about his dad without getting an emotional response? Does she care enough about him to leave him alone?

Carla gets back to the television station to check on a tape the length of a basketball game that was recorded that morning.

She walks down a hallway to the editing booths and turns left to where all the small rooms are lined up. Small televisions surround the closet space. The sliding door is open, so she steps inside. It's standing room only. "Kyle!" she says. "How did that game turn out? Do we have good footage of the winning basket? Ryan said it was a pretty shot."

Kyle pauses, one hand on the button, and turns his head. "Yeah, it was. Wanna see?"

"Yes, please."

"Let me finish this. Almost done."

Carla watches Kyle turn a wheel and press a couple of buttons. There's the basketball game on the screen, and Kyle visually runs through it to find the clip.

"Here you go," he says, his black parted hair sliding back and forth over his temples. He is wearing a faded KISS T-shirt and jeans.

Carla watches the screen and records the time so that she knows how long she has to talk about the game.

"Hard to believe about Elliot. His reporting was improving."

Carla's eyes narrow and she shakes her head. "What's wrong with him?"

"Nothing," Kyle says, focusing on the screen in front of him and pushing buttons without looking down at his hands. "He was let go."

Carla stares at the young rocker. "When did that happen?"

"This morning."

"I had no idea," she says, gasping. "Are you sure?"

"Yeah," he says, bobbing his head, staring at the screen, one hand on the dial. "Didn't you see your e-mail?"

"I must have missed that." She brings a finger to her lips, puzzled that she wasn't on top of the company news. "He's been here forever."

"I know."

"I wonder if it was a surprise. . . ." she says. "Who's going to cover the morning news?"

"I thought you were."

"You're joking!"

"I heard your name being passed around, but don't say anything. You didn't hear that from me."

"I won't say anything, but if Elliot's gone, Annalise will anchor by herself."

Kyle smirks. "She likes it that way. She probably had something to do with it."

"She doesn't have that much power. She's the morning news anchor!" Carla wants to laugh at her comment. She controls her voice and her thoughts, remembering the sliding door of the booth is open and anyone can eavesdrop.

"There you go. All done," Kyle says. The screen is black.

"Thank you." She stops, puts her hand out to hold the handle. "Have you heard anything about the sports department?" she asks wearily. Could they be cleaning shop? Freshening up the station with new faces? She likes this place and can't imagine being anywhere else, unless the Sports National position comes up, which would be an excellent opportunity to showcase what she has to offer.

"Well . . ." Kyle says, dragging out the word as if he's contemplating what to tell her.

"What is it?" she demands, stepping back into the booth. "You heard something? Really?"

"I'm sure it wasn't true. There's always talk going on, you know that."

"It's business, I know. Tell me!"

"I heard they want another guy reporting sports and want to move you to weekends."

"What?" she gasps. "They can't do that! I have seniority."

"Or do the morning news." Kyle gives her a sympathetic look. "You might have a choice."

"There's never a choice. Ever!" Carla brings her hand to her mouth. "Who did you hear this from?"

He pauses. "I can't say. He told me not to tell. It's all speculation anyway. You know how this business is. One minute someone gets fired, and then three or more follow."

"It's true. It starts that way and then it becomes real. I'm going to lose my job!" *They want to ax me and keep Ryan, I bet.* "What happens if they do get rid of me? Where will I go?" She faces him. "I like my job. I don't want to change positions."

They fall silent, and Carla thinks about it. Where would she go if she was fired? "Who else knows about this?"

"I thought everyone knew there was going to be a shake-up. The company newsletter said ratings were low. If we don't do better in the spring, then you bet there'll be a firing spree."

"You think?"

"You watch. It'll happen," Kyle says.

"You're speculating."

He shrugs. "I guess we'll see in a few weeks."

Carla returns to her desk. What if she gets fired? What if Ryan takes over her job? Was that why Timothy told her about that sports job back east? Is he looking out for her? Nobody wants to see someone get fired. Does he know something she doesn't?

Her stomach is uneasy. She can't think straight. Maybe she should apply for jobs just in case. She doesn't even know what's out there. Her job has been somewhat secure. She's been happy here. Content.

Her phone rings and she takes herself away from e-mail.

"Hi, Carla. It's Keith Miller."

"Oh, hi."

"When are you interviewing Devin?"

Do I tell him I tried, but Devin doesn't want to speak to me?

"I'd like to come with you."

"I don't think that's a good—"

"I really want to be there. To see him. . . ."

"I never allow tagalongs."

"I'm his dad! It's not as if he doesn't know who I am."

"Then why don't you talk to him yourself?"

She can hear his breath blow out, like he's going to get all teary-eyed on her. Then he recovers. "I haven't seen him for over twenty years. I don't want him to go into shock."

"Must be some story," Carla says, softening her voice.

"Not something I want to discuss."

"Why has it been so long?" She scribbles on her notebook. She'll have questions for Devin when she sees him.

"Time passes too quickly." He stops, as though he's thinking about what to say next. "I don't know where the time went."

"Why now? Why do you want to contact Devin?"

He sucks in a breath. "It takes courage when your son is more successful than you are."

"He didn't start off that way," she says.

"Well, no."

"If I had a child who was successful, I'd be proud of their accomplishments." Carla thinks about her mom. Was her mom proud of her? She didn't really know. Ever since she went off to college, she'd been on her own, working. Planning her life the way she saw fit, never needing her parents' okay because she was okay. She knew what she was doing with her life. She hadn't needed a road map to tell her that she had to climb the corporate ladder, get married and have babies. She married Timothy and expected pregnancy to just happen. After two years of marriage and two miscarriages, she'd panicked and thought something was wrong. She'd agonized about when her period was due, when she was most fertile, and kept track of when she and Timothy made love. Her life became a schedule. She wouldn't have surprises during her weeks; she wanted a baby and was trying everything in her power to make it happen. Carla had gotten caught up in controlling everything she ate, power foods to help with development, prenatal vitamins and eating only pure ingredients because she wanted the healthiest baby she could make. After three years of trying, Timothy had started to come home later, reheat his dinners and go to bed. They began to lose their connection, that spark that was so important. Working together in a demanding career had its consequences. They began to only talk about work. They didn't have time to socialize, to be a couple anymore. Their life fell apart, and Carla blamed herself for not trying harder when she loved Timothy but couldn't live with him.

"Let me talk to Devin and ask him," she suggests.

"No! Please don't! He doesn't want to speak with me."

"Then what do you want me to do?" Carla asks.

"I need to see him."

"But what if he doesn't want to see you?"

"I have something very important to talk to him about."

"Do you want me to relay the message?"

"No." His voice fades. "Can you give him my number? Tell him it's important. Tell him I've had twenty-four years to think about it."

Chapter 6

Devin holds the phone up to his ear, walking around his condo as though inspecting his place. His couch has barely been sat on, his stove never used. It's his washer and dryer he can't live without. "Look, Mom, I told you. I don't want to talk to him."

"But he's your dad."

"Technically, yes, but I haven't seen him in twenty-four years and I don't care if I ever do."

"You don't mean that! I think it's time to put everything behind you and at least meet with him."

"Why does he want to talk to me now?" Devin asks, a question that's been on his mind for weeks, ever since his mom first told him that his dad had been in contact with her. Was it because he was a well-known hockey player? Or because he's considered a celebrity in his new city? He's heard those stories before, relatives making contact to get free stuff or to tell people they know each other. Devin wasn't going to be a part of that scam.

"I have nothing to say to him."

"I'm sure you have lots to say," she says.

"Nothing nice."

"I'm sure if you thought about it, there are a lot of questions you have for him." Her voice was pleading and sincere.

"Why are you so forgiving?"

She sighs. Takes a breath and says, "I'm happy. I hope he is too."

"I wish I had that in me," Devin admits. "I can't let go of what he did to you, to us."

"One day you will. Healing takes time."

Those words lingered with Devin long after he hung up the phone.

He was curious as to why his dad wanted to talk to him. The only reason was because Devin was somebody now.

"I'll think about it," Devin says.

"That means no."

"Come on, Mom. I don't want to talk to him now, but I will. One day, I'm sure."

"Don't let it be too much longer. You need to talk to him; at least put that conversation behind you."

He knows his mom is right, but he can't get past the idea of asking his dad why he was such a jerk, why he hadn't fought for his family. Any good man should be able to fight for the people he loves and work to make their family proud. Not a coward, walking out and not coming back because he had issues. He never resolved them and made them Devin and his mom's problem.

The thought of his dad made him mad. His blood boiled. He was fierce, thinking about Keith Miller and what he might say to him if he ever met him.

What would be the first thing he'd want to say? That question sat in his mind for years. When he was younger, he wanted to ask, *Why did you miss my birthday?* Expecting him to walk in the door after dinner, Devin had dreamed of the day his dad asked for an apology. By the time he turned twelve, he refused to call him Dad. It was Keith. He didn't deserve to be called Dad. After all, dads didn't leave their kids.

"Okay, Mom," Devin says, changing the subject. "Are you planning on coming up for a game?"

"I'd like to."

"Let me know when you can make it and I'll get you tickets."

"Paul would like that. I'd like to see you. I miss you."

"Miss you too, Mom."

"Are you getting enough sleep?"

"For sure!"

"Eating right?"

"Always."

"Okay, son. Are you seeing anyone? You need a woman to take care of you."

"I can take care of myself," Devin says. "Come on, Mom. I've been on my own for twelve years."

"It's time for you to settle down and have home-cooked meals, someone to watch over you."

"One day."

"I've heard that enough. You need to find someone. You're thirty years old, time to find a nice woman to settle down with."

"I just got here. We'll see what Vancouver holds for me."

"A lot more, if you let it."

Devin drives to Children's Hospital to take part in the annual Warriors Heroes Campaign. He had only found out about the event while on the plane to Boston for their road trip. Anytime kids were involved with hockey organizations, it was a big event. He wonders if Carla will be there. His back straightens and he taps his hand hard on the steering wheel. How will she react to him now, since he didn't show up after practice for an interview? She probably had other players to interview and forgot about talking to him. He couldn't bring himself to talk to her. He didn't want his new team to get any ideas about the two of them. He can't help the silly grin on his face when he sees her. He's never been good at asking a girl out. Will she be mad about standing her up?

He feels stupid about the night at Buckley's, telling her he wants her when she just wants to talk to him, all because of his job.

He parks his Range Rover and heads into the nonemergency entrance, taking the elevator to see a little boy who gets excited with every visit Devin makes. He walks into the room. "Hey, buddy! How are you today?"

"Good," the boy answers. His eyes follow Devin to his bed.

"I brought you something," Devin says, handing him a bag.

The boy whips out the hockey magazine and a pack of trading cards. "Cool! Thanks," Jason says, his eyes skimming the gifts.

"I wasn't sure if you collected cards. I used to have boxes of them when I was young. I think my mom has them in her attic."

"That's cool."

Devin makes small talk and then heads downstairs, where he's needed.

"Miller!"

"Hey, Price, how's it going?" Devin asks. "You know where to go?"

"Yeah, follow me. I'm going that way."

"Perfect."

Devin strides through the hall wearing black dress pants and a button-down shirt. This was the dress code whenever making public appearances for work. Everyone who passes them smiles or looks at them as recognizable faces.

"In here," the player says, walking through the propped-open doors to a line of tables set up with phones and name cards for the people who will be answering the calls for pledges. It's busy, with people coming and going, clusters of them talking among themselves. There are cameras set up and a crowd of people from the organization, as well as from the media and the hospital.

"Devin?" a male reporter calls out. "Can I get a word with you?"

He saunters over to the camera crew. From a side glance, a woman with dirty blond hair and a booming voice makes Devin stop in his tracks. He watches how she flicks her hair behind her head and laughs with Alex Price, a veteran player who knows a thing or two about talking to the ladies.

"Devin?" the male reporter calls again, walking toward him with a microphone.

"Ah, yeah, yeah." Devin scratches his neck and looks once more at Carla before giving the guy his attention.

"Can we get a few words?"

Devin nods. He had to push himself to come today. He wasn't in the mood, knowing Carla would be here, but it's for sick kids, and that's what got him here today.

The reporter fiddles with the cord, straightening it out in front of him and bringing the microphone up to his mouth. "Good to have you with us today, Devin. The Warriors Heroes is a great cause, helping children and their families seek medical treatment when they don't have the funds."

Devin continues to nod.

"You gave one little boy your hockey stick after your last home game."

"That was something," Devin recalls, rubbing his chin.

"It was a generous thing to do," the reporter says, staring at the television set up beside the cameraman. "His name is Miles and he's an outpatient here."

"Is that right?"

"Before being diagnosed with type two diabetes, he was an active kid playing hockey; you're his hero."

Devin sucks in a breath as he sees the boy staring at him, with a missing front tooth displaying a smile so big it pulls at his heart. It always amazes him how kids react to him.

"Come here, Miles," the reporter says, pulling him closer with an extended arm. "You get to meet your hero."

Devin never thought of himself as a hero. All he does is play hockey. His stepbrother is a firefighter; he's a real hero.

What should I say to this boy? Devin thinks as he smiles back at the toothless grin and then at the reporter, who needs to fill in the silence. He could ask him about school or what he likes to do at home. Thankfully, the reporter saves him.

"Miles, what did you do with the hockey stick?" the reporter asks.

"It's in my room," he answers, staring at his shoes and then at Devin. "My dad put it up on my wall."

"Very good."

"My cousin wants it, but I told him he can't have it," the boy says, scuffing his feet.

Devin watches the boy's expression.

"You're doing better, Miles?" the reporter asks.

He nods and stares at the floor. "I have lots of homework."

"So you're back in school? That's great! You brought your parents here?"

Miles's mom and dad step up to the camera. His mom reaches out to touch her son's shoulder.

"How has the journey been for you as a family?" the reporter asks.

"It's been tough," the dad says. "Between doctor appointments and school . . ."

Devin side glances in Carla's direction but can't see her. He looks the other way as casually as possible, brushes his finger across his chin. His eyes wander past the parents, curious, wondering where she is and wanting one more look at her peach-colored lips.

"Isn't that right, Devin?" the reporter asks.

"Pardon?"

"You donated a sum of money to Warriors Heroes to help with families like Miles's to pay for accommodations while they're here from out of town."

"It's the least I can do."

"Thank you," the mother says, tearing up. "Without your help, I don't know what we would have done. You're our angel!" The lady throws her arms around Devin's middle. "Thank you," she says again, looking him in the eye before letting go. The dad gives Devin a firm handshake.

Devin holds out his hand to the little boy. "Hang in there." He doesn't know what else to say to Miles. He knows by the look on the child's face that he too was thankful for what Devin had done.

Devin walks away, shaken by the family he touched yet aware of the magnitude of his contribution, how much he has helped.

"Did I see a tear in your eye?"

Devin stops, looks sideways and beams at the blue-eyed beauty holding a clipboard by her side. "Do you want to do that interview now?"

"No way!" Carla protests. "You don't want to talk anyway. I respect that." She turns away.

"Carla! Wait! Sorry. I didn't mean to disappear on you after practice. You weren't waiting around just for me, right?"

Carla purses her lips.

"You didn't have anyone else to talk to?" He smirks. He notices her eyes drift past him. "I guess you did. Sorry."

"I won't ask you again about an interview," she says.

"We'll talk next practice. Promise."

She stares at him with uncertainty.

"Promise," he repeats.

"I know why you didn't want to talk."

Devin's eyes widen.

"People will start talking. They'll think I have a thing for you."

"I thought you did." He watches her cheeks deepen with color. He waits for her to clam up, and changes the subject now that he's put her on the spot.

"Just a little bit. It will pass with time."

He's tongue-tied. What can he say to that? He's always the one with the last word.

"And if it doesn't?" he asks, because his curiosity has gotten the better of him. What he would give to have one night with her. That's all it would be, though, he tells himself. She's too bossy and opinionated for there to be anything more.

"It will," she assures him. "Guaranteed!"

"Carla!" A voice catches her attention and she looks away. "I've got the family you were looking for."

"Perfect," she says to the director and shoots Devin heightened brows as she makes her escape.

Devin whispers "'Bye," staring at her legs where the hem of her skirt meets her thigh. His eyes follow her around the room, talking to some people and then moving on to the next.

"Devin?"

He quickly looks toward the voice calling him over.

"Are you ready? I need you over here," one of the campaign employees says. "You'll be answering the phone."

Devin scratches his head. Nobody told him he'd be taking pledges; he thought he was just showing up.

"Have you done this before?"

"Once, when I played in Carolina, I was a part of a telethon."

"Nothing to it," the guy says. "Here are the pledge forms, pens, and if you need help with anything, we'll be hanging around; just look for someone in an orange T-shirt."

"Thanks. When does this start? Do I have time to get a coffee?"

"If you can make it back here in ten minutes. Phone lines will be open then."

Devin looks at the tables beginning to fill up, mostly with women. "Are you Buckley's wife?"

"Yes," she says, holding out her hand. "I'm Jen." She sits down.

"Where's Mark?"

"He may pop by later."

Devin squints his eyes. "I'm the only player answering phones."

"You have to get yourself a girlfriend."

Devin laughs to himself as he walks off to find a cup of coffee; not that he needs one, but he doesn't know what to do with himself without staring at Carla interviewing a family across the room. He walks past her, his eyes fixated on her slender legs. He watches her bend down to the little girl, who is shy and cradling her teddy bear. She puts an arm around the girl and brings her in for a hug. Devin doesn't know why he freezes at that particular moment, but standing only ten feet from her, he can smell her ginger and fruity skin, or is that his imagination?

"Devin?" Carla asks, waving her hand, directing him over. "Come on over here!"

Devin does what he's told, cautiously stepping closer, aware of the big lights and the cameraman focusing on him.

"This is Shelby," Carla introduces. "She's a Warriors fan."

Naturally, Devin thinks. Or her parents are.

"Shelby is seven years old," Carla says, patting the girl's shoulder. "She's had a heart transplant and is doing well today, thanks to the Warriors Heroes Campaign. Shelby was able to get treatment while her mom stayed with her."

Devin stares at this little girl, who in his mind doesn't really seem like a seven-year-old; but then, what did he know? He was just thankful his organization could help.

"Shelby has something for you to sign," Carla says.

The girl looks to her mom, who hands her a rolled-up Warriors T-shirt.

Devin takes the shirt as Carla signs off the air. "I'll have to find a pen," he says, checking his pants pockets.

"Here you go," the mom says, pulling a Sharpie out of her purse.

Devin bends his leg and uses it as a table as he signs.

"Thank you," the girl says, taking it from him.

"My pleasure." Devin looks at his watch and then at the tables full of volunteers answering phones. "I guess I should get to my seat," he says with a grin. "Are you going to be here a while?"

"Maybe for just a little bit longer."

"I might see you around then," he says and walks to his seat. Damn! Why did he walk away? Why didn't he ask her to dinner or something? She was standing there, as if waiting for the question. Or maybe she wanted an interview. His phone is lighting up by the time he pulls in his chair. Why can't he ask a girl out? Why does Carla make him feel like he needs to beg?

Chapter 7

"Carla, I've got some news!" her brother exclaims on the phone.

"Is this for the six o'clock?" she jokes, holding the receiver on her shoulder as she types.

"I did it! I asked Mia to marry me."

She stops typing. "You did what?" Carla squeezes her phone between her shoulder and her cheek, preventing it from slipping. "What made you decide? I mean, I hardly see the two of you together; didn't know things were that serious."

"Of course we're serious. We've been together two years."

Carla hovers over her desk. "Congratulations!" she says, swallowing. "I assume she said yes."

"She did."

"I can't wait to see the ring."

"There's no ring yet," Gavin says.

"You proposed without a ring? Why?"

"She's picking it out. She's the one who's going to wear it."

"But still . . . it's a gift. You don't go picking out your own gift, do you?"

"Mia's happy."

"I guess that's all that matters. So, when's the wedding?"

"Next year. We're thinking of doing it in her parents' backyard. They have an acreage."

"Carla!"

Carla looks up at Ryan rushing toward her. "Gavin, I've got to go. Congrats again!" She hangs up and throws her phone into her purse. "What is it?"

"Alex Price won't be at practice."

"Why?"

"Last practice he took a slap shot to his knee. Might need surgery."

"You're kidding."

Ryan shakes his head.

"How did I miss that? I didn't see anything. Why do these things happen a month before play-offs?"

"I called media relations to see if they're holding a press conference."

"How did you find out about Price?"

"I, uh, swung by the rink at the start of practice."

"I told you I was there."

"I had an interview to do at the aquatic center down the street. I thought I'd stop in at the rink to—"

"See if I needed help with the interview?" she mocks.

"No, not at all."

"What is it, then? Why were you there?"

He's slow to answer. "I wanted to see them practice. Steve Morrow is changing up the lines for Saturday's game; wanted to ask him a few questions."

"I could have done that," she says. "You knew I was there. Do you not trust me?"

Ryan sighs and shrugs. "It's not that."

Carla places her hands on her thighs, looking up at the young reporter. "Then what is it?"

"I was asked to come."

She hangs her head. "Who asked you?"

"Steve."

"You know him on a first-name basis now?" she asks, referring to the Warriors' head coach, Steve Morrow.

Ryan cracks a grin. "I guess."

"Did Steve call you to invite you personally? How did you manage to work that out?"

"Yeah, Steve knows me now. He called me to invite me. I couldn't turn it down."

"Why didn't you tell me?" She glares at him, hurt that this was happening and she hadn't seen it.

"I don't want to lose my contacts."

Carla understands where he's coming from. She'd wanted a name for herself too. There was a time when she was twenty-five and working hard to gain respect, but she never would have gone behind her superior.

"You won't lose them."

"Steve trusts me," he says, thrusting his hands into his pants pockets. "I figure if he wants to give me a story, why not?"

"Why not?" she mutters.

"It's not a competition."

Maybe for Ryan it's not, but how will she get a new job if she's not showing all her talent and reporting too? She doesn't want to be just an anchor, she wants to prove she can handle a live report. Anything to add to her résumé that will get her to the next step.

"I know," she says.

"It's just one of those things," he says with a shrug. "You have better luck talking to the Giants and the Heat than I do."

"Our junior teams?" She laughs. "That's all good, but I still should be able to talk to the Warriors anytime I want. I've been doing this for a long time. I'm no beginner."

"Maybe that's the problem," Ryan says. "Have you tried approaching them like you don't know who and what you're talking about?"

"Seriously?" She squints her eyes. "I've been sports reporting here for six years. People know what I do."

"It's worth a try."

"Is that what you did?"

"No," he says and laughs. "Guys don't have that problem. At least I don't." He smirks.

"Right." She exhales and lowers her shoulders. "Why is that?"

"People need to know you're approachable."

She gasps. "I am!"

"Sure, sometimes," he falters. "We all have those days. Don't worry about it."

"I'm not!" A twinge of nerves fire up her body like a flag going up in flames. Could that be the reason she gets forgotten by the Warriors?

What if Kyle is right and she gets fired? Her nerves are making her stomach flutter. If they want to get rid of her, it's best to leave the job first, before the termination letter is issued.

"Do you know if Steve drinks coffee?"

"I think so. I saw him once with a Starbucks cup," Ryan says.

"Perfect! I'll surprise him tomorrow."

"Hey, sorry I'm late," Devin says, taking an open bottle of beer from Mark Buckley's hand.

"No sweat. You can play the next game of pool. I think they're just about done," Mark says. "Were you at Children's today?"

Devin nods. "My weekly visit."

"I was there yesterday," Mark says. "A little girl had heart surgery and a five-year-old boy was having a brain tumor removed. I couldn't stay long." He brings his beer to his chest. "Makes me thankful for what I have."

"For sure!" Devin says. "I was visiting Jason again; he's excited to see me every week, asks me if I brought Price or Carter and tells me who should be traded, but today he didn't say much. . . ."

"It could be the medication he's on, or maybe he was tired," Mark says. "You know those kids are always tested, poked at and talked to by doctors, I'm sure he was just having a rough day."

Devin thinks for a second. "Maybe. You know, that kid is battling leukemia and still tells me he's going to play hockey next season."

"Kid's got hope; that's what will help him get through his treatment."

"Can't help thinking that when I was eight years old I was trading hockey cards and building a tree fort."

"You're up," Alex says, handing Devin a pool stick.

He throws back his beer and sets the half-filled bottle down on a nearby table.

"Were you with Carla?" Alex asks, digging the balls out to reset the table. "Did she give you a private interview?"

"Nah," Devin says, playing it cool. The conversation should blow over and then they can talk about sports or cars, anything but women, where opinions are important.

"I bet she's hard to handle," Alex taunts him, leaning against the pool table to support his balance because of his bandaged knee.

"It's not like that. What are you talking about?"

"Come on! She wants your attention. She wants you!" Alex says, laughing. "Never seen a reporter so determined to speak with a player. Can't tell me there's nothing there; you'd be stupid not to hit that."

"There's nothing between . . . between Carla and me," he says, wishing he could tell him different, but the way things were going, the chances of persuading her for a night out were looking slim. Why was she so difficult?

"Okay," Alex says and takes the first shot to break. "Have you checked out her ass?" He whistles. "It's as hard as a rock. Wow! A hot woman with an attitude; you need some of that. You haven't been getting it from groupies. I expect you're trying too hard to score with Carla."

Devin takes a shot and then says, "You should know by now that it's not my thing."

"Right; you're not looking for a hookup, you want a real relationship." Alex begins to laugh, watching his teammate line up a shot. "I've heard that one before. So you're not going for her? Not asking her out?"

"I don't think so," Devin says, leaning on his pool stick, waiting for Alex's friend to finish his shot.

"No?"

"No." Devin surprised himself, not expecting to answer so quickly, but if the guys knew he was even interested, they'd be all over him with embarrassing comments, razzing him about what he and Carla did. The thought was entertaining, though: thinking about her and what she'd be like in bed.

"She seems like a Goody Two-shoes." Alex's shaved head reflects the track lighting and his eyes squint as he watches the ball roll into a pocket.

Devin chuckles and finishes his beer. It was refreshing and light, exactly what he needed to unwind.

"How are you settling in?" Mark asks.

"Fine. The city is great and the people . . . I was warned you had a lot of fans."

"It's good here. It can be crazy at times."

"And I'm slowly learning my way around," Devin says, taking a shot.

"Wow, that was close!" Alex says with a click of his tongue against the roof of his mouth.

"Have you had a chance to check out the city?" Mark asks.

"Here and there."

"How's it working out with Brittany?" Mark asks, walking to the beer fridge and taking out a bottle. "Another beer?" Mark asks as he hands Devin a cold one.

"Sure, one more."

"She's always asking about you."

"Is that right?" Devin asks, chugging his beer. For the first time he doesn't care about getting to know any other woman. He wants Carla, and he isn't about to give up on scoring with her. He was intrigued. She was different, wasn't after him for the obvious reasons. She was her own person, with a career, and her edginess turned him on.

"Interested?"

"Not really."

Alex looks up. "Something's wrong with you, man. I've never known a player to say no to a freebie."

"It's not about a one-nighter," Devin says, placing his beer bottle on a nearby table.

"Okay, a fling," Alex says.

Devin shakes his head. The guys all look at him as though he has a secret.

"Are you gay?" Alex asks with apprehension. "It's fine if you are."

"No! I just haven't found someone I'm interested in. I want a relationship where I know what she's about and what she does for a living. You should know, Buckley. It's where you're at."

"It keeps me honest," Mark says.

"We'll see how long you last," Alex chirps and then takes a shot. The cue hits the ball hard, making a loud popping sound over the music playing. The room is larger than most people's houses and has all the necessities for a man cave: bar, flat-screen TV, stereo system and a row of recliners. The walls are decorated with framed jerseys and shelves of trophies.

"I'm sure I'll last longer than you," Devin says.

"Probably," Alex agrees. "I like variety. Hey, Henrik!" he calls across the room. "Do ya wanna pass me another beer?"

Devin ignores the big talk. No wonder he was hard-pressed for friends; Alex's attitude will only get him one-night stands. What woman would want to stay with him?

Devin turns his head. He doesn't want to live an unfulfilling life, without someone to care about and have a family with. He's more ready now than ever. He's more than a hockey player and a brand name; he's setting an example that will take time to see results, but he knows it's worth the journey, and Carla might be the perfect person to start it with, even though she doesn't know it yet.

Chapter 8

Carla gets to the rink before the practice starts. She had sent the PR department a request for an interview with Steve, but he hadn't gotten back to her, so with two coffees in hand and a paper bag loaded with cream and sugar hanging off her fingers, she decides to play nice to get Steve talking to her.

"Where are we supposed to meet?" Gary asks, following behind her as she searches for the coach.

"Uh, here, somewhere," she says, glancing every which way.

"He's not expecting you, is he?"

"Why do you think that?" she asks, turning around to face him.

"You're usually more organized."

"This spot looks good for the interview with Devin," she says.

"Does he know we're interviewing him?"

"As far as I know, unless he's changed his mind. He did promise," Carla says.

"If he stands you up this time, I'd give up on him. He's not worth your time."

"Steve!" Carla calls when she spots him moseying along the outside rink in skates and a team jacket.

He makes eye contact. Carla hustles toward him with a raised cup in her hand.

"Hi!" she says, clearing her throat. "I'm Carla Sinclair from Channel Five."

"Yes, we've met before. A few times."

"Right. Well, I brought you a cup of coffee."

"You're not trying to poison me before practice, are you? Or get me to say something I shouldn't?"

Carla shakes her head and laughs.

"I'm kidding." He takes the cup. "Thanks. I suppose you want something from me."

"Answer a couple of questions."

"Question period is after the game. We have one tomorrow night."

"Yeah, but there are always so many people. I'm talking to Miller after practice; thought I'd talk to you first, just five minutes," she says, holding up a hand.

"Two questions?" he asks, eyeing her.

"Four."

"Two. I have to get on the ice."

"Okay," she says, giving in. "Two."

"Shoot." He blows steam from his cup and takes a sip.

Carla takes out her pad and flips to the questions that are most important. Gary gives her a microphone and tells Steve to sidestep so that the plexiglass is behind him. Players trickle onto the ice and Carla takes her position. She counts down and gives Steve a nod of reassurance. "We're close to play-offs," she says. "What is the team focusing on to ensure a good run?"

"We have a good team. It's that simple," Steve says with a half smirk. "We acquired Devin Miller and Jared Landry, two outstanding players who have made a difference for our team."

"Come on," Carla taunts. "Why do you think they've made an impact? The team was doing fine without them."

"Really? Stats don't lie." Steve puts a hand on his hip.

"Couldn't it have happened without paying a big price tag?"

"And get what we have? Not at all," he says. "Miller has exceptional intuition. When the puck's coming his way, he gets control of the play. And Landry, he's been scoring almost every game. They're great additions."

"If you're so confident of Landry's scoring, why don't you use him for shoot-outs?"

"Some players do better in a game," he says and pauses. "Now that's four questions. I have a practice to run." He steps past her. "Thanks for the coffee."

Carla wanders over to the boards, watching the players filter onto the ice one by one. Carla spots Devin stepping onto the ice with his white helmet in hand and then scooping it onto his head, not bothering to snap on the chin strap. She watches him skate a lap and then carry a puck to one corner of the ice, stopping to chat with another player. Their group is getting bigger and Steve makes his way to them, talking and telling them what to do.

Devin stays in his place with the other defensemen while the others split up into groups and begin their drills.

"Do you want me to get some shots of this?" Gary asks, adjusting his camera.

"That would be great." She doesn't bother to look at him, staring through the plexiglass at the guy whose lips she would love to taste. She takes a deep breath and exhales, causing the glass to steam up. She can't have him. She *shouldn't* want him. He's not good for her. He travels all the time, doesn't seem to want to be a husband, not like she's looking for one right now. She pouts. Carla had that chance with Timothy; who's going to want her now? She doesn't even know if she can have children. It kills her to think about it.

Carla watches Devin skate around the ice. As he passes the corner where she's standing, he catches a glimpse of her and smiles.

Her toes arch in her pumps. A tingle runs through her body. He skates by again and smiles again. She smiles back, trying to keep her lips closed, but she feels all goofy and immature. Her insides turn. She can't have him, she reminds herself. *Get over it! Nothing will become of it.*

After practice, Carla waits for Devin by the bench. Players walk off the ice, saying hello to her as they pass by. She is oblivious to the men walking by. She has no interest in any of them right now, except for Devin.

"Hi!" he says, catching her attention.

She looks up at him with a cheery grin and puts her hands in her coat pockets.

"Where do you want me?" he asks.

"I have a spot over here, away from the crowd."

"Not as crowded as our last practice. There were people standing all around the rink, and the stands were pretty much full."

"How do you like playing in Vancouver?" she asks, leading him around the corner where two chairs await them.

"So far so good." He stops at a chair. "Is this my spot?" Devin asks, helmetless, standing tall in his white practice jersey, leaning on his hockey stick and sweating profusely.

Carla hands him a fresh towel with the station's logo on it. It's amazing what she can stash in her purse. She doesn't want to carry two separate bags, one holding a hand recorder, notes and pens.

"Right here," Carla says, pointing with her notebook and taking a seat. Devin dries his face and neck, keeping it in his hand while Gary takes his stick and leans it up against the wall beside him.

Carla sits up straighter, making sure her skirt is covering her thighs and that her blouse isn't revealing any skin. She adjusts her two neck-laces and combs her fingers through her hair to fluff it up. "Thanks for doing the interview."

Devin sits in the chair beside her. "As long as you play fair, I'm all yours."

Carla freezes, digesting his comment. "I do play fair."

Devin gives her a smirk. He sits down, legs spread apart, his hands between them against the chair.

Carla hands him a water bottle.

"Thanks." Devin unscrews the top and drinks half of it.

"How was practice?" she asks, watching him move the bottle away from his wet lips. His face is clean shaven, and the sweat runs down his face to his chin.

"Are we starting already?"

"No, just warming up."

"I'm good to go," he presses. "Practice was good."

Carla nods at Gary, who's playing around with the lights. He steps behind the camera and counts down, holding up his index finger until he's ready, and then flags his hand to indicate that he's taping.

Carla looks into the camera with her hand on the microphone. "The Warriors are back from a week-long road trip, finishing with two wins and two losses. Coach Steve Morrow says they needed to tighten up on defense. I have Devin Miller with me." Carla turns her legs slightly.

"Devin, obviously you're not the only defenseman responsible for how the team played. What do you think was lacking in your team's performance?"

"Well, I don't think anything was lacking. I think we just needed to score goals. That's what wins games."

"I noticed that practice went a little smoother than the last time; is that because you're gelling as a team?"

Devin smirks. "Anytime you throw in a player with a developed team, it's going to take a bit to get used to." He shrugs a padded shoulder and takes a sip from his water bottle.

"There's good indication that your team will make the play-offs. How prepared are you?"

"I'm as prepared as the rest of my team. It's a mental game. Right now, we're focusing on each practice and game. When the play-offs happen, then we'll concentrate on what we need to do to win," he says, making eye contact before looking at the camera and then at his almost empty water bottle.

"You came here with thirty-three points and you're already at thirty-seven points."

"You sound surprised," he says.

"I am! Do you think being traded is what's helped you refocus your game?"

He laughs. "No, I think getting chances with the puck has helped."

"I want to switch gears and talk about growing up." Carla pauses, looking down at her notes and then at Devin, who swallows hard. He plays with the bottle, putting the lid on and then taking it off, and repeating it.

"Your mom," Carla continues, "has been an inspiration to you. How so?"

"She's always been there for me, even when hockey wasn't a popular sport. I loved the game then as much as I do now, and she helped me achieve my goals. She was a single mom and made sure that I played hockey. She didn't have to. It was a sacrifice, but we made it."

Carla watches Devin take his last sip and tighten the lid on the empty bottle. A question about Keith is on the tip of her tongue, but she can't bring herself to ask about him.

"Who influenced you to play hockey?"

He shakes his head. "I love the game. . . ." He pauses. His mouth moves sideways. "I learned to skate early on. There was a rink advertising they needed players. My mom thought it would be good for me to join." Devin fiddles with the bottle.

"Did you have a male influence for playing hockey?"

He shakes his head. "Family." He presses his lips together.

"Not an uncle? Your dad?"

She watches Devin shake the empty bottle in his hands like he's drumming a beat. Has she made Devin uncomfortable?

Devin shakes his head slowly, avoiding her gaze.

Carla ends the interview with a quick sign-off.

"What the hell was that?" he asks, throwing the empty water bottle down.

She watches him stand, taller in skates, over six foot two inches.

"What?" Her eyes widen with worry.

"What's the fascination with my personal life?"

"I don't really care."

"Sounds like you do, or you wouldn't have asked."

"Sorry." She lifts a shoulder. "It's easier for fans to connect when they know more about a player."

"Nobody needs to know my business. I'm here to play hockey."

She nods to agree, even though it would be better if he was more relaxed.

His face softens and he musters a grin. "Okay?" he says, all friendly, and then walks off, taking long steps toward the dressing room.

Carla observes him with a twist of her lips. "What just happened?" she asks Gary.

Gary flicks off the lights and walks with a hunch, picking up the black cord as he moves toward the outlet to unplug it. "I guess the guy doesn't want to talk about his private life."

"No way!" She hands him her microphone. "One reporter asked him about his relationship with some girl he was seeing and he was happy to tell her that the relationship was going well."

Gary shrugs and carries on with his cleanup while Carla scrolls her cell phone, checking for messages. She helps pack up by making a pile of stuff to take to the station vehicle. She makes a couple of trips, carrying out the small cooler of water, a bag of extra cords and her microphone.

"Carla! Wait!"

She turns around to face Devin, showered and dressed in a suit and tie. How did he get ready so fast? His hair is still damp and she can smell his shampoo.

"I'm sorry. I didn't mean to offend you," he says, walking toward her in shiny black leather shoes. He stops, puffs out his chest. "It's just that I want to focus on hockey and not my past, you know?"

He's incredibly hot, Carla thinks, looking past him to see who is around them. The hall is crowded with people and players are walking every which way. "We all have a past," she says, choosing her words carefully. "But fair enough." Her eyes wander past him and she spots his coach giving him a quick nod as he passes.

"Now that you have your interview, when are you free to take me out on the town?"

Carla looks at the dirty mat beneath their feet, avoiding Gary, who is unraveling cords and looking her way every few seconds. "Oh."

"That was the deal."

"Okay. Remember the night at Buckley's? What do you want to see?" she asks.

"Your city." He laughs. "I'm dying to see it. I've heard about the big ball."

She laughs. "Science World."

"Okay. And Gastown, is it?"

Her face flushes. "Anything specific?"

"You know, the landmarks."

She stares at him, blinking.

"Look, you need to get to know me; then you might change your mind about me."

What did he want her to think about him? "I'm not sure about that."

"Come on."

"Even if the fans don't like you, you're playing on their team. What does it matter, anyway? It's hockey; you're not being adopted into a family."

Devin takes a sidestep, wipes his brow with his finger.

"Acceptance paves the way," he says.

Suddenly she thinks of her mom. If her mom accepted that she didn't have a family, there would be no pressure and no remorse in their relationship.

Carla smiles tightly. He has a point. Maybe he knew something she didn't.

"Does one night this week work for you?"

"Friday. I'm off work at seven."

"Text me your address."

She watches him saunter away, his gold necklace shining on the back of his neck. He's sexy in every possible way. She can't bring herself to admit that his sex appeal is more tempting with every encounter. So how does she stay away from him? Or not, and ignore her attraction?

Chapter 9

Carla flips through a parenting magazine as she waits for her doctor in the examining room. Advertisements for pregnancy tests, prepacked applesauces and diapers: Her life will forever change when or if she has children. How she wants to be part of the mom conversations at work and be able to relate to three A.M. feedings and how little Johnny scored his first goal in soccer. The list goes on, and Carla has never felt more ready to have a baby than now.

The doorknob turns; Carla puts down the magazine on the chair beside her and sits up straighter, her hands resting on her lap.

"Why, hello there, Carla. How are you today?"

"I'm great." Her mouth stretches into a bigger smile.

"What can I help you with? You look well." Her family doctor takes a seat on the swivel stool and wheels himself over to get closer for the conversation.

"Thanks. Actually, I wanted to talk to you again about my plans for conceiving."

"Are you sure you're ready for this?" He places his hands on his knees, sitting in a V-shape position. "Parenthood is a big decision, never mind being a single parent," Dr. Rogers advises. "It's a big step."

"I know. It's just that I want a baby so bad." She drops her head. "I thought I'd be a mom by now and it hasn't happened."

"You can't put a date on kids," he says, skimming Carla's medical records. "What did Dr. Fossett say? Did she run tests? I haven't received anything."

"No, she said it might be me. She won't know unless I'm trying, but I want to know if I can or can't. She wants me to be with someone before crossing that bridge. And I'm not with anyone," Carla says, her lips wrinkling as she makes a face. "I want to know what my options are. What happens if I don't meet anyone for ten years? Then I'm done! I won't be able to have any kids, even if there is a chance." If only Timothy had wanted it as much as she did.

The doctor stands and opens a drawer. "Do you want to adopt?"

She shakes her head. "No."

"Are you thinking about artificial insemination?" he asks as he thumbs through the drawer.

"I haven't decided yet. I'm considering it," she admits. "I'd like to have my own child if I can."

"If you're worried about your age—"

"I'm only thirty-one," she says, straightening her back. "I just had a birthday."

He hands her a pamphlet and a freshly printed paper with more information.

"You have plenty of time to find a mate and procreate." His voice is gentle. "These things do take time." He eyes the papers in her hands. "And there's no guarantee, even if you do artificial insemination."

"Maybe I should adopt. People do it all the time. It's not a big deal, right? There are thousands of children who need to be loved. I could be that parent."

"Carla?" Dr. Rogers's eyes narrow. "There's a process for that too."

She exhales and pouts. What can she do? Would Timothy consider being a dad now? Maybe it would work this time. Friends have children together. . . .

"You need to relax about the whole thing. Give yourself a few months to think about it. Consider your options. You never know; by then you could meet someone and be relieved you didn't jump at your idea."

"You don't think it's a good idea?" Her voice is filled with worry.

He shakes his head. "Not right now, no. You're not in a relationship, so you would be starting a family alone."

She stares at the papers.

"It's probably not the answer you were hoping for. It's a big step. Trust me on this."

Carla can't get the thought of pregnancy out of her mind. She knows it will be hard, but her mom will help her. Could she have her mom around every day? And would she want to be? They don't get along on the best of days. Would it be different with a child?

Carla drives to an outdoor mall and decides to check out a baby store.

"Hi. How are you today?" the salesclerk asks the moment Carla walks into the store.

"Fine, thanks."

"Anything I can help you find?"

"No, just looking," Carla says softly, and wanders off to the baby section, where bassinets and crib bedding are displayed. She takes in the cute patterns and bright nursery colors. How would she decorate her child's room? She loves pale yellow with either a splash of blue or pink. Would she have a boy or a girl? Trying hard to envision the sex of her child, she knows she'd be happy with either. To be a mom would be the best experience, no matter what her child was.

Carla goes over to the clothes. The tiny sleepers remind her of her childhood dolls. The hats, the onesies and socks make her squeal with hope. She takes the items in her hands, all neutral colors, fit for a girl or boy. It's not a waste buying now, she decides; it's either now or later.

She places the items on the counter to pay.

"Is this a gift?" the salesclerk asks. "Or for yourself?"

"Ah . . ." What does it matter?

It's like the clerk can read her mind. "I can give you a gift receipt."

Why not ask that in the first place? "No, that's okay." Carla sweeps hair away from her face and leans her hand on the counter, watching the woman scan each piece. Her fingers are jittery as she reaches into her purse to pull out her wallet and takes out her bank card to complete the transaction.

Carla's phone rings as she exits the store.

Mom.

She sighs and answers in a trying voice.

"Care Bear! Where are you?"

"Shopping."

"Oh! Great. I'm leaving Nana's."

"How is she?"

"Her arthritis is bothering her. She has a lot of pain when she walks."

"Oh, no."

"And her memory is going. She forgets the day of the week and what medicines she's taking. I think she has the beginning of Alzheimer's."

"How can anyone remember what pills they take when they're getting them shoved down their throats?"

"The nurses don't shove them down Nana's throat. They tell her what she's taking."

Carla puts her phone between her ear and shoulder to unlock her door. "It's not important. She's taken care of."

"Are you coming for dinner?"

"When?" Carla asks, throwing her bag in the passenger seat and slamming the door.

"Tonight. It's Dad's birthday!"

"I know," Carla says, bringing her hand to her forehead. She forgot. Nana probably has a better memory. It's easy to forget something when you're trying to remember it the hardest.

She slides into her seat. It's even written on her calendar. "I don't remember you telling me about dinner. I thought we were celebrating it on Monday, the actual date."

"Tonight works for everyone. I told you about it last week when you were over."

"What time's dinner?"

"Between five-thirty and six. Keep it early since you have to work tomorrow."

Carla scans the shops, looking for a sports store. Her dad is always happy with a new Warriors shirt or hat. Tickets are hard to come by for the game, especially at the end of the season when they're heading into the play-offs.

She hangs up the phone and looks at the clock on the screen. Three o'clock. She bites her bottom lip, looking for a store to buy her dad's gift. There's a Sports Junkies at the corner. They'll have something. She stuffs her baby clothes bag under the passenger seat and trots off down the sidewalk with a bounce in her step. A last-minute gift idea may just work out perfectly. Too bad she didn't know Devin better; her dad would love a signed jersey.

She walks up to the door and stops. Devin. Could she call him and ask if he'll sign it? Or would he laugh at her? Would he think she was just another fan? But then, what's wrong with that? She's Carla Sinclair, the sports reporter.

Carla pulls her phone from her purse and scrolls her contacts list for Devin's number. What happens if he doesn't answer? How will she get him to sign it before dinner tonight? She could buy it now and have Devin sign it later. She taps his name to make the call, stopping between the entrance and the window. Her feet can't stay still, but she can't walk around; there are too many people around. She lowers her head and faces the wall to keep her voice low. She has to be cool. Why is she nervous?

"Hello," his voice answers, smooth and friendly. She closes her eyes as she collects her thoughts.

"Devin!" she says with new excitement. "It's Carla Sinclair. How are you?"

"Hi, Carla. This is a surprise."

She rubs her lips together. "I knew you would be surprised."

"What's up?"

His abrupt question stings. Was she taking him away from something important? "I hope I didn't catch you at a bad time," she says.

"I'm on my way home from a workout."

"That's great, ah, perfect." There's a pause. She's not sure how to ask him. Does he get these requests all the time? "I have a favor to ask you."

"I don't know if I can do another interview."

"Oh no, it's not that. It's a personal request. You can say no, I'm just putting it out there, if it's a possibility."

"What is it?"

"Well, it's my dad's birthday, and I'm wondering if you wouldn't mind signing his jersey."

"Bring it to practice Tuesday and I'll sign it. No problem."

"Okay . . . great . . . thanks. I don't want to seem unprofessional, I mean, coming to practice with merchandise and wanting you to sign."

"I can meet you before. Call me Tuesday morning and we'll meet up," he says simply.

He's done this before.

"Um, okay."

"When's your dad's birthday?"

"The party's today."

"I'll be around. Where do your parents live?"

"In Richmond."

"Is that where the airport is?"

"Yes."

"Okay. I'm sure I can get there."

"To my parents' house?" she asks, holding in her excitement. Wouldn't her dad be shocked?

"I can make it."

"Tonight?" she asks, making sure he hears her right.

"Sure. I'm not doing much."

"That's very nice of you, but I don't expect you to—"

"What's the address?"

She rambles off the address and gives him directions.

"What time do you want me there?"

"Well," she thinks, "I'll be there at around five-thirty."

"I'll see you then."

The thought of Devin showing up to her parents' house is not quite sinking in, even after she buys a jersey with his number nineteen on it and drives home to shower and change into a new pair of jeans and a top. She puts hoops in her ears and slips on a pair of ankle boots.

Jittery and unable to calm her nerves, she fingers some strands, trying to fix her hair just right. It looks the same, but it's not perfect. After a last look in the mirror, she grabs the gift bag with the jersey in it and heads off to see her parents.

Did she give Devin good directions? Will he find their house? It's not easy to navigate; most of the streets are names, not numbers. Thankfully, the house is close to the hospital, a landmark he can identify.

Carla parks on the street and wanders up the driveway. Thinking about Devin on his way over makes her knees want to give out. Her sister and brother are already there and it's not even five-thirty. She turns the door handle and walks right in. The house is loud with conversation and laughter. She can't remember the last time the house was filled with such joy.

"Aunt Marie!" Carla says, scurrying over with open arms. "I didn't know you were going to be here."

"I couldn't miss your dad's sixtieth." Marie gives her a once-over. "You look fantastic! What's your secret for keeping trim and polished? You carry yourself well." She squints tightly, like she's about to explode with a question, and all Carla can see is her silver eye shadow and ruby, high cheekbones that she too inherited. "Sooo . . . who's the guy?"

"There's no guy," Carla answers happily. "I'm single."

"You've got to be kidding! You? Single?" She laughs. "You have to be seeing someone." Marie stops, holds Carla's arms and stares into her eyes. "Unless you don't want your mother to know," she whispers. "We all know how she gets with other people's relationships."

Carla giggles because she knows her aunt is impressed and doesn't mean any harm; they both love gossip.

"What's this?" Carla's mom asks, walking into the living room. "Hi, Care Bear!"

"I was just asking Carla if she's dating anyone."

Mom huffs, carrying a tray of hot wings and setting them down on the coffee table. "I keep asking, but I get the same answer."

Marie flashes Carla a smile. "Don't worry, you'll find someone. You're probably more cautious after the divorce."

"Oh, I don't know. . . ."

"It can't be easy," Marie says.

"Come eat!" her mom shouts, standing at the table. "It's getting cold." She picks up a wing and bites into it.

"Happy birthday, Dad!" Carla says, walking over to the couch, interrupting his conversation. She bends down to give him a squeeze, says hi to her uncle and backs up to find a seat near the circle that's been created around the television.

"Mia, hi!" Carla says, dragging a chair from the dining room over to the adjoining living room where her brother, his girlfriend and uncle have a seat. "It's been a while."

"Busy," she responds. Her black straight hair, parted in the middle, accents her dark, heavy eyelashes. She's wearing jeans with studs that run down the outside leg and a shirt that's a bit too small.

"With what?" Carla presses. There must be something important taking her away from family visits.

"I've been working weekends."

"Last I spoke to you, you were working as a receptionist."

"That was a long time ago," she says.

"Mia's working on a fashion show," Gavin says, placing a hand on his fiancée's knee. "She's been working really hard. All those early mornings and late nights." He gazes at her with pride. "It's going to be worth it."

Mia grins. "I'm hoping it will be a success."

"What is it for?" Carla asks, eyeballing an orange stain on the cream carpet.

"It's new designers. All of them graduates and wanting to show their fashions."

"Why are you involved?" Carla asks, trying to piece together exactly what Mia does. She's been with her brother for two years, yet Carla has no idea what his fiancée does or anything about her.

"I have a fashion degree. Haven't done anything with it for some time, and then some college graduates and I decided to showcase what we've done. There are amazing designers who live here, and we don't ever get to see their designs."

"You'll have to let me know. I'm interested," Carla says, standing up and grabbing hold of a tall houseplant by its basket and dragging it over to cover up the stain.

"What are you doing?" Gavin asks.

"The plant looks better here." Carla steps back to look at it and sits down.

"So, you're interested?" Mia asks.

Carla nods, pleased by the position of the plant.

"Do you think Channel Five would come, give us some exposure?" Mia asks.

"I'm not sure. I can give you the person to talk to."

"That would be great. Thank you!"

"Oh! Congratulations on your engagement!" Carla tells Mia.

She grins.

Carla looks at Mia's left hand. Still no ring. That's disappointing. "Any wedding plans?"

Mia shakes her head.

Carla might regret saying this, but as a friendly gesture, she suggests, "If you need any help or want someone to go shoe shopping with, I'd be happy to come with you."

"Okay."

"Carla has a thing for shoes," Sadie says. "She owns something like fifty pairs."

"Hard to resist, aren't they?" Mia says. "I have eighty."

Carla's eyes pop. "Lucky!"

"Dinner's almost ready!" her mom shouts.

Carla pulls out her cell phone to check the time and to see if Devin has left any messages. It's after six. He should be here any time, Carla thinks, placing her phone back in her purse. Her stomach feels rocky.

"Carla, do you want something to drink?" Mom asks.

"I can get it," she says, eyeing the baby picture of herself on the fireplace. She stands up, her legs jumpy. She can't stay still, knowing Devin will be here in her parents' house. Nonchalantly, she walks by the fireplace and with a gentle hand folds over the frame and walks into the kitchen, where Sadie is holding Brinley and talking to Aunt Marie.

"Hi, Sadie," Carla says, taking a glass out of the cupboard. She goes over to her sister and offers her finger to her niece. "Hi, Brin." The baby smiles back and blows a string of bubbles with her lips.

"I think she's teething. The drool is unbelievable," Sadie says, wiping her daughter's mouth.

"You teethed early," Mom says, stirring the spaghetti sauce over the stove. "Give her a cold cloth. That always used to help you guys. I didn't buy those fancy teethers they have out now."

Sadie goes into the drawer to pull out a cloth and turns on the tap.

"It's so good to have you kids here," her mom says, putting a cookie sheet of garlic toast into the oven. "You've made your dad's day."

Carla pours a glass of ginger ale, hoping it will settle her stomach. Why is she so nervous? It's Devin, the guy with the attitude. She's not interested in him. He's just surprising her dad for his birthday, no big deal. He'll sign the jersey and then leave. Devin just wants her to make positive comments about him so he gains more public support. It's a competition off the ice. The one with the most attention sells the most product. Not that they would know or even check, but the more they're favored, the chances are they'll stay and make a bigger name for themselves.

Her mom stares into the sauce. "I look forward to when there will be more grandchildren." She smiles. "I love a full house."

"Maybe Mia and Gavin will have kids right away. He's always talking about being a dad," Sadie says.

"I want them," Carla snaps, taking another sip.

"I know you do," her sister says.

"Well, one day," Mom says. "Will you have any more?"

Sadie's eyes are fixated on her mother. "Maybe when Brin's five."

Mom wipes her dry hands on her apron. "Don't wait that long. Brin needs someone to grow up with, have someone to play with. If you wait that long, they won't be close."

"Who says?" Sadie brings her daughter to her shoulder.

"That's the way it is."

"Gavin and I are five years apart and we're close. I think," Sadie says.

"Sure. Now that you're adults."

"The time has to be right," Sadie says, looking at her sister.

"You'll know," Carla says, peeking at the pot of boiling pasta. "I think you should add more noodles."

Her mom stirs more noodles into the pot.

"It's a lot of work," Sadie says, giving Brin a squeeze.

"Right now it is," Mom agrees. "It doesn't matter how many children you have, it's not an easy job, but it does get easier. Think of the joy children bring."

"Are you trying to convince me?" Carla asks, taking note of how many times her mom has looked into her eyes.

"No! You have to find a guy first," she says, moving the pot of sauce to the counter. "Sadie? Can you tell everyone dinner is ready?"

"Can I cut the bread?" Carla asks, opening up the oven door.

"It's not ready yet," Mom says, pulling out a cutting board and handing it to her. "Is that the doorbell?"

Carla's stomach sinks. Her body is all shaky again. She pats her hands on the tea towel on the counter. "I'll get it!" And dashes out of the kitchen to the front door. She glances in the mirror, wipes a strand of hair away from her face and exhales as her hand touches the knob. Slowly, she opens the door, takes a peek to see if it's really him. Devin. All six feet of him, with broad shoulders and a thick neck, wearing faded jeans and a black V-neck shirt; he smiles, making her stomach sink.

She swallows hard. Even his dark eyes are smiling. They look past her and he lets out a smirk: Carla's family has crowded into the foyer.

"Hi!" Carla says, opening the door wider. "Come in. You found it!"

He takes a big step inside and says hello.

Carla spins around.

"This is quite a welcome," he says to the gathering at the door.

Carla blushes. "They're excited to meet you," she says. "Everyone, Devin Miller!"

Her brother steps forward and extends his hand. "I'm Gavin. Pleasure to meet you. I'm a huge fan."

"Come in!" Carla says again, closing the door.

Devin walks past her and she gets a whiff of his soap, a mix of sweetness and cinnamon or something earthy, she can't quite tell.

"I heard it was somebody's birthday," Devin says, walking into the room.

Her dad gets off the couch and walks toward the hockey player. "I wondered what all the fuss was about at the door," he says. He pats Devin's arm and shakes his hand.

"Happy birthday!" Devin says. "I brought you something."

"You did?" Carla and Dad ask in unison. Her eyebrows come together, watching Devin rush to the door, open it and bring back a hockey stick.

"Carla told me you're a Warriors fan. Thought you might like the stick I used to score against Chicago the other night."

"The game Saturday?" her dad asks, pointing in midair. "Wow!" He's staring at the stick like it's made of gold. Devin hands it over.

"For me?" Dad asks. "Are you sure?"

"Yeah."

"This is something! Thank you!" He holds it up, studying the markings on the shaft. The top of the stick is numbered nineteen. "And you don't want it?" he asks, as if it's a crazy gesture.

"Nah, it's yours."

"Thank you," Dad says again. The guys all come together to take a look at his prize.

"You didn't have to do that," Carla whispers.

Devin smiles.

"Thank you," Carla says, looking up into his eyes, getting lost in them. They suck her in and she can't seem to pull herself away. Finally, she bends down and grabs the gift bag. Remembering she brought a black marker for Devin's signature, she grabs her purse as well. "Here, Dad. Happy birthday!"

"Thanks, honey." He takes the gift, reads the card and pulls out the white jersey while Carla and Devin watch patiently. Her dad lets out a rambling thank you. He focuses on the jersey for a minute, collecting his thoughts.

"Do you like it?" Carla asks. "If you prefer the blue jersey, I can return it."

"No, no, this is great." He puts it over his head. "What do you think?"

"Looks good!" Carla tells him. "Did you want Devin to sign it?" She gets out her marker, waiting for a response.

"Would you do that?" Dad asks.

"Of course!" Devin grins and takes the marker, his fingers grazing Carla's. He braces his hand on her dad's back and signs by his silk-stitched number.

"Care Bear! You didn't tell me you were bringing someone for dinner," her mom says, wiping her hands on her apron. "That's why you were checking to see how much food I was making."

Devin throws out his hand. "I'm not staying."

"You must! I made lots."

Devin looks at Carla.

"You can stay if you want," she says, her stomach spinning around like a washing machine. She can't quite believe that he's here either.

"I don't want to impose."

"If you don't have plans," she says, "my dad would love for you to stay." *I'd love for you to stay.*

"Come on!" Mom says. "Sadie? Can you grab another place setting? We have room." Her mom returns to the kitchen.

Her sister waltzes into the kitchen. "Anything else need to be on the table?"

"No. Let's eat," Mom says and leads them to the table. "Dinner!" she calls out, and everyone slowly makes their way to the table.

"Well, this is certainly a surprise," Dad says, wiggling a chair out for Devin and gesturing for him to sit down. "I wasn't expecting this."

"I wasn't expecting Carla to bring a date," Gavin says, laughing.

Carla's face heats up as she takes a seat beside Devin. "We're not together," she starts to say, and then her mother's voice takes over, like a bomb has gone off.

"Help yourself! There's lots. I'm taking out another bread from the oven. Do you have a plate, Devin?"

"Yes. Thanks!"

"Well, then, start eating!" She claps her hands and sits down, eyeing everyone's plate, waiting, making sure everyone has food.

Carla uses the tongs to plop pasta on her plate and passes it to Devin.

"Devin? Take more!" Mom says.

"Mom?" Carla says, glaring, and then bites her lip. She decides not to tell her to leave him alone, to mind her own business.

"Here!" Mom says, passing the salad bowl to Carla. "Do you want to give this to Devin? He needs salad."

Carla doesn't acknowledge her mom; she takes the bowl in one hand and moves it to Devin.

"Devin?" her dad asks. "I heard Mario Visconti is a real prick."

"No. He's a nice guy," Devin says, lowering his fork to his plate. He gives her dad his full attention, but everyone at the table is interested in the conversation, all eyes in Devin's direction. "He was traded from Pittsburgh to Carolina. I played with him for a season until I was traded. He's an enforcer."

"Is that a tough guy?" Mom asks.

Devin nods and Dad springs on to another question.

"It must be hard to settle into a city and then have to move away," he comments. "Where are you from originally?"

"Seattle."

"You're close to home, then. You must have been to Vancouver growing up."

Devin swirls his pasta on his fork. "A few times."

"Let him eat!" Mom says. "His food is getting cold. Sadie, can you pass the bread?"

"How did you two meet?" Sadie asks, looking at her sister from across the table as though she's waiting for a juicy story. "Did I miss that conversation, because having a child will do that. A kid takes away brain cells; I'm sure of it."

"I agree," her husband says, reaching for his glass of water. "She's not as sharp as she used to be."

Sadie turns her head and glares at him.

"Hey, you started it," he says. "Sadie used to remember what bills needed to be paid before we got the bill!" he exclaims. "Now we get a bill and she leaves it in the drawer. I have to remember to pay them or we'll be getting late charges."

Sadie breaks apart the bread before putting it into her mouth. "It's called being sleep deprived. Who can function with hardly any sleep?"

"Brin should be sleeping through the night," Mom states.

"Most of the time. She still gets up once or twice. My days are tiring. Who would have thought a little person could be so much work?"

Carla pours salad dressing on her greens. She can't even eat, knowing Devin is sitting beside her, watching her and listening to every word she says.

"Wait until you experience it," Sadie says to her sister. "It's like nothing you're prepared for."

"But it's worth it," Carla says.

"Yes, it's worth it."

"Where's Brinley?"

"Napping."

"At six-thirty?"

"She goes to bed at ten."

"Past my bedtime." Carla laughs. "That's why you're tired."

"Kids suck the energy out of you. Anyway," Sadie says, "I didn't know you were seeing each other. How did you two meet?"

Carla takes a breath, looks at Devin and then at her sister. "We're not together," she says, watching everyone's face fixated on her. She twirls her pasta, not sure what to do with the sudden jitters in her fingers. Meanwhile he appears to be relaxed, smirking at her like he's interested in what she's about to say.

"I met Devin when he was with Carolina and was here playing. It was after a game. I took him aside to interview him. He'd just scored two goals and Carolina was winning." She pauses, gathering her thoughts. "That was the first time." She gulps. "When he was traded here, I had some questions for him and set up an interview."

"Did you catch that first interview?" Devin asks everyone.

He doesn't wait for an answer; he starts talking. "Some questions!" He looks at her and then at the table. "She wanted to know if I was planning on staying in Carolina or if I was going to be traded." He looks at her, and for a moment she is awestruck by his sensitivity. "I don't know how she knew, but she knew. I didn't want to let the cat out of the bag. How did you know?"

"I followed you and . . . and others who were ending their contracts." Carla feels her face warming. "I thought it was an honest question."

"Honest, yes," Gavin says, "but leave the guy alone."

Devin laughs and takes a bite of his dinner.

"So, Devin, have you had a chance to see the city?"

"Not as much as I'd like."

"Carla should show you around."

"She promised me she would," he says.

Carla sucks in her lips, feeling all eyes on her. She glares at her brother and then turns her head toward Devin. "I'd love to."

He sits back and places his hands on his lap, giving everyone his full attention, like he's on display. He's probably used to it.

"Tickets are hard to get," Uncle Bob chimes in. "I tried to get tickets to the game against Detroit, but there were none available."

"Never are," Dad says. "They're hard to get unless you're lucky and work for a company that has box seats or season tickets."

Devin shakes his head. "Hard to believe."

"You're playing in a hockey-obsessed city. That's just the way it is here," Dad says.

Mom stands and collects dirty plates. Carla jumps to her feet to help.

"I'll put the kettle on. We'll have tea with cake?" Mom asks, walking with an armful of dishes to the kitchen. Devin and the men are making small talk at the table while the women are in the kitchen getting dessert.

Sadie leans over Carla's shoulder and whispers, "Are you sure there's nothing between you two?"

"No!" Carla snaps. She opens the dishwasher and loads it.

"I don't believe it."

Mom looks their way, listening as she takes out a box of tea from the cupboard and places four bags in the pot.

"Seriously, there's nothing," Carla says, reaching for a dirty plate.

Sadie arches an eyebrow. "He definitely likes you."

Carla can't keep the smile from her lips. They start to twitch and she bends down to place forks in the cutlery slot to save herself from her sister's quizzical gaze.

"You should go for him, then," Sadie says. "He likes you and you're single." She shrugs and opens the drawer to take out the dessert forks. Sadie stares. "You're not interested, are you?"

"Nope."

"That's why you're still single," Mom says. "You're not giving yourself a chance."

"A chance to what? Get my heart broken? Get wrapped up in an affair and be the one hurt when it's over? No way. I'm not doing it."

"Is that what this is about? You don't want to date because you're scared of getting hurt?" Sadie asks, stepping closer.

Carla can feel her eyes sting. She won't allow herself to cry. Not here. Never.

Her mom comes in close. They're both surrounding her.

"Who's to say you'll get hurt?"

"I always do!" Carla says, holding back from lashing out. She doesn't want the guys to hear her. She doesn't want Devin to hear her. It's best if, after tonight, they go their separate ways and meet each other again at a game or practice. It's best for both of them. It's best for Carla.

"I've been divorced," she begins, once she's collected her thoughts. "Nobody wants a divorcée."

"What does that have to do with being in love?"

"I told Timothy I loved him. We said our vows. How can I fall in love with someone else and say those vows again? It doesn't seem right. How would someone know I was telling them the truth?"

"Why are you worried about something that hasn't happened?" Mom asks.

Carla taps her fingernails on the counter, thinking about it. "I don't want to go down that road again."

"I know," Sadie says, reaching her arm out for comfort.

"I believed in us," Carla whispers. "I might have fallen out of love, but I still care for Timothy a lot and every day when I see him I think, should I have tried harder? Should I have done something to save us? What could I have done?"

"Nothing," Sadie says softly. "You did everything you could."

"Did I?"

Sadie nods with strained eyes. "You did. I was there. I heard it all and saw it all. You and Tim tried. It just didn't work, but that's not to say it can't work with someone else. Stop beating yourself up. It was two years ago. It's time to move on. You've had enough time to mourn and to come to grips with it being over. But *you're* not over. You need to live. Find someone to live with."

"Thanks," Carla says. Her sister wraps her arms around her. It feels good to have a hug and feel the love.

"Where's the cake?" Gavin says, coming into the kitchen. "Dad says it's chocolate."

"His favorite," Mom says, handing Gavin the cake. She lights the candles and Gavin walks out of the kitchen with a loud introduction of "Happy Birthday."

They have their cake and drink tea, laughing and talking. Dad tells the story about when he and Gavin tried to make an ice rink in the backyard and it wasn't cold enough to freeze solid and the ice cracked, getting his foot stuck.

"Carla didn't try skating on it?" Devin wants to know.

"She was smart," Dad says. "She warned us it would happen. I guess I wanted to at least try so I could say we played ice hockey in our backyard."

"You'd have to go back east for that," Gavin says.

"I'm fine here," Dad says, lifting his teacup to his mouth.

There's a lull in the conversation until Sadie clears her and her husband's plates and cups and says, "We should get going. I have to put Brinley to bed." She puts her dishes in the kitchen and comes back out to give her dad a hug and a kiss on his cheek. "Happy birthday, Dad."

"Thanks, honey."

"Nice meeting you, Devin," she says, shaking his hand.

Devin rises to his feet. "I should get going too. I have to pack. We're in Anaheim tomorrow night."

Of course, just as Carla was starting to feel comfortable. But the evening did have to come to a close. She had work tomorrow and it would be a good idea to get a decent night's sleep.

"I'll walk you out," Carla tells Devin. He eyes her with a skeptical gaze. "I'm leaving too," she manages to say.

Carla stands and hugs her parents. She puts on her shoes, Devin standing patiently beside her. She likes that he's waiting for her, as though they'd be going home together.

"All set?" he asks her.

A smile perks her lips. He opens the door, stops and shouts out, "It was nice meeting you!"

Her parents both wave. "It was good to have you."

"Happy birthday," Devin says and steps outside.

Carla shuts the door behind them. "Thank you for coming," she says, walking in stride to their cars.

"My pleasure. Thanks for the invite. It was fun."

"It was the best birthday my dad has had," Carla says. "Because you showed up."

She stops in front of her car.

"I don't think it was me. He had his family there. That's what made it."

A light in Devin's eye captures Carla, and she wonders what it would be like if she could get closer to him and smell his sweet scent.

"He's a family guy," she says happily.

"I noticed. And why not? It's the best."

"What?"

"Family. Kids. You know, the whole package."

"Wife." Carla bit her lip. Why did she say that word? She wasn't trying to put words in his mouth, and damn her for thinking it. The last thing she wants is for Devin to think she's coming on to him, because she's not. She doesn't want him. She's made up her mind.

"Of course."

Her stomach flops. Devin does have a sensitive side. She stands on her tippy toes and then relaxes her feet.

"You know how to get back?" she asks.

"I have GPS."

"Right."

"I'll be okay, thanks." He takes a step back. "Will I see you Friday night at the game?"

He's not going to kiss her . . . he wants to leave. Devin doesn't want her . . . probably a good thing, she thinks. Why would he want her?

"No. I'm working at the station." She fumbles with her purse, trying to pull out her keys. "I'll see you around."

"Yeah." He's walking backward. "Thanks for dinner."

"Anytime."

"You don't want to tell me that; you might not get rid of me. That was the best spaghetti dinner I've ever had."

"My mom would be happy to hear that."

"I told her. She said I could come over next Sunday night for dinner."

"She did, did she?" Carla opens her car door. "My mom would love to cook for you. She complains that no one comes over anymore. She forgets we're all working and have our own lives."

"If I had a family like yours, I'd make a point of coming for dinner."

"We try," she says, not sure what to do with her keys. Should she get in and start her car or keep talking and hope that he'll kiss her?

"I better get going," Devin says. A sharp smile shows off his white teeth.

Everything about him makes him gorgeous and easy to look at.

He holds up his hand and does a quick wave. "Catch you at a game, I'm sure." And walks away.

Carla stands at her car with the door open. That's it? *When will we get to talk again?*

She watches him saunter to his Range Rover down the street. He clicks his remote and hops in.

He is so hot and yet so cold.

She lets him drive away first so she can feel sorry for herself and not worry about him looking in his rearview mirror and see her pout. It's dark, but surely she could be spotted under a streetlight or at an intersection.

It's not meant to be.

Devin doesn't want her.

He can't have her anyway because . . . because she *doesn't want him*.

Chapter 10

"He's not interested in me," Carla tells Gabby as they trot down the hallway from the graphics department to the studio.

"Come on, really? You don't think he'd want a sexy babe as a girlfriend?"

Carla bursts out laughing.

"You talk a lot about him," Gabby says.

"No, I don't. I see him a lot, that's the difference." Carla bites her tongue. "I mean, I don't see him that much."

"You should ask him out."

Carla bites her bottom lip, holding back a smile. "I'm really not interested. He likes himself too much, and besides, he's kind of cold."

"Really?"

"Well, yeah. I don't think he's a happy person."

"That's because he's single and not getting any."

Carla bursts out with a laugh. "I'm sure he's getting some."

They turn the corner and head down the stairs. "He's always perplexed and comes off edgy, like I'm going to ask him something he's not comfortable with." Carla stops and faces her friend. "Tell me, am I overbearing? Too persuasive? Strong-minded?"

"Your mother is overbearing. You? You're good at doing what you do. You've been single for too long. That's the problem. It's time for you to date again. You need to start caring about a guy, get to know him."

Carla gives it some thought, and the two start walking again to the bottom level. "I don't want to be with another anxious guy, you know? Or one who's boring . . . all he does is work. You know what that does to a relationship?" Carla raises an eyebrow. If she ever were to marry again, she would make sure that not only was there a physical connection but he had to be her best friend too. She'd learned from marrying Timothy that marriage was more than two people creating a life together. It was a friendship that needed to be strong from the beginning.

"Why don't we head out to a club or something this weekend? Get dressed up, wear our leopard-print heels. Pick up some guys."

Carla bursts out laughing. "And do what? We're not twenty, and aren't you seeing that guy?" Carla snaps her fingers. "From the dealership? What's his name?"

Gabby rolls her eyes. "One date. It's over. Tried selling me a car on our first date. That's grounds for 'see-ya!'"

They enter a newsroom bursting with activity. Phones are ringing, people shouting. "I guess I should get back to work," Carla says. "I have to file a story for six."

"Don't forget about this weekend."

"We'll see."

"That means no," Gabby says.

"Can't we do something that doesn't remind me of my age? Like going to a show?"

Gabby sighs. "We always go to a show. We didn't like the last one."

"Interested in going to see the Warriors play?" Carla asks hopefully. It's not very often they hang out at a game unless it's a double date, and even then, tickets are hard to come by.

"Or go to a club?" her friend pouts.

Carla makes a face.

"Do you have Warriors tickets?"

"I can get you a media pass," Carla says.

"And stand the whole game at the boards? Not fun."

"I can try for box seats."

Pamela races toward them. "Carla? You have a phone call. Line two." She holds up two fingers and passes them in a rush.

"Thanks." Carla turns to her friend. "Gotta go! We'll catch up later."

Carla gets to her desk and answers abruptly before sitting down in her chair.

"Hi, it's Keith Miller."

"Hi, Keith."

"I'll be at the game. Do you think you can make arrangements to meet?"

She bites her bottom lip. Why can't she tell Keith she's not interested in getting involved with his family reunion? What would Devin say about her talking to his dad behind his back?

"I don't know. . . ."

"I live in Seattle. I'm coming up for the game. You have my number? I'll meet you at the media box."

"Have you been there before?"

"I've been to a few games. It's the only way I get to see my son."

Carla swallows. How sad. "I'll see. I don't know if I'll be at the game. . . ."

"I have to see Devin." His voice comes alive.

"I don't see how. Don't you have a family member who can be there?"

"You interviewed him last year and said something to him that made me think of what's been missing in our lives."

"I did?"

"You asked him about his contract."

"I guess he wasn't expecting my question."

"It wasn't that. He had a sparkle in his eye, I remember. Sure, you caught him off guard, but did you see how he reacted?"

"That's why he doesn't like me."

"You're good for him. Any woman who can stand up to Devin is a good match. He's not easy to get along with, and that's my point. He's stubborn. Devin gets that from me, but you can be there as mediator."

"That's not my job, Keith," Carla says, head down and holding her head. *Why did he pick me?* "My job is to report on sports. I can't do it." Carla sees Timothy making eyes at her, probably wondering who she's talking to. She lowers her voice. "I understand your situation. I'm sorry, but I can't get involved. It's unprofessional."

Keith makes a sound like he's about to say something, then pauses. "I think you're the only one who can help," he says gently. "He'll listen to you."

Carla laughs. "If he won't listen to his father, he won't listen to me."

"I wish it were that way."

"Look, I could get into trouble," she whispers into the phone. "If things went sideways. I have a job to do and I don't want to jeopardize it." Why is she making excuses? She doesn't need to explain herself to a guy she doesn't know.

"I'll be sitting in section D, row one forty. I'll be waiting there during second period for you. If you change your mind, call. If you get a hold of Devin, be sure to tell him there's someone at the game who's been dying to meet him. He might like it. He always was a proud and determined kid. I guess that's why he's made it as far as he has. Never thought playing street hockey would lead him to the NHL. . . ."

"Keith? I have to go. I have work to do."

"Right. Well, if by chance I could meet you, even if I won't be seeing Devin, at least I could thank you in person."

"Thank me for what?"

"For not hanging up on me. Listening to me. I haven't spoken about Devin to a stranger in years, and now that I have, I'm ready to face him. I'm ready to move on to a better place."

Carla slumps back in her chair, holding the phone without any strength. Her heart aches for Devin. To not know his dad, not have a relationship with one of the most important people in his life. As much as Carla disagrees with her mom and sometimes has the feeling she loves Sadie more for staying married and being a mom, she can't imagine not being part of a family. Maybe she should call her mom just to say hi. Reassure herself that even though there's a strain between them at times, she still loves her.

Carla hangs up with Keith and is finishing the story she's writing for the evening news when Timothy approaches, laying a hand on her desk. Her eyes follow the long fingers, up to the bridge of his nose. Has he always been so tall? He has sideburns now and thin-rim glasses. He's a different man than he was five, six years ago. Older, possibly wiser. She doesn't know what it is, but he certainly has changed.

"Is everything okay?" he asks.

"Just finishing up this story. Can you believe Price is out again with another knee injury? He won't be playing any road-trip games. What's wrong with that guy? He's been on the injury list more times than he's played."

"How long is he out for?"

"I'll know more tomorrow. It's possible he'll miss the play-offs."

Timothy whistles. "Tough break."

Carla leans back in her chair. "Everything fine with you?"

"Great."

"Good," Carla says, staring into his eyes. Even though they aren't together and haven't been for three years, she still has an attachment to Timothy, like if her car broke down, she knows she could count on him to help her. Could they have worked it out? Guilt replaces the agony of what she could have done. It could have been better. Giving up wasn't what she did, but, at the time, divorce seemed like the logical thing to do.

"If you need me, to talk, whatever, you know I'm here."

"I know. Thanks," she says and lets out a sigh. If only she could ask him about having a baby.

"What is it?"

"Nothing." She waves him away and focuses on her computer screen. She's saving her story and clicking off the page when Pamela rushes toward her.

"What's up?" Carla asks.

Pamela's eyes are full of worry. She crouches down. "Taya just got fired. They called her into the office. She walked out carrying her coat and purse and told me she was fired! Can you believe that? I can't."

Carla puts her lips together. Kyle is right; they are firing people. Could it be because the ratings fell?

"Who's next?" Pamela asks, throwing her hand to her forehead. "It's like a horror movie, people getting killed off and nobody knowing when it's going to be them."

"Don't panic. Taya was in . . . graphics." Carla stops herself. Is Gabby in trouble? Her pulse quickens and she clutches her jaw. "Did she say why?"

Pamela shakes her head.

"Maybe she did something and we don't know." Carla shrugs.

"I'm scared. I've had this job forever."

"They'll keep you. They'd be foolish to get rid of their best employee," Carla says with a twist of her lips. Will there be more firings?

"Taya was good. She and Gabby were a team up there," Pamela says.

"I hope I'm not next," Carla mutters.

"Boss!" Ryan shouts, running toward her.

"I've gotta go," Pamela says and hurries off.

"What's up?" she asks her coworker.

"First thing tomorrow I'm heading over to UBC to interview the coach of the women's hockey team."

"Okay."

"After that, I've been invited to check out the guy's hockey team. They're also practicing. There are some new players, and I'm told the coach has a lot to say about them."

"You're getting a lot of calls lately," Carla says.

Ryan throws a hand on his hip. He raises his chin. "I'm making good connections. They seem to like me there."

"Where?"

"Anywhere a team is practicing. I've had no problems getting on the field or in the offices."

"We're Channel Five. We shouldn't have a problem." Carla wonders why she doesn't get these types of phone calls. They don't come as often as they should. She has to be the one to track down the story.

Ryan moves his body with an uncomfortable wiggle. "I guess. I get along with the guys. They treat me like one of their own."

Carla purses her lips. She's not going to let Ryan think any less of her. She's paid her dues. She's one of them. She's the sports anchor. She wouldn't have gotten the job if they didn't think she could do it. She's good, she tries telling herself, but the other part of her gnaws at her, telling her it's only a matter of time before she's fired, and if she is, will she get the Sports National job? She hasn't heard anything yet.

"Well, good luck, then. Keep me posted."

"I will!"

She watches him leave and is stuck in self-pity. She sulks. What can she do to keep her job? Ryan is good at what he does. She doesn't doubt that he gets phone calls. He may even have invites for dinner and drinks with the guys.

Carla picks up the phone and calls her mom.

"Care Bear! This is a surprise. Everything okay?"

"Just fine." Carla twirls the phone cord between her fingers. "Just checking in. How are you?"

"Good! Aunt Marie and I just got in from shopping. There's a sale on at Target. I needed some new bathroom things. Your dad has started to rip out the tub and toilet. We're upgrading! Can't wait to have a rainfall shower."

"Okay, well, I won't keep you, since Aunt Marie is there."

"Dad really liked his birthday," she keeps talking. "He's been wearing that jersey every day."

"I hope not while he's doing renovations."

"Oh, no. No. He's so proud of that. What a good gift for him, and to bring Devin to dinner; your dad is still talking about it. Thanks for making his day special. Devin is a nice man. He and Dad get along perfectly, like they'd known each other for years," she says with giddiness. "And his manners! You can tell his mom brought him up right. What's going on with you two? Are you dating? Aunt Marie wants to know."

"And you don't?" Carla teases.

"I always want to know."

"Nothing," Carla says simply.

"You can't tell me that! Nothing? I don't believe it."

"It's true."

"Are you friends?"

"I don't think I can call it that," Carla says, gathering the cord and releasing it and gathering it again unconsciously. "We're not even friends. We know each other. I asked him to do me a favor and stop by the house for Dad's birthday. I didn't know he'd stay for dinner," Carla adds. "I was hoping he would; for Dad, that is."

"You should be. I saw light in your eyes when he was here. I haven't seen that since you married Timothy."

"Please don't talk about it."

"Happy. You being happy."

"I am happy!" Carla says, letting the cord go and resting her hand on her desk.

"Of course you are," her mom says. "But you're happier when you're with someone."

"I'm always happy, regardless." Her voice fades.

"I guess it's been a while," Mom says.

Carla says good-bye and hangs up the phone, telling herself that happiness is a state of mind, yet anxiety fills her like an overflowing sink. Suddenly she remembers that tomorrow Keith will be there. So many what-ifs enter her mind, like what if Keith isn't who he says is? And how will she know?

Chapter 11

Carla makes her way to the press box, appearing taller in black pants and pumps. She stays away from wearing anything higher than quarter-inch heels to be steady on her feet, ready for a quick interview if necessary.

"Shouldn't you be out on a Friday night, partying with your friends?" Gary asks, stepping away from the tripod and straightening the cord. His salt-and-pepper hair falls to the side.

"I'd rather watch the game."

"You're going to make some guy lucky one day."

"I did, remember? We divorced."

"We all make mistakes."

"Yeah," she says.

"What are you doing here, anyway? You're not working, are you?"

"No. I'm here if anyone needs me," she lies. Secretly, she scans the stadium, getting her feel for where section D is. Carla stands at the edge of the box, staring out into the packed seats. She will have to wander downstairs once the game starts to find where Keith may be sitting, if he's here at all.

"Carla!"

She turns around to see Ryan.

"Hi. I didn't know you were here tonight," he says.

"I, um . . . wanted to come by to see if . . ."

"You're here to watch the game, aren't you?" he asks with a lingering smirk.

"Well, yeah," she says, looking around. She spots unfamiliar faces talking to the crew. Squinting, she tries to read their badges, and then something strange happens. The one guy wearing a suit, an open-button dress shirt at the base of his neck, steps beside Ryan, who gives him his full attention.

Carla hangs her hands over the glass railing, widening her fingers, pretending to look at her manicured nails, as she listens to their conversation.

"A young guy like you wouldn't have a problem moving to a new city," the executive says. "It's a good way to build your career."

"I'm not sure what I want to do," Ryan says.

The anthem begins and the box fills with media personnel. Carla loses the conversation. Is Ryan thinking about leaving the station? He jolts, making eye contact with her. Her insides twist in a knot, as though she's heard something she wasn't supposed to.

The anthem is over, and Ryan turns to her and asks, "Are you here to check up on me?"

"No. I wouldn't do that," she says, holding a hand on the railing. What does it matter that she's here? It's not the first time she's shown up to watch a game without working. "Do you have your interviews set up?" she asks, taking control, reminding him that she has seniority over him.

"Yeah. Alex Price," he snaps. "He's back today from a recurring knee injury."

"Okay," she says, pressing her lips together.

"Puck's going to drop," he says and walks to an empty seat reserved for him. It's a long counter set up for commentators and reporters. The view is spectacular for watching the game. Every angle of the ice is clear. Her dad would appreciate that.

Carla remains standing. She'll wait until the period is over and escape to find Keith. The game is intense. She listens to the guys behind her do the play-by-play, then glances at Ryan, who has headphones on, watching the game and taking notes. She looks up at the Jumbotron. With five minutes left in the first period, Carla decides to venture out to find Keith. Is she doing the right thing by tracking him down? What happens if he's some crazy guy, not who he says he is? At least she's in a public place.

As she strolls the arena, she glances up at the seating signage. She keeps walking.

"I knew you would be here," a voice says, distracting her under the section D sign.

Carla bats her eyelashes at the man with the heavy gaze.

"I'm Keith," he says, extending his hand.

Carla holds out her hand, studying this man who resembles Devin in so many ways: the light brown skin, dark eyes and short black hair. He isn't as tall and sports a mustache.

"Keith, hi," Carla says, shaking his hand. "Nice to meet you. Look, I don't have plans to talk to Devin today. I'm not even working."

"That's okay. It's asking a lot from a stranger, I know. You'll probably see Devin before I do." He clutches his jaw and breathes in, as though bracing to say something emotional. "Can you give him something from me?" Keith reaches into his jacket pocket and pulls out a white envelope with Devin's named printed on it. He hands it to her.

"I've sent him letters in the past, but he's never responded. I hope this one will get through to him." He bows his head and hands the envelope over.

"What do you want me to say? I'm going to have to tell him how I got this letter."

"Tell him the truth. That's something I should have done years ago."

"Won't he be mad that you contacted me?"

"Nah. He's past the anger, I think. Once he reads my letter, he'll understand."

Carla takes the envelope, placing it in an inside pocket of her purse.

"You're doing me a huge favor. Thank you." His stare lingers on hers.

How terrible it must be to lose contact with your child and have this be the only way to get in touch. A letter? A stranger intervening because the two can't do it on their own.

"I'm going to get back to the game. I'm sure we'll see each other again," Keith says.

"Did you want me to see if I can flag Devin down after the game so you can meet him face-to-face?" Carla blurts out. She bites her lower lip. Her insides are all knotted again. Can she make this promise? How will she get Keith downstairs without a media badge? Her hair starts to tingle at the roots. Her arms prickle and her heart races at the thought of getting caught.

Keith's face lights up. "Can you do it? That would be excellent." He blows out a breath, shakes his head and puts his hand on his hip, then takes it off and puts it back. "I can't tell you how much that would mean to me. Thank you. Thank you. I don't know what to say. I've wanted to see him for so long." His eyes close slightly. He clears his throat, a fist over his mouth, looks away and then says, "I owe you."

"You don't owe me anything," she says. "I can't make promises, but I can try. Okay?"

Keith nods.

"Meet me here ten minutes before the third period ends," she says, "and I'll do my best to get you downstairs."

Keith clutches his jaw. "What happens if we go into overtime? A shoot-out?"

"We won't. We beat Toronto every time." She pauses. "But regardless, I'll be here before the end of the third period."

They part ways and Carla's brain is racing with ideas of how she'll get Keith downstairs.

Carla makes her way back to the top floor to hang out in the press box.

The loud horn blows and people are going crazy. The Warriors score.

"Awesome goal!" one of the sports reporters says. He claps his hands in the air. "Good start to the game." He looks over. "Carla! Jimmy's sick. He had to leave. He's supposed to be doing center-ice interviews. Can you do it?"

"Sure! Looks like you have enough people here." She looks around her.

"I'm doing replay after first period," he says, referring to the live show during the break.

"When do you need me?" Carla asks, not familiar with the protocol of this kind of reporting.

"Go downstairs and you'll see Mac. Tell him you're taking Jimmy's place."

Carla takes off, finding her way down to center ice to find Mac, the weekend cameraman. Thankfully, she knows where she's going. It's a maze finding the entrance, but once through the double doors, security is waiting.

Carla flashes her media badge and the security guard takes a long look.

He opens the door for her. She feels the presence of somebody behind her.

"Mac?"

"That's me!"

"Jimmy's sick. I'm replacing him."

"Done this before?"

"Never."

"Should be fun then," he says, and the two walk down the hallway. "Here's your headset." He pulls one from his belt clip. "Do you know which player you want to talk to?"

"Nope."

"Good luck," Mac says, stops and leans against the cold brick wall in close proximity to the bench. He hands her a long microphone. "You'll need this."

"Thanks." She clears her throat, thinking about questions she can ask any player. Unfortunately, she hasn't been watching the game, so she can't comment on most of the first period. She bites her bottom lip, trying to wrack her brain for questions. She is so close to the players, she can reach out her hand and touch them. The smell of sweat and rubber mats makes her rub the top of her nose.

Carla adjusts her headset while looking up at the clock. Four minutes. She eyes the bench to see who is close to her. As she makes contact with Landry and Price, they both seem to look down the bench at Devin, who is too preoccupied by the game to look their way.

The referee blows his whistle and the play stops while they skate to a new face-off, giving her an extra minute to think of questions.

She listens to her headset. The guys upstairs are talking until she hears one of them say, "We're going live in thirty."

Her hands go clammy. Less than a minute. She swallows hard, trying to think of questions. Why is this difficult all of a sudden? She can do this, she tells herself. Her eyes scan the bench, taking note of which players are on the ice.

"Carla?" A voice in her headset gets her attention as she steps toward the bench and cups her hand around the headset.

"Yes?"

"Whenever you're ready, we can go," the voice says, pressuring her to start the interviews.

She takes a deep breath, swings her body around to face the guys. It's between Landry and Price. Her mind is zigzagging back and forth. Who should she ask? Landry's a friendly guy, easy to talk to, while Price has been out with a knee injury and is back playing. There's not much to talk about with him.

"Ready, Carla?" the voice asks. "In ten."

She looks at Mac, who is listening to the same conversation through his headset. He nods, balancing the camera on his shoulders and focusing his lens. He scurries closer. Carla has to make a move or she'll be pushed over.

"Ready in five," she says into her headset and positions herself in the corner of the cold plexiglass and the boards. She takes a breath. "Jared?" she says his name with authority. "Question for you."

"In three, two, one, you're on."

"Jared, you've had a goal a game for the past four games; do you feel pressured to keep up the streak?"

"Nah," he says, sweat dripping down this face. "It's not every game you get opportunities. I just happened to have the chance."

"You're two goals away from breaking your scoring record. Would you say playing on a new line is the reason?"

He brings his ear to his shoulder, stretching his neck. "It doesn't hurt. We seem to be gelling and making plays. . . ."

There is a commotion on the bench. Carla steps back as the guys make a line change. The interview is over. Mac already has his camera off his shoulder. The buzzer goes off and the period comes to an end. She leans against the low-bearing wall that separates the crowd from the players, letting the guys walk past her to the dressing room.

"Hey, there," Devin says.

Carla smiles. Her cheeks grow warm and her heart feels like it's stopped for a second. What has gotten into her? She can't even say hello. He's already gone.

She hangs around with Mac until the game resumes, interviewing one more player.

When Carla finishes, she heads upstairs to watch the remainder of the game before going to find Keith. How is she going to get him downstairs? There are so many media personnel and security, she'll have a tough time getting him through without a badge. Who can she ask to borrow from? She'd ask Ryan, but he's already downstairs, and the cameramen need theirs.

She shuffles through the gathering of media in the press box. She stands in the corner, resting her wrists on the ledge, watching the third period. Devin is on the ice. It's hard not to pay attention to his number nineteen.

Carla feels the vibration of her phone. She sweeps it up from her purse. "Hey, Gab!"

"You're at the game, aren't you?" Gabby asks, disappointed.

"It's a good thing I'm here. I did a fill-in." Carla plugs her opposite ear with her middle finger. "Where are you?"

"At the Midnight Oil. You should come. They're playing good music," she yells. "There are hot guys, too. I met someone."

Carla giggles. "Probably another one-date wonder."

"What's that?" Gabby yells into the phone.

"Nothing," Carla says.

"Are you coming out?"

"Not tonight."

"Aw," Gabby whines. "Come on. You'll have fun, I promise."

"I'm working."

"That's what happens when you show up to games."

"I'll call you tomorrow," Carla says and hangs up. She feels somebody getting close to her. It's Kip, the weekend sports reporter.

"A bunch of us are heading to Buckley's after the game. You're welcome to join us," he says.

"Thanks," she says, trying to keep an eye on the Jumbotron to count down until the last ten minutes of the game before meeting up with Keith. "I'll see."

"I'll buy you a drink," he says, stepping closer and leaning his arms over the railing. "Damn! He almost had it!" The crowd erupts at the play. "If he passed the puck to Landry, he probably would have had it."

"He never passes when he has the chance," Carla says, eyeing the game.

"Selfish play," Kip mutters.

She watches Devin skate from the bench to take his position. He's in the play at center ice, and as the play moves toward the Warriors' net, Devin skates backward, stick out in front of him, ready to poke check his opponent. With a flick of his stick, Devin manages to knock the puck off the blade and out, letting his winger scoop it up and head down the ice for a rush to score.

Carla makes fists with both hands, grinding her teeth for the chance to score again in the last seconds of play. The player misses the net and Carla throws her head back. "So close," she squeals and looks up at Kip, who is staring back at her.

He smiles. "Thanks for filling in tonight."

"No problem. I'm glad I was able to. It was a first for me." This is the longest conversation she's ever had with Kip.

"You're a pro. Nobody would ever think it was your first time reporting live on the ice."

"With our schedules, it's a wonder we haven't worked together more often," she says, glancing up at him. She likes his laid-back attitude. He would be good for her. Someone easy to talk to, ready to jump at the chance to socialize. She shoots her fluttery eyes and smiles.

"Or at least bump into each other. I heard the average person meets at least ten thousand people in a lifetime. So, yeah, it is amazing we haven't run into each other."

"That many, really?"

"I didn't make it up." He throws his hands outward. "I swear."

"And to think there are people at work I've never met before. It's possible." She looks up at the clock and gasps. "I gotta go."

"See you at Buckley's?"

"Maybe!" She runs out into the hall. Panic sets in as she hurries to meet Keith. How is she going to pull this off? She runs into the elevator just before the door closes and spots Ryan chatting with the executive he was talking to earlier.

"I think you have a chance," Executive Guy says. Ryan spots Carla and closes his mouth.

She stands in front of them. Her hands come together and then come to rest at her sides; she stares straight ahead, her feet wiggling around in her flats. She has to find Keith before the game is over or she'll have a tough time spotting him in the crowd. She gets off the elevator on the main floor and dashes to section D. As she passes an opening to a section of seats, she can see the game is close to ending. Five minutes left. Her heart's racing. She has to find Keith, get downstairs and through security before the players disperse into interviews or leave the rink.

"Carla!" Keith shouts, waving his hand above his head.

She sees him and rushes over. "If anyone asks, you're with Channel Five."

"Okay."

They start walking fast to the elevators. "And you're new to the station and forgot your media badge."

"Will they buy it?"

"I don't know," she says, ducking between people, trying to stay in pace with Keith. "I'll go first, and when security tells you that you can't enter without media credentials, tell them I can vouch for you."

"Okay."

"And stand tall, confident and believe that you're supposed to be here."

"Got it!"

"Let's take the stairs; it's faster." She leads him down a hallway to the door where security is standing. They still have to go downstairs and through another set of guards. She forgot how much security was there. She comes and goes as she pleases and never thinks about who is watching her. They walk past the first security guard with no problem and hurry down the stairwell to the next floor. She opens the metal door and another security guard is there, smiling.

"Hi, Carla."

"Hi!" she says, not knowing who the person is, but she has been there enough times to be a recognizable face.

"Whoa! Buddy! Stop!" security yells after Keith.

Keith turns around.

"Badge?" security asks.

Keith pauses.

"He's with me!" Carla says.

"Okay," the guard says, and Keith catches up to Carla before the guard calls him back.

"I'm going through those doors up ahead," she says. "I'll go first," she instructs, "and you follow me."

Carla gets to the door where security is checking every person. Once through the doors, she looks back to see where Keith is.

"I didn't think you were doing an interview," Ryan says, approaching her.

"I, uh, I'm—" She looks behind her. Keith is having a word with security. She wanders over. "He's with me," she says nonchalantly.

"He needs a badge. Can't go through without one," a male security guard with a bright blue jacket says. He takes up the doorway with his beefy arms and chest.

"I know," Carla says with gritted teeth. "He had one, but I forgot it. Sorry."

"Can't let you through," the guard says, shaking his head. His double chin bobbles with every motion.

"Just this once?" she asks. "Please?" If only the guard knew the story, she was sure he'd let Keith in.

"Nope. Can't do," he says, and waves the people behind Keith through.

"Not even if he's with me the whole time?" she asks.

"You know the rules," he says gruffly.

Carla lets out an exhausted breath like a deflated balloon. She looks at Keith, telepaths a *sorry* as she walks back to the doors. She looks behind her, remembering Ryan is standing there, probably wondering what she's doing with this old guy.

"He's helping me do an interview."

"Is that right?" the guard asks, rocking on his heels and with one hand on his hip.

"He's with Channel Five," she says, regretting her words. She knows she's abusing her position, but what else can she do? "He's an editor, and I wanted him to come down and get a sense of what I'm doing."

"Who are you interviewing?"

"Devin Miller," she answers without giving it a second thought.

"You'll have to show your editor out and make other arrangements," the security guard says. "And you'll have to move it along. The players are expected to come out any minute and there's going to be a rush in this doorway."

She hangs her head and does what she's told, exiting the area without further action. She doesn't want the guard to remember her as a difficult one but rather as easy to get along with, so he remembers her in the future.

Once she gets back through the hallway, she spots Keith waiting. "I'm really sorry, Keith. I thought I could get you in."

"Don't worry. Thanks for trying. You've already gone out of your way for me. I appreciate it. If you can get that letter to Devin, that's all I really care about. Seeing him tonight might be too much for me. I just wrote the letter," he says and grins.

She purses her lips. "I wish I could have done more tonight." And she does. If that guard only knew the story, he would have been willing to help; she was sure of it. Now she has the letter that she must give to Devin. It's in her hands now. She has to pull through for both men.

* * *

Carla drives the short distance to Buckley's.

"Got a seat for you here," Kip yells out with a wave of his hand as she wanders around the pub, looking for a seat.

Kip pulls out a chair for her, using his foot. She takes a seat with the guys and orders a light beer.

"You're a talented woman," Kip says. "Filling in like you did. I knew you could do it."

The waitress sets down her beer and Carla is quick to grab it and take a drink.

"And look who just walked in," Kip says to the table, pointing his bottle toward the door.

Carla scans the entrance. Her heart picks up its pace and her fingers slide around the bottle, flicking the label with a nail.

Devin saunters in wearing a dark suit, no tie, just like the other two guys he's with. They're laughing, talking, as they find their place at a reserved table hidden away from everyone else.

His jacket hugs his broad shoulders, fitting him in all the right places. She watches him pucker his lips with his fingers and drops them when talking to his teammates.

"I guess the guys changed their minds," Kip says. "Or some of them."

She can't help staring at him. Breathtaking. He is good to look at, but that's as far as she'll take it. Not like she has a chance. He's probably happy with puck bunnies.

She catches his eye.

"Hey!" Devin says with a raised chin.

"Hi," Carla answers. Like an awkward teenager, she looks down at the table and then back at him and smiles. What does she say to him? She tries to collect her thoughts and, for what feels like forever, it's like everyone is staring at the two of them, waiting for the next step. "Good game," she says, still smiling. What more can she say without people speculating and talking?

Devin smiles, his brown eyes bright and carefree. He pauses, gives her a half grin and keeps walking with his friends. *What just happened?* He didn't even say anything. Why not say hello? Is he scared to be among the media? Is he too good to stop for a minute and talk? Does he not want his friends to know he knows her?

Kip puts down his beer bottle. His chin and the skin beneath his cheek is razor burned. He has light brown reddish hair and untamed eyebrows. "You know Miller?" he asks, rocking his bottle back and forth on the table.

"Kind of," she says. "I've interviewed him a few times."

"So it's not like an old boyfriend."

She bursts out laughing. "No." She laughs a little more. "He just moved here."

"Anything is possible," he says coolly. "Are you seeing anyone?"

Carla puts down her half-empty beer. "No."

"That surprises me."

"Why?"

"Someone like you . . ."

"Like what?" Her eyebrows come together and she stares at Kip, guessing his age. He can't be much older than her.

"Well, you know . . ." He shifts in his seat. "You're known as the woman of sports."

"Am I now?" This amuses her.

He nods. "You are."

"Good to know people think of me as a professional and not some woman reading off a teleprompter."

"Definitely not."

"I like what I do."

"It shows." He takes in a breath. "You may not remember this, but the first time we met I was working at Q-News Radio, collecting stories for the evening shift, and you were working as the weather girl."

She laughs. "Some weather girl. I was reporting what was given to me. How many times can you say it's raining and the weather is going to suck all weekend?"

"It's a talent."

"I didn't know we worked together. I wasn't there for long."

"I used to leave *Fashion* magazine on your desk."

"That was you?" Her eyes open inquisitively. "I always wondered who did that."

"You had a thing for shoes," he says, lowering his head.

"I still do. I'm the proud owner of fifty pairs."

Gary the cameraman sits down at their table and the waitress comes by to offer him a drink.

"I left you a daisy once," Kips says, "but you were dating Andy and you thought it was from him."

"Oh, yeah, Andy." She grabs her bottle. "He didn't deny it." She sipped the last of her beer. "I asked him, and he didn't say it wasn't from him."

"Andy was a joker, wasn't he? I didn't know when he was telling the truth."

"I couldn't." She pushes her bottle away. "Thankfully, it didn't last. He got a promotion and moved across the country."

"Last I heard, he was doing the morning show at some local radio station."

"Funny where we end up," she says, looking past Kip. She can barely see Devin at the other side of the pub. He's probably waiting for the rest of his teammates, maybe even some strays looking for a good time. There's no doubt the team has their fair share of women, although so far, Carla hasn't noticed anybody else joining their table.

"Hard to believe we used to work together," she says. "You look different."

"I had longer hair back then," he says, picking up the bottle and then placing it back down. He stares at the table.

"Maybe that was it."

"I had a crush on you." Kip fidgets with the empty bottle, tapping it on the table as though trying to think of something else to say.

"You did?"

"You were always nice to me. Nice to everyone. One day in the lunchroom, I came in and you were arguing about a trade the Warriors made. You were right, and I was amazed at your facts. They were dead on."

"I wouldn't say it unless I was right."

The waitress sets down a bottle in front of Kip. He swipes the cold bottle and brings it to his mouth.

"Why didn't you ask me out?" Carla wants to know.

"Because you were with Andy."

"Oh."

"You wouldn't have gone out with me, anyway."

"No? Why's that?"

"I wasn't your type."

"And Andy was?" she says, laughing, remembering her boyfriend breaking out in a dance whenever he finished on air. It was like a ritual for him. Loved the attention and loved making people laugh, although Carla never got his jokes.

"Do you want another drink?" the waitress asks.

"No, thanks." Carla looks at what's left of her beer. She should probably get going, unless Kip plans to be here longer. She can use the company on a Friday night.

"Do you like Chinese food?" Kip asks.

"Yeah." *Is he going to ask me out?*

"There's a really good Chinese restaurant that just opened up by the Dome. Awesome food."

"Really?" she asks, interested.

"Lined up out the door."

"I'd love to try it." Carla leans forward, batting her eyes.

"You should. It's worth the wait," Kip says, knocking back his beer. "I'd better get going. My wife will start to wonder who I've run off with." He laughs nervously.

"Wife? You're married?" Carla looks at his hand for a ring but doesn't see one.

"Yeah. I've got twin boys too."

"Congratulations. How old?"

"They just turned three."

She swallows hard. "You must be proud."

"They're amazing little guys. They can build a fort out of cushions and blankets and play pirates for hours." Kip grins and takes a sip from his new beer, as though his mind is stuck on the memory. "Do you have kids?"

"No."

"Most rewarding experience."

Carla tucks in her lips. "I hope one day . . ."

She watches Kip get up and throw money on the table. "There's enough here to cover one of your beers."

"Thanks," she says softly and watches him walk away. Her eyes are fixated on Kip walking away as Devin comes into view. Her heartbeat quickens. "Hi."

"Hi." His stare shoots right through her. "Can I join you?"

"Sure."

He pulls out a chair and sits beside her, resting his arm on the table. "Is your guy friend coming back?"

She purses her lips. "Kip? No. We used to work together. Hardly a friend."

"And there's nothing between the two of you?"

She laughs. "No, why?"

"He kept trying to touch you."

"He's married." She tilts her bottle toward her. "Some people just like talking with their hands."

"That explains it."

"Explains what?"

"You said he's married? Then he's looking for some side action."

"What are you talking about?" Her look is half mischievous, half flirtatious.

"I know those types of guys. Is he coming back?"

"No!" she says and her mouth freezes in position until she takes a quick sip from her bottle. "Why aren't you sitting with your teammates?"

"I thought I'd see what you were up to. Friday night . . . you by yourself . . . no date?"

She shakes her head, staring into those dark eyes of his.

"Who did you go to the game with, or were you working?"

She sucks in a breath. Should she tell him she met his dad and that he was at the game? How will she explain why she met him? And the letter?

"Working," she lies. "Always on call."

She casually reaches into her purse, opening the inside zipper for the white envelope addressed to Devin. She can feel those intense eyes watching her every move. What should she say? That she ran into his dad and he gave her this to give him? What happens if he says he doesn't know what she's talking about? Her fingers stop at the feel of the paper, unsure how to approach him. She likes looking at him. Right now he's easy to talk to. Giving him the letter will intensify it, maybe change the way he talks to her. A split decision; she grabs her cell phone instead. She takes it out of her purse and says, "I thought I heard it ring." She fakes a laugh and shoves it back into her purse.

"Have you toured the city much since the last time we talked?" she asks, taking the last sip of her beer.

"Not as much as I'd like. What do you say we get out of here?"

Her eyebrow lifts and her lips come together, unsure of what he's asking. "And go where?"

He shrugs. "I dunno. You still need to show me your city."

"Right. I promised."

"You don't keep promises very well."

"I never make them," she says.

"Except?"

"Except to you."

He brings a hand to his chest. "I feel so privileged."

"Don't be." She grins. "Aren't you having another drink?"

"No. One beer's enough."

"Is that what your dietician suggests?"

"It's my preference. I come to sit with the guys and have a drink. I'm not one to sit around all night in a bar."

"Me neither. I don't know why I'm here," she says, thinking of Gabby and passing up a club for a game, something she wouldn't think twice about. A game is always more entertaining. Carla stands up.

"Have you heard of Westminster Quay?"

She laughs.

"I guess you have."

"Haven't been there in years."

"Do you want to go?"

"When?"

"Now."

"There's not much to do there at this hour. The casino." She digs for her phone and clicks it on so she can read the time. "It's late."

"You're probably right."

"I should go," she says. "Good luck on Tuesday."

"Tuesday?"

"You're playing the Blackhawks."

Devin stands up. "Are you sure you don't want to go for a drive?"

"I'm sure. It's late and I need to get home." She takes her keys in her hand. "Good night." She waves and heads out the door.

"I'll walk you out." He chases her out of the bar.

She stops, turns around, her nose inches from his broad chest. He smells of soap mixed with cologne. "I . . . I'm fine. My car is right there," she says, flinging her arm over her shoulder with her keys in hand. She doesn't bother to look.

"What do you drive?" he asks, glancing past her.

"Mercedes." She turns her head. "Huh." Carla puts a hand on her hip. "Where did I park? Oh, yeah. Right there!" She points and glares. It doesn't look like her car, but it's ten o'clock at night. It's dark. "Hard to see."

"Let me walk with you," he says.

"Suddenly you're Mr. Nice Guy?"

"I am nice! I don't know where you get the idea I'm not. Where do you get your information, anyway?"

"My research and"—she looks ahead but doesn't recognize her car—"people talk."

"They shouldn't. It's bad information."

"Not if it's true." She clicks her button for her alarm and nothing. Again. Nothing. "Batteries," she mutters. She stops at the parking stall. "What the hell? My car. I parked it right here!" She frantically looks around her. "I'm sure I parked here."

Devin looks at the building and points with his thumb. "Where it says loading zone?"

"What? No! I didn't park in a loading zone."

"Are you sure it's not on the other side of the building? There's a back entrance. Maybe you came in that way."

"I never go that way. I always park here . . . well, on this side." Carla digs in her purse for her phone.

"Who are you calling?"

"Mark Buckley, to tell him his parking rules suck. I'm calling the towing company." She exhales to relax and puts a hand on her hip. When the operator answers, she asks very calmly if they have her car.

"Yes. Jack is dropping it in the yard right now."

Carla blows out a bigger breath. "Seriously? Jack didn't have anything better to do on a Friday night than tow a woman's car? Single woman, I might add, and I'm by myself." She exhales. What happened to the days when you parked in the wrong spot and someone came into the place and yelled out to ask who was parked in the spot? Jeez! "Nobody gives anybody a break anymore?"

"You can come down and pick up your car. Cash is preferred."

"Of course it is." Carla hangs up the phone and turns to Devin.

"You're not alone. I'll drive you."

"You don't have to."

"How else will you get your car?"

She thinks for a second. "Okay, I guess. Thanks." She pouts. Who would she call if Devin wasn't here? Gabby was probably in no shape to drive. It's too late to call her dad, but she would have if she had to. She could call Timothy, but he's the last resort.

"Just tell me where to go," he says.

She follows him around the building to his Range Rover. She hops in the passenger seat, throws her purse on the floor and tightens her seat belt.

"Do you know where we're going?" he asks, turning the ignition.

"Yeah." She sits back. "Been there before."

"How often?" He laughs.

"Just once. I parked in a no-parking zone after four. Didn't think it meant holiday Mondays."

Devin chuckles as he turns onto the main street. "You thought they would make you the exception?"

"I was in a hurry to park and make it to an event. I overlooked the sign." Carla watches the streets as they pass intersections. "Keep going straight."

Devin looks up at every street number as he drives through it.

"At the next light, make a right, and instead of going over the bridge, make a right and it will take you underneath to the yard."

"You know where you're going for only having been towed once." He has a half smile on his face as he looks over.

Devin pulls up in the dirt parking lot. Carla jumps out, clutching her purse and marching up the steps of the portable office. She swings open the door. "I'm here to pick up my car," she tells the lady, who gets up from her desk like it's an inconvenience and brings her glasses to her face.

"License plate?" she asks and takes the invoice papers in her hands.

Carla runs off her plate number.

"White Mercedes?" the woman asks, searching the papers for the right one. "That'll be seventy dollars."

"What? For a no-parking zone?"

"It's a violation."

"So is the price," Carla says, getting out her wallet and handing over the cash.

The woman ignores her as she rings up the charge and hands her the invoice to sign.

Carla's hand is trembling as she signs her name. She puts the paper in her purse and takes out her keys.

"Your car is parked by the gate."

Carla storms out of the portable, slamming the door behind her. She gets down the steps and walks over to the gate, where she can barely see her car.

Devin jumps out of his Range Rover and runs over to her. "Did they tell you where your car is?"

"Yeah, right here." She presses the unlock button on her remote.

"Okay, well, good . . . glad you got it." He runs his hand through his hair, the other hand on his hip. "They didn't do any damage?" He steps closer to her car so he's standing right beside her.

"I didn't think to look." She gets close to her car and examines her driver's side window, slides her hand around the frame. "Nope. I don't see anything." She turns around and is caught with her nose in his chest, inhaling his cologne. Her insides go frail at his scent, imagining how his arms would feel wrapped around her. She envisions his hard abs. She swallows and looks up to meet his uneasy stare.

"Looks good, then?"

"It does." She nods swiftly.

Devin doesn't step back; instead he bows his head to hers and stares into her eyes.

She swallows again to moisten her throat. "What?" she whispers.

"You," he says, bringing his hand to her chin and leaning in to kiss her.

She opens her mouth to his as a reaction to his lips closing in on hers. The kiss is slow enough to taste his sweet lips. She shouldn't do this. She can't. He'll regret this when he finds out what she's done. What will he say when he gets the letter? Will he feel the same about her? Devin wraps his arm around her waist like an anchor to keep her still. He kisses her tenderly. Her body presses against his. She brings her hand up to his open suit jacket, feeling the firmness and well-worked muscles underneath his shirt. What is happening? She kisses him back. His lips tug at hers, eager for more, and then he gently sweeps her lips with one last kiss before letting go.

She can't let this happen. *He doesn't want me.* He wants the recognition, for her to forget how she feels about his career, doesn't he?

"What are you doing?" she asks.

"Kissing you."

"W-why?"

"I was tempted and . . . well, the moment felt right." He pauses, staring into her eyes.

He takes two steps back. "I just thought . . . that you . . . that I . . ." He scratches the back of his neck and keeps his hand there while staring at the crushed gravel. "I don't know what came over me." His eyes find hers. There's a pull of desire in his gaze that captures her.

She doesn't want him this way.

"Thank you for driving me here. I appreciate it," she says, matter-of-fact.

"No problem." He thrusts his hands into his pants pockets. "Glad I was there. You're safe."

"Yes. Thank you. Well, good night." She opens her car door.

"Oh, Carla?"

She pivots before sitting down in her seat.

"I didn't mean to upset you."

"I'm not upset." She tightens her mouth. Why couldn't he be a lousy kisser? It would make this easier.

"I wanted to see if there was something there." His eyelids crease and he tilts his head slightly. "You're not?"

"No . . . no . . . I . . . um . . . I'm not looking for a fling. I don't do that. And I'm not what you're looking for. Trust me." She sits and starts up her car, watching Devin kick rocks as he makes his way to his vehicle.

She can't fall for this guy. If he only knew she was looking for a guy wanting to commit and start a family together. . . .

Chapter 12

Carla gets ready for work, throwing a granola bar into her purse. She freezes when she spots the white envelope. She should have given it to Devin last night at the tow yard. What should she tell him? If she keeps the letter for a bit longer, maybe there will be an opportunity to slip it in his car, or somehow tell him she found it and hand it to him. So many stories go through her head. Any of them would be easier than telling Devin she's been in touch with his dad.

Her cell phone rings. She slides her finger across the screen to accept the call and braces the phone between her ear and shoulder as she takes out a pair of her favorite black flats from her hall closet.

"Carla, it's Mike Donald from Sports National."

She drops her shoes and purse on the floor. "Oh, hi!" Carla moves to the couch to sit so she can think and listen to Mike tell her she has the job. She'll have to find a place to move to, sell her car, hire movers. . . .

"You're still at Channel Five?"

"That's right," she says, beaming. Her heart races.

"How's it going there?"

"Fine. Yes, it's good, you know, but—"

"Is Russ still there? Last time I heard he was station manager."

"He is."

"Good for him. Russ has a way of getting people to do things for him. I'm sure he's excelling at it." He laughs. "That's great. That's great. Listen, the reason I'm calling is we've had a huge response for our reporter position."

"Yes! Yes!"

"And we've narrowed it down to twenty. Phew. I tell you, it's been the hardest position to cover yet. We don't know why. We had a Web reporter position posted and didn't get nearly as much response as this."

"It's a great company," she says off the top of her head. "It's the top position for any sports reporter, working with retired players, seasoned media professionals. . . ."

He laughs. "It's a hard decision, no doubt. We want to hire the right person, so you can imagine how tough this has been."

"Uh-huh." She flexes her toes. The excitement is too much. Maybe this is it. Maybe she's destined to move across the country, start a new life and find the person she needs to settle down with.

"Ryan Peller listed you as a reference. What can you tell me about Ryan? Is he a good employee?"

"Oh." She sinks into her couch. "Yes, he's good."

"How good is he at his job? And I'm not talking about a pretty face." Mike bursts out laughing. "He sent us a picture on his résumé."

"Ryan's good," she says again, feeling the excitement disperse like a deflated balloon. "He does his job well. Aims to please."

"I like that! Would you say he's independent and can work on his own, without supervision?"

"I'd say so."

"How is he to get along with?"

"Good." She pouts.

"All right, then. Thanks."

Does Ryan have the same intentions? Is he reaching for similar goals? He's young and energetic. He has a better chance because he's a guy.

"He loves what he does and doesn't want to disappoint, so you'd be getting a great employee if you hired Ryan."

"That makes my decision easier. Thank you!"

"Mike, by any chance did you see my résumé?"

"You applied for this job?"

"I did."

He shuffles papers. "I don't see you in the pile. I have the top twenty applicants; sorry. I don't have it here. It was for this position?"

"Yes."

"Nope. Sorry. Don't see it. We do keep résumés on hand for six months. You never know. We'll contact you if there are new positions to apply for."

"Thank you," she manages to say and hangs up the phone. It's time to head to work, where she gets a call from her mom as soon as she sits down.

"Did you hear from Gavin?"

"No, not lately. What's up?"

"They booked the day."

"Great."

"I heard Gavin wants you as one of the bridesmaids."

"I hardly know Mia."

"What do you mean? She's at every family function. Christmas, birthdays—"

"I don't know her. Isn't that strange to you?"

"Not really. You and Gavin are close. Anyway, I'm planning on an engagement dinner. Next Saturday. I already checked, the Warriors aren't playing, so you and your dad won't be itching to go."

"Where are you having it?"

"I thought I'd have it here or at the Olive Garden. Apparently it's where they had their first date."

"How nice."

"I'm inviting family and some friends. You can bring a date if you want."

"Probably not."

"No date? How about Devin?"

"I knew you'd say that."

"Well, you have a week to change your mind."

"Mom, I'm fine being by myself."

"We all are, Care Bear, but no one likes eating alone."

"I live by myself and I'm fine with it."

"Sure you are. I'd better go. I have a list of people I have to call, and then I'll make the reservations."

"Do you know what they need for an engagement gift?"

"Oh, right. I'd better ask if Sadie can bring her minivan to haul the gifts back from the restaurant. Thanks for reminding me. Why don't you bring Timothy, then?" she asks as an afterthought.

"Are you out of your mind? No, I'm not. We're divorced, and divorced couples don't socialize with each other."

"But you're still friends."

"We work together. We have to get along," Carla says. "We're civil people."

"It would be nice to see him. You know, he was part of our family."

"Not anymore. Maybe I'll ask Gabby to come," Carla suggests.

"Sure. Didn't Gavin and she used to date?"

"No, that was Michelle. I have to go. I'm at work." She hangs up as she turns into the parking lot and loads her arms with an oversize bag, her purse and a travel cup of coffee.

Carla gets to her desk, fires up her computer and takes a tin of mints out of her purse.

"Ryan," she says, watching him walk through the studio. She holds up her hand, motioning him to come over to her.

"Hey!"

"I didn't know you used me as a reference." She pops a mint into her mouth.

"I was going to tell you about that." He cups his hands together. "Did they call?" He gives her a sideways grin, just enough so she can see his white front teeth. "They did, didn't they?"

She nods. "Yes." She breaks off a piece of granola bar and pops it into her mouth. "You didn't tell me you were looking for another job."

He presses his hand down in the air. "I don't want anyone to know," he says quietly.

"Okay. I won't say anything."

"I'm not worried about you."

She pushes her face in and brings her hand to her chest. "About me? What's there to worry about?"

"Jay applied for the same job. He's sure he's got it because of his experience."

"That doesn't mean anything," Carla says, deciding that she would keep her application a secret as well. "A big part of what they hire on is personality."

"Jay has personality."

"So do you." Ryan had that cool swagger that made him seem older than his twenty-five years.

"Jay has more experience than me. He worked for sports radio before this. What did they ask you?"

She breaks apart another piece of granola bar. "The usual. Do you need supervision? Can you work on your own? That sort of thing."

"What did you tell them?"

"I said you're a good employee. You work hard." She chews her snack.

"Thanks, Carla. I really need this."

"You're not happy here?"

"I am. It's just that I'm from Toronto and it would be nice living in the same city as my family. If I stay here, it would be nice to get higher up on the food chain. I may be considered a junior reporter longer than I like."

"I see. Well, good luck. I hope you get it."

Ryan walks off and Carla clicks on her e-mail. She filters through the messages and writes down story ideas as she goes. As she replies to an e-mail, the lanky legs of a guy in jeans distract her. She looks up. "Hi," she says softly to her ex.

"I need to ask you something."

"Shoot." She sits back in her chair, staring up at him.

"I didn't know when to ask you this, but I'm stuck." He folds his arms to his chest. "I don't know what to do about Freddie."

She drops her chin. "Your cat? Is he okay? He's only five. He's healthy, isn't he?"

"Yeah, yeah. Freddie's good. Healthy. It's just that I need to find him a home, and I thought that you might—"

"A home? I bought Freddie for you. He's your cat."

Timothy grits his teeth so that his cheeks puff out and his eyes start to squint. "I know, but I'm hardly home."

"Cats are self-sufficient." She talks with her hands. "If he moves, that will really mess him up. You know cats aren't good with change. They hate moving. Where are you moving to?"

"I'm not."

"Then why don't you want him?"

There's a pause, and Carla's eyes grow bigger. She sucks in a breath. "You're getting rid of Freddie because he reminds you of me, is that it? The cat. We've been apart for three years and now it's the cat that's bothering you? I still have our kitchen table and I use it. I'm not getting rid of it."

"It's solid oak."

"So?"

"So it's a good piece of furniture. I told you if you ever wanted to get rid of it, I'd take it back."

"And how about the glass vase from your aunt? The one with frosted glass ribbons around it?" They divided up their possessions when they divorced. She didn't think there was anything left.

"You liked it. I didn't." He clears his throat. "Will you take Freddie? If not, I'll find him a good home."

"You wanted that cat because he reminded you of Sniffles, your childhood cat."

He snickers. "We both wanted a pet, and a cat seemed like the best choice since we were both out of the house for extended periods of time," he says coolly.

She stands and lets out a breath. "Where else can he go?"

"I don't know who will want him."

"I don't want a pet, but I guess if nobody will take him—"

"Thanks." He nods his head with approval. "I knew you would."

She walks off with the realization that she has inherited a cat when it's the last thing she wants. If only adopting a baby was easier.

Chapter 13

The kiss. It has been on Devin's mind since he left the tow yard. Carla was incredible. Why did he want her so badly? She was probably used to relationships and had expectations. It was clear she didn't want anything to do with him, but there was one thing for certain: He wanted more of her. The kiss was a tease for something more. She wouldn't let him get close to her, he was sure.

Devin skates hard around the ice until he gets to a pile of pucks. He picks one up with the blade of his stick and skates with it to the other end, taking a shot at his goal.

"Nice one," Devin says about the glove save and slows down as he skates back toward the bench.

"Miller!" Coach Steve calls. "Try that again. This time shoot blocker side. I bet you'll get it."

Devin takes his advice and skates for the blue line to pick up a puck. He flicks a couple of practice shots off the boards before skating hard to the net. He looks at the goalie and winds up and shoots. The puck skips over the blocker and in.

"That'll do it!" Steve yells and blows his whistle. "We've got a game against the Hawks tomorrow. I want lots of shots on net and defense. Remember, do your job and take your man. Last time they killed us. We let them walk right in."

Devin steps off the ice and into the locker room to shower and dress. He walks outside in the afternoon sun and is greeted by five young women, all wearing tight tops and big smiles.

"Hi, ladies," Devin says. Does he stay or leave? It's tempting to invite them for a drink and, if all goes well, invite them back to his house. But how is he ever going to settle down if that's the only way he's going to meet women? He takes another glance at the woman with long curly brown hair and a miniskirt. Her legs are as long and lean as a cheerleader he used to date. Tempting. Where would that get him? It's short-term. It's not like Carla will be knocking at his door anytime soon.

"What are you doing here, hanging out at the back of the building?" he asks the curly-haired woman among the few kids with Sharpie pens and paper.

"Waiting for you," she says, shifting her weight to one side. "What do you say we grab a drink?"

"Are you old enough to drink?"

"I'm of age, if that's what you're asking. My girl Tina here has a thing for Alex Price. Any chance you can call him over, and maybe the four of us can hang out?"

He clears his throat. An elbow taps his arm. "Pricey, we were just talking about you."

"Oh, yeah?" he asks with a raised chin. The two-inch scar on his cheek creases when he smiles. "Are we going somewhere?"

"You're taking us for a drink," Tina says.

"We are?" Alex asks.

"My friend and I want to have fun. You guys are fun." The one woman takes a closer step toward Devin and licks her bottom lip, playing with a long curl, wrapping it around her finger.

Devin knows what it means when women hang out at the rink. Their only purpose is to hook up with one of them and then tell everyone about it. Devin thinks about Carla.

Alex steps closer to Devin and whispers in his ear. "What do you say we head out for a drink with these hotties?"

"Nah, I'm going to pass."

"You have something better in mind?" Alex snickers.

"I'm going home."

"Ah, someone's waiting for you." He gives him a thumbs-up. "Got it. Right. See you at the game."

Devin grins and saunters through the parking lot. It was too easy to hook up with one of those women. Why can't he stop thinking about Carla? She doesn't want him, but why? He has everything going for him: single, wealthy, a good job and hasn't disappointed a lady as far as he knows. What will change her mind?

Devin starts his Range Rover when it hits him: She hasn't given him a tour of the city like she promised. A bottle of wine, a blanket and a little place he just discovered on the North Shore. A smile forms. Time to step up his game.

But right now he has something important to do before dinner: visit his sick little friend Jason, who has been on his mind. Devin doesn't enjoy hospitals and everything they expose him to, like the smell. He doesn't know exactly what that cool air brings, like an attic with a trunk of old clothes. It's unsettling because outcomes are unknown and people's lives are at risk.

Since moving to Vancouver, he was told this was one of the expectations for every player. He tried to be committed to every charity his hockey team supported, but sometimes they hit him harder than others. Devin remembers when he broke his arm playing on the school playground. Sitting in the cast room hadn't been that bad. He knew he'd be bandaged up and sent home, a minor injury. Even when he got boarded in a hockey game when he was younger and had a separated shoulder, he knew he would just be out of the game for six weeks. He would heal and be back playing.

Nothing could prepare him for the Children's Hospital. It got to him every time. It was never easy making the trip—it was sometimes a battle to step inside—but when the time was up, Devin was glad he'd gone. Seeing the smile on the kids' faces was worth it.

Devin is chaperoned by a nurse through an open door.

"There he is!" the nurse says. "Still fighting the bad guys?" she asks Jason, who is holding a computer game up to his face.

"I lost. I'm on a new game."

"I wouldn't even know what to do with it," she admits.

"It's easy!" Jason says and pauses his game, bringing it down to his lap.

The nurse turns to Devin. "You know how to use those things?"

"I can probably figure it out." Devin grins at the eight-year-old with pale skin. "How are you doing, buddy?"

"Good," the boy answers, turning off his game.

Devin takes a seat at his bedside. The boy, with a bald head and no eyebrows, makes Devin sad with worry. The more Devin sees Jason, the more attached he feels, always wondering how he's holding up and getting through chemotherapy.

"I brought you something." Devin hands him a sports bag.

The boy's face lights up, and he takes the bag from Devin and pulls out a Warriors hat. "Wow! Thanks! It's super!" He places the hat on his head, turning and nodding to feel the new accessory.

"Looks good." Devin rises from his seat. "Here, I'll take the tags off."

"No, I wanna keep them. I wanna show my mom and dad."

Devin nods and sits back in his seat.

"I guess you won't be visiting me as much when play-offs start," Jason says.

"I don't know about that. I'll still come to see you. It just might be once a week instead of twice. I'll do my best."

"You will?"

"Why not?"

"You won't have time."

"I'll make time," Devin says, watching the boy's smile broaden.

"Mom says I'm here till September."

Devin nods somberly. He had no idea that acute myeloid leukemia could keep a child in the hospital for half a year.

"Are you sad you're missing school?"

It takes a minute for Jason to answer. "I miss my friends."

"I bet."

"I miss playing on the playground."

Devin's not sure what to say. Nothing he can do will make Jason better, yet he wants to be an inspiration and give only words of encouragement. That's the whole point of the visits, but Devin is really stuck for what to say.

"I'll tell you what," Devin says, making a promise he knows he has to keep. "When you're out of the hospital and if it's okay with your parents, I'll have tickets for you and your family to come to a Warriors game."

"Really? I've never been to a game before!"

"Never?"

"No. My mom says it's too much money."

"Well, I'll have tickets with your name on them."

"I can't wait!" the boy shrieks, padding his hands on his lap. "I can't wait," he says firmly and with strength. Devin can see the determination in his eyes.

"I can't wait either," Devin says.

Chapter 14

Carla is busily typing, preparing for the six o'clock news, when her desk phone rings. She hits SAVE. "Newsroom, Carla speaking."

"Hey, Carla, it's Devin."

Her heart feels like it's stopped beating. A hot flash fills her body as she pictures him as he looked the other night, in his Armani suit, smelling like macadamia nuts, buttery and warm. His lips were the same. Smooth and lush, making her body seize up with emotion. How can Devin, a guy she barely knows, have that effect on her? That tenderness about him, making her think there's much more under the glass case than meets the eye. And back to those lips, and desperately wanting to taste more of him. "Oh, hi."

"Hi. I wasn't sure how to reach you."

"You have my cell . . . but this is fine. . . ." *More than fine.*

"I left a message. I know you're busy."

"Do you have a news story?" she asks jokingly to break the ice.

"It could be, I guess." He laughs and then turns serious. "I'm going out to a new restaurant, ah, Flourish? Flamingo?" He laughs. "I can't remember now."

She gushes. "Flavors? They just opened on Robson Street."

"That sounds right. See? I don't even know where it is. I'm hoping you can show me."

"You just want to see where they're located?" she asks, giving him a hard time. "'Cause I can just tell you. It would make it easier. . . .'"

There's a pause, and she's not sure what he's getting at.

"Well, it's supposed to be a great place for dinner. That's what I hear, and I have the number of the manager. I can make reservations. I'm told that's probably best since it's so busy and hard to get a table. . . ."

"Dinner?" Why can't he just say it? What is he afraid of?

"Dinner. Do you want to try it?"

"I've been. Great food."

"Oh."

She can imagine his broad shoulders sinking like a barge. Disappointed? What did he have in mind? "I'd love to go there again sometime."

"Okay. Tomorrow night?"

"Sorry, I work until seven, weekends off."

"I have a game Saturday."

"I know." She stares at her computer screen.

"How 'bout lunch?"

"I'm scheduled to do the noon news tomorrow."

"Okay. We could make it another night or day. . . ."

"I'm free for breakfast?" *Breakfast?* She makes a face and clutches her hands on her desk.

"Breakfast? All right. Tomorrow?"

"Sure," she says, smiling.

"Meet you at IHOP?"

"Okay."

"Okay! Great!" he says. "I'll see you then."

"Yes, see you then." She hangs up. Why is she so excited about breakfast? This is new for her. Nothing can come from the most important meal of the day, can it? She calms herself by rereading her script.

"Carla!" a boisterous voice yells.

Her head pops up from the screen. Russ, the station manager. Her stomach sinks like she's ridden in an elevator dropping to the ground floor.

"Can I see you in my office? Now."

Her stomach is in the basement now. She squeezes her fingers together and releases, doing this several times as she gets to her feet.

His hand is in his front pocket, jingling his keys. It's nerve-racking being called to the attention of many. Eyes in the newsroom stare, and some pretend they're not listening as they work.

Carla's face is flushed with uncertainty. Is she getting fired?

Demoted? Did she say something in a story she shouldn't have? Will he give her a warning?

"Russ!" she exclaims. It's a good confidence booster to be positive, Carla decides. If this is her last day, then she might as well go out with a bang.

"I hope I'm not taking you away from anything too pressing," he says, opening his office door. "Have a seat." He pulls out the chair as he walks to his desk and sits down. Russ folds his hands on his desk.

Carla notices his gold band on his left hand and a mustache that's well trimmed above his lip.

"I'm just finishing up a news story. I can be done in five minutes," she says, pushing her back to the seat.

"What's the story? The Warriors not making the play-offs?"

"No, they'll make it."

"They have Devin Miller. He's been making some good plays for offense."

"Actually, Alex Price is out indefinitely. He needs knee surgery and won't be well enough to make the play-offs."

"Sucks for him." Russ looks at loose white sheets of paper.

Carla can't tell what they are. Perhaps notes of evidence for letting her go?

"I wanted to see you and talk to you about the sports department." He pauses. "It's come to my attention that the department is struggling with having enough staff on hand. I wasn't aware of the issue."

"There's no issue. I'm not sure who told you that. We seem to be fine." Even if there is a staffing problem, she isn't going to say it. She wants to keep her job. The last thing to do is complain in the middle of reconstruction.

Russ clears his throat. "You're doing a fine job. But . . ."

But? There's a *but?* She plays with her fingers. Her heart races. Here it is. She shifts in her seat.

"I want to see Ryan do more anchoring shifts. Not every night; Monday and Tuesday nights. You can do mornings."

She lowers her head. "Monday and Tuesday mornings?" she asks.

"It would be better for you."

"It would? What about Jay? Where is he going? He usually does mornings."

"I let him go."

"You fired him? When?"

"Just now. He told me he got a job at Sports National."

Her head drops. A cold twinge rises up her spine. "So you let him go? Why? We need him," she tells him in a mere whisper, trying to comprehend the news. "Jay is great at what he does. We need him back. You didn't tell him he should stay?"

He shakes his head. "Jay is good, but he'll do better elsewhere."

"But why?" As much as Jay thinks he's better than the rest, she needs him and his talent. Who can she count on besides Ryan?

A smirk comes across his face. "No need to worry. We do what we have to do."

"I counted on Jay. He worked whenever and did what needed to be done. Now what are we going to do?"

"Use Edson."

"He's so green! I can't put him just anywhere." She tries not to panic.

"He'll get experience," Russ says passively. "He'll learn."

Why does this bother her more than the general manager? "And what about the late news? Who's covering sports?"

"Edson."

Carla exhales. What's the reason behind this? she wants to ask. She can't ask because that will cause tension, and when there's tension, jobs are jeopardized.

"You guys will be fine," he says, pushing the papers that are in front of him into a pile.

He doesn't know Ryan is browsing for a new job. She sinks in her chair. Then what will happen?

"I don't know," she says, worried. "What happens if someone else leaves? We'll have no one."

"Is someone leaving?"

"Well, no, no, not that I'm aware of, but I'm saying we'll be short-staffed if someone does."

"No, you won't," he says.

Her eyebrows furrow.

"I hired a new reporter. Kip—"

Her eyes can't stretch any wider.

She returns to her desk pale-faced and angry. She can't wrap her mind around it.

"Boss!" Ryan says, running toward her.

Carla plunks herself down.

"Jay got fired."

"I just found out."

"What happened? Do you know?"

Carla shakes her head. "I don't."

"That sucks," Ryan says. "I mean for you. What's going to happen?"

"I don't know." Carla stops herself from telling him what Russ told her, at least for now. It's good for him to be uncertain. She doesn't know what's going on either.

Chapter 15

Carla sips her coffee, holding it with both hands, sitting across from Devin at a restaurant table at nine-thirty in the morning. She's never had a breakfast date before. In fact, meeting someone of the opposite sex at a restaurant before noon doesn't feel like a date at all.

"Have you ever been on a breakfast date?" he asks, pouring syrup on his buttermilk pancakes.

"No. Never. Not even with my ex-husband." She cautiously puts down her cup and smiles. "Timothy wasn't much of a breakfast guy."

"Most important meal of the day!"

"He considered noon early."

"It's all about your daily schedule. I prefer mornings, but playing hockey at night pushes me to wake up late." He cuts into his pancakes. "How 'bout you? Do you like working nights?" He takes a bite.

She shrugs. "I'm used to it. My days are sometimes long, depending on what's going on. What do you do when you're not playing or training?"

"I'm still trying to get settled. I have boxes to unpack." He sips his coffee.

"Do you have a lot? I mean, moving from city to city, how much do you bring with you?"

"A fair share. I'm going to be here for six years, so I'm putting things away and not leaving them in boxes like I did in the past."

His past, Carla thinks, and is reminded that she has the letter in her purse. She has to give it to him. It's Devin's.

The waitress refills their coffees.

"Are you free tonight after work? I've been doing my own touring."

She grins. "I'd like to see what you've found."

"It's just a view of the water. I'm sure you've seen it before."

"I can always see it again."

"How about tonight?"

Her phone rings and she reaches into her purse, pulls it out and looks at the number. "It's my sister."

"Carla. It's Sadie," she says, panicked.

"Is everything okay?" Carla combs her hair away from her face with her fingers.

"I'm sick," Sadie whines. "I have a horrible head cold and need to lie down. Brin's been up all night. . . . I can't get hold of Mom and I need help."

"I'm on my way!" Carla says, hangs up and tosses her phone back into her purse. "Sorry. I have to go."

"Everything okay?"

"My sister is sick and needs a hand with her daughter." Carla downs the last of her coffee and pushes it aside, taking out cash from her wallet.

"I'll walk you out."

"You don't have to. You're still eating."

"No. I'm done." He wipes his lips with a napkin and drops it on his plate. He leans up and takes out his wallet from his back pocket, throws down money and slides out of the booth.

"Devin Miller!" a guy at a table yells.

Devin looks behind him and grins.

"That's him!" someone says as he walks past a booth. They get outside before people approach him and head over to Carla's car.

"So, about tonight . . ." Carla says, getting out her keys. "I can be out of work by seven-thirty."

"That's good." Devin stands beside her car. "Text me your address. I'll pick you up."

"I can pick you up. Isn't that the deal? I show you the city?"

"I like to drive. It will help me learn the roads."

"All right," Carla says, opening her car door.

"Devin! Devin! Is that you?" someone says, rushing toward him, with another guy trailing behind.

"I have to go." Carla gets into her car. "Sorry I can't save you."

"See you tonight," he says and turns to face hockey fans, who are in his face with pens and papers to sign.

Carla looks in her rearview mirror. He handles it just fine, she thinks, driving off.

It's a twenty-minute drive to her sister's town house. There used to be a time when shopping and lunch dates were a weekly event. Now they're lucky if coffee is on the go and the sandwiches are premade.

Sadie answers the door, holding her head with one hand and a baby on her hip with the other.

Automatically, Carla reaches out to take Brinley, who is crying and fussing.

"I think she's teething," Sadie says, shutting the door and locking it. "I haven't seen a tooth yet, but she's been gnawing on her fingers."

"At six months?" Carla pats her niece's back and bounces. The little girl is sucking on her hand.

"Did you try a teether?"

Sadie raises an eyebrow.

"I know a little bit about children."

Sadie lets out a breath. "Yes."

"How about a cold washcloth like Mom suggested?" When her sister doesn't answer, Carla goes into the bathroom and grabs a cotton facecloth from the drawer. She wets it down with one hand, squeezes it, leaves it in a tight roll and hands it to Brinley. "There you go, princess."

The little girl sucks on the cloth and coos.

"Go have a hot bath and lay down," Carla instructs. "I'm fine. Did you get hold of Mom?"

"She's on her way."

"Good."

"If she doesn't get here when you have to get to work, wake me."

"Okay. Shut your door and don't worry. If I run into trouble, I'll get you."

Sadie turns around. "Thanks. Brian would have stayed home if he could, but he had some important meetings to get to."

"You have me. Any time." Carla looks at her niece. "Let's give Mommy a break and go read a story." She carries her niece into her room to pick out a book and sits on the rocking chair with Brinley curled up on her shoulder. Carla closes her eyes and takes in the smell of the baby and rubs her cheek against hers, feeling the firm skin and button lips. So perfect. Would her children be as beautiful? What would they have looked like had she had them with Timothy? She often wonders because it was the closest chance she had with someone. Would her eyes light up with joy every time she said his name? Could she love her baby just as much as she loved Brinley?

Carla rocks, opens the book and begins to read. "'Guess how much I love you?'" she says, letting her head settle gently against the baby's. It is quiet and peaceful. Getting the situation under control, she lowers her voice, noticing the baby is almost asleep.

Brinley's light brown eyelashes flutter as her eyes get heavy, and when her lids finally close, Carla's voice gets softer until Brinley falls asleep.

"'. . . To the moon and back,'" Carla says and gently puts the book down on the dresser beside her, wraps both arms around the baby and stands, careful not to disturb her position. At the crib, she extends her arms and places Brinley down on her back. Slowly, she takes the cloth away and tiptoes out of the room. Mission accomplished. She can do this!

A cry stops her in her tracks. She probably wants her pacifier. When Carla walks back into the room to peek in on her, Brinley is staring back at her through the wooden slats of the crib. Then her bottom lip curls and an outburst of a cry makes Carla scoop her up and take her in her arms, bouncing her and hushing her back to sleep.

"You're okay," she whispers. "It's nap time. Auntie needs to go to work shortly and Grandma will be here. You get to see Grandma." Carla's words run into one another as she fears her sister will come into the room and take over. "Shhh." She bounces. "You must be really tired . . . shhh . . . you need your beauty sleep . . . shhh." The baby starts to calm. Carla relaxes her shoulders and holds her firmly to her chest. She takes a seat on a large chair in the living room and sits mindlessly holding the sleepy baby. Her phone rings. Carla gets up and sidesteps to her purse, careful not to move the baby. She reaches in and takes it out to answer it.

"Hey, Carla, it's Devin."

"Hi!"

"About tonight, sorry; I can't make it."

"Oh, okay." Her heart slows and she presses her lips together.

Devin doesn't want me. He doesn't know how to say it. Probably like a lot of things in his life, his dad being one of them.

She sits back down in the chair, staring at the abstract painting on the wall. She still can't figure out what it's supposed to be. Her mind is wandering. Why did she think Devin liked her? He didn't care for her from the first time they met. Why is now any different?

"Something came up," he says.

"Oh?"

Who is she? Where did he meet her?

"Maybe this weekend? If you're not busy."

"We'll see. . . . I might be working," she lies, looking at Brinley's eyes fluttering.

He doesn't want me.

"Okay. Let me know. Sunday works for me. Game Saturday night."

Who does he think he is?

"I have to go; my niece is waking up." She hangs up and enjoys the cuddles with Brinley until a tap sounds at the door. Carla carefully gets up, the baby snuggled into her neck. She opens the door.

"Hi! Oh, she's asleep?" her mom says, stepping in and taking off her shoes. She pulls the blanket back to peek at her granddaughter. "Looks like you have it under control. A baby looks good on you."

Carla looks at her niece and kisses the top of her head. "It's a good feeling, holding a baby."

"Yes, it is. The best feeling in the world. You should think about it."

"About being a mom?"

They look at each other with hesitation.

"I always think about it," Carla admits, giving her niece a squeeze.

"Don't think about it for too much longer."

"Then what?"

"How about that Devin guy?"

"What about him?"

"He seems like he'd make a good dad. I saw how he smiled when he met Brin."

Carla looks at her mom, thinking about Devin. "I'm not falling for that."

"For what?" her mom asks, her forehead wrinkled.

Carla hands over her niece to her mom so she can get her shoes on. "For just any guy."

"He's not just any guy. He's Devin Miller."

Carla grins, liking the sound of his name. "I don't know how he feels about me."

"He likes you! What are you talking about?"

"I don't know." Carla picks up her purse. "Mom, you have to stop pressuring me." She shakes her head and secures her purse on her shoulder. "You know I want kids. Always have. If and when that day comes, I want to be with the person I love. And until that day comes, I need my space. Please. Give me a break. I need it."

"Oh, Care Bear," her mom says, taking a free arm and bringing her daughter in for a hug so they're cheek to cheek. Her mom gives her a peck before letting go. "I love you." She stares into Carla's eyes. "I'm sorry. I didn't mean to pressure you. I'm trying to help."

"Pressuring me isn't helping."

Her mom lowers her head, her eyes droopy. "I'm sorry."

Carla nods. "I gotta get to work." She opens the door and turns back to say, "I love you," and runs to her car.

Chapter 16

Carla agreed to see Devin on Sunday afternoon. What are his intentions? He cancels without an explanation and then calls to say he wants to meet up. What does he want?

"I could have driven," Carla says as she climbs into his silver Maserati. It isn't every day she rides around in luxury cars, but today is different. Today she'll judge Devin for herself. She clicks her seat belt and brushes her hair back off her shoulders and stretches her legs as far as they will go. She tucks one leg over the other and glances at him.

"Nah, this way I can get used to navigating myself around."

"Where are you taking me?"

Devin glances over, one hand on the wheel, one relaxed on his thigh. "Granville Island. I'm intrigued by the name."

She laughs. "You're not the only one. It attracts ten million people a year."

"Do we have to take a ferry?"

"No, but parking is always a challenge."

His flexed arm catches her attention as he spins the wheel and steps on the gas.

"You're going to want that lane." She points. "Are we getting out or is it just a scenic tour?"

"That depends on what you're offering."

"We won't have time to see everything if we get out every five minutes."

"Let's drive. Maybe next time we can stop at your favorite place."

"There's going to be a next time? I thought this was the deal."

"It is," he says. "But if it works out, we can do this again."

Carla represses a smile and looks out her window.

"What?"

"I didn't say anything," she says, smiling, looking at him.

Devin's arm is extended on the wheel, relaxed, and he seems to be enjoying the drive. His T-shirt is tight around his biceps. He's wearing a gold chain around his thick neck.

"That's my point," he says.

"You want to take that turnoff!" she shouts, pointing.

He eases into the lane and turns off. "Nice." He seems to be trying to look out his window as he pays attention to the traffic in front of him.

"It is," she says. "It's an enjoyable walk."

"Wow, it's busy."

"Always is. There's parking over there," she points out. "And tons of shops, but you have to walk through the buildings. The market is constantly busy."

"I'm used to that."

"I guess so. Being from Seattle."

"Yeah." He raises his head.

He takes it all in. When they've driven as far as they can, Devin exits and turns back onto the main road. "Where to next?"

"Well, if you keep going, there's Granville Street. High-end shops. Again, a good place to walk and browse around. And if you drive straight, over the bridge, there's the mall."

"Was it hard playing in a city that wasn't crazy about hockey?" She looks at him.

"It was all right," he says with a shrug. "By the time I played junior, I was living in Spokane and then Portland. That's where I learned about hockey fans."

She smiles.

"What about you? Have you always lived here?"

She bobs her head. "Pretty much. I moved up north for a couple of years for work, and then I got a job in Kamloops before a job opened up here. That was when I met my husband."

"You didn't tell me you're married." The corner of his mouth arches.

"I'm not," she says, letting her mouth widen into a grin, realizing she hasn't told Devin her story. "I was. Didn't work out." She looks at her hands and then out her window.

"Sorry."

"Ah. It was one of those things. We rushed into it. Thought we wanted the same things."

"You didn't?"

"No. I didn't think it through."

"What's there to think about?"

She looks at him with curiosity. She did think it through when Timothy asked her. It felt right at the time. He wanted to be married too. He wanted to work and give them a comfortable place to live, a condo he still lives in. He talked about having a child and a vacation in Hawaii every year. Everything came true except the baby. They didn't talk about spending Saturdays together, going on hikes and out for dinner or taking day trips to Grouse Mountain. "We wanted different things. We drifted apart and didn't see eye to eye." Is that where they went wrong? Is that why they didn't understand each other?

"I don't know," he says. "I've never been in that situation. How does one know?"

Carla sucks in her breath. "They say you just know." There was that unsteadiness in her that told her to wait, but she wanted to get married and settle down so bad. She couldn't wait. She looks out her window. "I didn't know. I didn't follow my heart."

"Kids?"

Her head turns toward him. Her stomach flips like it always does when she thinks about being a mom. "Nope."

There's a brief moment of silence before they try talking at the same time.

"How 'bout you?" she asks, curious and prying.

"Me? Never been married, no kids." He shakes his head slowly, staring at the road.

"And I've been separated for a year, divorced for two," she adds, although she doesn't know why she's telling him this. He's going to think she's unsteady and difficult to be with, or worse, she has a problem that affected her marriage.

"Must be hard."

Her eyes soften as she stares ahead. "Sometimes," she whispers and pulls herself together to grin widely. "I've moved on." She taps her hands on her lap.

"Are you with someone now?"

"Nope. How about you? Did you leave a girlfriend in Raleigh?"

He chuckles. "I suppose I did."

"Why is that funny?"

"It's not. I'm glad I was traded so I can forget about her." He chuckles again. "She was something else." He swipes a finger down his nose and says, "I'd been trying to break it off for a while, but it wasn't easy. It was nothing serious, if that's what you're wondering."

"I wasn't, but now I'm curious. Was she one of those puck bunny types?" Carla raises an eyebrow.

"Nah. I met her through someone."

"And it didn't work out?"

"It wasn't a close friend."

"Oh."

"She lied. A lot." He sucks his teeth. "She'd tell me she was out with a girlfriend and I found out she was at the casino with some guy friends. She swore they were gay, but I don't care, I don't like being lied to."

"No one does. So what happened?"

"She expected me to show up at every party she went to, just so she wasn't alone. I was used." He lets out a breath. "I was hardly around anyway. I shouldn't have expected anything more."

"Have you spoken to her since?"

"Once when I arrived here. Never again," he says, turning the corner.

Carla's phone vibrates and she takes it out of her purse and scrolls through her e-mail.

"You're not taking notes, are you?"

"No." She puts her phone back into her purse. "I'm waiting on someone to get back to me."

They drive farther and Carla tells him about the street they're on and where it leads.

"I could get used to living here."

"You're here for six years."

"It goes by fast."

"Does it?" she asks. Will he stay after his contract is up? "Turn here. Follow the sign."

"We're going to Stanley Park?"

"Sure. We can drive through it."

"You get settled and then have to move again."

"Maybe this time you won't have to."

"We'll see."

"You need more points. You need to show people you're of value, that you make a difference to the team."

"You don't think I'm up to par, do you?"

"Honestly? I think you need to play like you did two seasons ago. You have the will."

"I still do!"

Carla silences herself. She wants to tell him that right now he's not worth the millions he's paid but decides it's none of her business.

"What happened? You used to have forty-, forty-five-point seasons. You're not that guy anymore. Something must have happened."

Devin clears his throat. "Maybe it's age."

She laughs. "It's not age."

They watch the shoreline.

"Not all years are good."

"But you've been declining instead of improving, or at least staying average."

"Do you always point out people's faults?"

Carla's head pops back. "I don't do that!"

"Or is it just to me?"

"You can play better. That's all I'm saying. I know your potential."

Devin pulls over and parks in a stall. "I bet you kick some serious ass in hockey pools."

"I usually do okay."

He turns off the ignition. "Do you wanna walk for a bit?"

She nods, and they get out and walk until they see an opening to the seawall. It's a short distance to the public access, where they can walk down a steep embankment. Carla stops at the edge of the path. She's not wearing proper shoes. There are branches and exposed tree roots on the dirt path.

Carla stands at the top, looks at her slip-on shoes and then at Devin. His jeans are fitted in all the right places. She doesn't have to see it to know that under a layer of clothing is a sculpted, well-defined body she only dreams of.

"Maybe there's another way," she says, eyebrows furrowed. It would be safer to walk through the ferns than the dirt.

Devin stops and turns around. "It's a little steep. You can make it. Take my hand."

She bites her bottom lip.

"Come on." He waves his hand, as though getting her to hurry up. "You won't fall. I promise."

The look in his eyes reassures her that if she does lose her balance, she'll be falling right into his arms. Wouldn't that be dreadful?

She shakes her head to clear the fantasies away and holds out her hand for his. His fingers are inches from hers. One more step and she'll feel his thick fingers between hers. She eyes them as the target. Another step and her body is slanted forward. She's going to fall. Her foot is wiggling out from the dry dirt and as she puts it in front of her, she looks at Devin's rounded jawline and luscious lips. The ones she kissed. He's so easy on the eyes that she forgets to step over the raised root. Her pointed toe gets caught, pulling her forward. Her arms fling outward as gravity takes her down. She sucks in a breath so hard that she can't scream, or even try. Like a flash, Devin grabs her arm, his other hand latching onto her side. He catches her before she hits the ground. Her hand rests on his broad shoulder, firm and with such power that she feels light on her feet.

He holds her there and finds her eyes. "Are you okay?"

She can't say anything. Her throat is dry. Being in Devin's arms has made her insides all mushy, and she doesn't pull away from him holding her.

"I'm okay," she says, breathless, feeling his body separate from hers and wishing he would hold her for a minute longer. He smells so good and his hand is strong enough to keep her standing. Surprisingly, he takes her hand. "Walk with me. Hold on to me if you need to." He tightens his grip.

Carla's other hand is on his back; in case she falls forward, she has him to stop her. Her hand feels like it's on a hard mattress, with little cushion. Even his back muscles are impressive.

They get to the base of the path.

"I guess we'll find another way back to the car," he says, releasing her hand. "Are we walking the whole park?"

She snickers as she realizes he's serious. "No. Not today. It's over eight kilometers long. I'd need my running shoes."

"I'd like to do that one day. It looks like a nice walk or run, depending . . ." He looks at her with wonder.

"What?" she asks with a smile.

He smiles back.

Why do her insides feel like they're being charged up every time he looks at her and makes eye contact?

"Nothing." He turns away.

She decides not to press him.

Bicycles speed past them and people running try to go around without bumping into them. It's a steady flow of people for an afternoon in March.

"I can't remember the last time I walked the seawall. It's been a long time," she says.

"I'll have to remember to come here. I like it."

"As long as you don't get recognized, you'll be fine."

"I'll wear a hat and sunglasses."

She laughs. "That'll work."

"You were saying about my points earlier. I haven't reached my personal best?"

"I don't know. I'm just saying I've seen you do better."

He smirks. "There you go again. Being critical."

"Opinionated," she snaps, raising an eyebrow.

"Bossy?"

"No!" she says playfully. Her lips pull at the sides of her mouth into a grin. "Absolutely not."

"Just with me?"

She breathes in the saltwater mist from the waves crashing against the stone wall. Her stomach is unsettled; it feels like the crashing waves. Uncontrollable.

"Not just you," she manages to say.

"Who else is on your list of players to critique?"

"There is no list. I pay attention to the newbies." Carla shrugs. "I have to. It helps to know. I also have a memory for numbers."

"So you're not bossy?" Devin asks. "Hard to believe."

"Come on!" She rolls her eyes. "It depends on the situation. I'm opinionated at work. It's natural."

"And you're not at any other time?"

"I don't think so."

"Describe yourself."

"I'm devoted to what I love. I'm caring, compassionate and strong-minded."

"What do you love?" he asks, glancing her way.

She bats an eye.

He shrugs. "I assume your job. That's undeniable."

"It is?" Why is she so surprised?

"Yeah, it shows."

She can't wipe the smile off her face. "I can't help it."

"Nothing wrong with it. I love hockey. What can I say?"

"I guess."

"And you love your family. That's obvious. What else?"

It takes a minute for Carla to think about it. "Belgian chocolate, red wine . . ."

Relationships.

"Nature walks, sunny afternoons . . ."

Being married.

"The spa." She laughs.

Babies.

"Tell me, what do you love to do?" She doesn't take her eyes off him.

"Besides hockey?" he asks with a quick glance. "Hanging out with friends, lounging on the beach, going to concerts . . ." He stares at her. It feels like a second too long. Enough time to observe the slightly angled eyeteeth that are symmetrical. His dark eyes appear to have a fleck of gold in them, twinkling like stars at night. She closes her eyes for a second to control the sexual desires she has for him.

"I like this. Fresh air. Nature."

"Devin Miller?" a voice cries out.

They're approached by two young people, making it hard to keep walking.

"Hi, there!" Devin says.

"Can I get an autograph?" The teenager pats at his pockets. "How 'bout a picture?" He takes out his smartphone and hands it to Carla. "Do you mind taking a picture of us?"

"No problem." She takes his phone and clicks away. Carla hands his phone back to him. They say good-bye and are stopped again before they can even start a conversation.

"Devin Miller! No way!" the young twentysomething shrieks as he stops. Devin shakes his hand. "Welcome to Vancouver."

"Thank you," Devin says.

The guy asks for a picture too, and Devin agrees. As they finish up with him, more people swarm to them like bees to honey. Graciously, Devin honors his fans by signing autographs and posing for photos.

"We better get going," he says to Carla. "I'll have to put more time on the meter."

It's the only way he can escape the crowd and head back toward the steep path.

"There's another way up," she says and rushes to an opening. Devin is right behind her. She hears his name being called again and again, but they ignore it and hurry to the top, where the path leads to street parking.

Carla starts to laugh. This is too much. It is common for her to get recognized and to speak with people on a community level, but not like this. Not like a celebrity, where she has to fear having her clothes ripped off or being mauled.

She holds her stomach, the muscles tightening and contracting from the enjoyment of his company and the adventure they're on together.

Devin steps to the top, laughing too. "That was something else." He pushes his hand over his forehead to the back of his head.

"The hat and sunglasses might be a good idea," she teases as they get into his car. The doors lock and she feels safe again. No one will come close. It's just her and Devin. She takes in a deep breath, exhales and looks over at him.

"Where to now?" He starts his car.

"I don't know, but we should get moving unless you'd like to talk to those people." Carla looks ahead at the group rushing toward them.

Devin puts his car in reverse. "I don't feel like it."

They drive around the park. Carla points out the sights. Her cell phone buzzes.

"Your city is beautiful," he says.

Carla picks up her purse and slips her hand inside to grab her phone. Her fingers touch the envelope and a jolt of guilt hits her. She should give him the letter. Now? He'd have to pull over. The news is too big to deliver while driving.

"I like it." Her words are meek. She looks out her window. She has to give him the letter today. Where? "Have you seen Science World?"

"I've driven by."

"How about the mountains? Whistler? Grouse?"

He shifts his lips while staring ahead. "Grouse? No." He glances at her and then back on the road. "Do you feel like a drive?"

"Sure. How long will it take?"

"Twenty minutes? Half an hour?"

"Let's go."

There will be an opportunity to give him the letter at the base of the mountain. She has to. This is her only chance. What will he say? Will he be angry Keith contacted her? Will he be sad his dad didn't contact him first? Will Devin be mad at her for getting involved?

They drive out of the park and make their way to the mountain, following signs and making small talk as they go.

"Amazing how close the mountains are," Devin comments. "I missed the West Coast."

"We take it for granted. Surrounded by mountains and ocean."

"I don't know why anyone would want to leave."

She bites her bottom lip. If only she'd gotten the job in Toronto.

"Turn here," she says. The paved road turns to gravel. "I wasn't thinking. Maybe we shouldn't go up the mountain. You don't have the proper wheels for it."

"I should have driven my Range Rover."

"That would have been a better choice. There's snow up ahead."

He pulls over and puts the car in park. "What do you say we head up the mountain another time?"

"I've seen it, been there lots. Sure. . . ."

He looks around at the trees surrounding them and then at her. "I can drive farther. I'm sure it's fine. It's a car," he says gruffly and starts. "What can happen, right?"

She smiles and leans her head on her hand, resting it on the door. "Up to you." The time is close for her to give him the letter. She can tell him to pull over again and talk to him. Get it over with. Her stomach flips as they reach the parking lot.

"I guess it wasn't that bad, after all," he says, pulling into the closest parking spot, leaving lots of room between his car and the next spot beside them.

She gets out of his silver, two-door prize possession and already there are people coming close.

An older man approaches them. "Nice car. Jeez, you don't see many of these around," he says, scratching his head. The man walks around the car, checking out every detail.

Another person walks up to the car, asking Devin if he likes driving it, and a third guy asks if he really is who he thinks he is.

"Yes, I am," Devin says proudly. Suddenly it's like a windstorm, the guys are taking pictures of Devin and his car and getting autographs.

"Thanks, guys," Devin says. "I hope it will be okay here while we take a little walk."

"I'll keep my eye on it for you," the older of the guys says. "I'm waiting for my wife. She's not going to believe you're here. Our kids are big fans too. They won't believe the picture of us." The guy is smiling and gushing like a boy.

"Nice meeting you," Devin says and gives him a wave. He grabs Carla's hand and puts an extra bounce in his steps to hurry along.

She looks up at him. The feel of his strong, thick hand wrapped around hers makes her petite hand feel smaller.

"Where should we go?" he asks.

"There's a coffee shop," she suggests. "I'll grab us some drinks."

"I'll come with you," he says.

"Are you sure? I don't want you hounded by people before we can get out the door."

"It'll be fine."

"Okay, then."

He drops her hand and she walks ahead, opening the coffee shop door. Devin follows.

Carla stands in line and as the line moves, she notices Devin is no longer behind her. He is talking to a couple of girls who are shaking a hip and playing with their long hair and laughing.

"What can I get for you?" the barista asks, her hands on the till, waiting to punch in the order.

"I'll have a large coffee."

"Is that everything?"

"No," Carla says and looks over at Devin to get his attention. He takes a step forward and then is caught in the conversation. He is not making eye contact with Carla.

Can't he be considerate? He didn't come here alone. She blows out a breath. "Okay, make that two large coffees, room for milk, please."

Carla steps to the side to wait for their drinks.

Devin walks briskly to her. He takes out his wallet. "How much is it?"

"Don't worry about it," she says hastily, picking up the paper cups from the counter. "You don't know what I ordered for you." She hands him one of the cups.

"Coffee. That's what I like." His voice is so full of sarcasm it makes Carla snicker.

"That's what I like too."

"How did you know?" he asks, handing her a lid from the dispenser and placing a lid on his. Devin opens the door and allows Carla to walk through before following.

"A guess." She brings the cup up to her nose to smell the aroma. It's too hot to drink. "We'll walk up here," she says, eyeing a spot to give him the letter. This is too much. How should she start the conversation? Is he going to get so mad at her that he'll leave her stranded here? Will he hug her and thank her for helping him? Her chest is tight as she thinks of the possibilities. Will he hate her? He will, she thinks. She will never be able to interview the team again. He'll make it a living nightmare for her. She'll have no choice but to move away; but then, bad news follows. How will this affect her career?

She has to take a drink to moisten her throat. She needs a warm-up. How can she talk about his family? Her mind is racing as she thinks of possible questions.

"Those girls you were talking to . . . did you know them?" she asks, trying to think of anything to ask to get him to start talking.

He gives her a smile that makes her forget what she was about to ask. His lips are so rich-looking, lush and large, that she only wants to feel them on hers. What has gotten into her? She can't stop thinking about him sexually. It's been too long since she's been held by someone who wants her, and she craves that affection like a forbidden dessert.

"Those girls?" he says with a chuckle. "They thought I was someone else."

Carla lets out a giggle. She can't help it. "And did you tell them who you are?"

"Oh, yeah."

Carla attempts a sip of her coffee as they walk under the Skyride, away from everyone.

Devin looks up. "We should ride that. I bet it's a great view."

"It is," she says, sipping her coffee. She could give him the letter on the tram. There's nowhere to run. . . .

They walk a circle around the base of the mountain. There's not much to see, except a quieter spot by the fence.

"I don't think it matters where we go," she says, her voice a bit shaky as she thinks about the letter. If only she had the guts to spit it out and be done with it. She's enjoying her time with Devin and it would be a shame to ruin such a pleasant afternoon. "You're like a magnet, attracting all sorts of people."

Devin leans over the fence, coffee in hand. "Are you attracted to me?"

Her throat is dry and she tries to moisten it by gulping the very hot coffee. She gives a little cough. When that fails, she breathes out, focusing on each breath. "I . . . uh . . . well, sure! I think you're all right." Her top lip twitches and she can't hold back a grin. She looks away into the forest, where hikers are making their way on the Grouse Grind, a difficult hike up the mountain but worth the view at the top. Her hands are shaking and she doesn't know what to do with them, so she shoves one of them into her jean pockets, which are small and made for style, not hands while the other one is holding the cup. Then she puts her hand on her hip, turning her body slightly in his direction. "You think you're something else, don't you? Just 'cause you're a hockey player and own a really nice car?" she asks, half-joking, half-serious. *Who does he think he is?*

"No, I—"

"Well, there's more to being attracted to someone than what they have."

"I know."

"Do you, really?" she questions guiltily.

He stares at her blankly. "Yeah. Yeah, I do."

"Okay, then." She tries hard to sound friendly enough. She wouldn't want Devin to take her the wrong way. "I hope you understand I'm only hanging out with you because we agreed at the interview that I would show you around."

"You have and we settled our agreement."

"You don't have anyone here to show you around." She gasps air. This is it. She's ready to give him the letter. "Family?" she throws out the word, expecting him to say no, but instead he steps closer and puts his hand on her arm, giving her a shot of adrenaline, which only makes her heart beat faster. It feels out of control. She doesn't know what he's going to do but has a good idea, since he's so close and she can smell his clean, earthy scent.

"Nobody." His hand is still on her arm.

"I'm sure you've met people here."

"Yeah, you."

She sighs. "I'm sure you've met someone. . . ."

He gives her a perplexed look. "You mean a girlfriend?"

"Well . . ."

"That's what you meant," he says, as though he's had a lightbulb moment.

"I wasn't sure." How could he not?

"No."

"Okay, maybe not a girlfriend but a friend?"

He laughs. "What are you talking about?"

"When you canceled the other day, I just thought you had a date, that's all. It's not a big deal."

"Well, it is!"

"No. If you have a date or something," she says, rambling, unsure of where she's taking this. She should change the subject now, before she looks like a desperate woman looking to settle down.

"I didn't. You thought I did?" His voice is getting excited.

She squeezes her lips together and nods. Why does she care anyway?

"I had to go to Seattle," he says, calmly. "There was a family function."

"Family you haven't seen in a long time?" she asks with innocent eyes.

"I guess so."

Suddenly her knees tingle like she's having a hard time standing. His dad! He met his dad!

"How was it?" she asks, searching his eyes. She's smiling, trying to encourage the conversation. Maybe she can surrender now. Tell him the truth about the letter and the worry will be over.

"Good. A visit with my mom."

"You didn't have uncles and aunts tell you how cute you were as a baby?" She's working hard for a smile from Devin. "Or what you did when you were in kindergarten? Hate those stories. I swear, my mom and dad remember embarrassing events and bank them, then let them out when they have an audience to share them with. Does that ever happen to you?"

She holds still, taking in his steady gaze. His eyes are like molten steel, making her body ache with desire to feel his lips on hers. Her cheeks warm from the uncertain approach and she wonders what exactly is crossing his mind.

"I want to kiss you," he says playfully. "But I don't want you to hate me."

"I can't hate you," she says. *You'll hate me when I tell you about the letter.*

His lips tighten in the corners. "The other night . . . at the tow yard . . . you didn't seem impressed by me."

"I had a lot on my mind," she says, trying to find an excuse as to why she brushed him off. "It was bad timing. . . ."

"I guess you're right. It's different now, between us. I feel like I know you, yet we hardly do. It's weird."

She smiles and looks at her coffee, then back at him, trying to find the words to tell him it won't work out between them. "If you're looking for a woman, a one-time thing, it's not me. You don't want me," she says with the realization that they can't be together. She can't allow it because, because . . .

"You don't know what I'm looking for," Devin says, dropping his arm. "I like you, Carla. I like hanging out with you. I don't need to be anybody but myself, and you seem to know that and accept me for me. You know about my past. You haven't judged me for where I came from."

She furrows her eyebrows. "Why do I care where you came from?"

"I don't know. You just might. I see how your parents are together, and live in a decent neighborhood. . . ."

"I'm not privileged, if that's what you're getting at."

"It's not that. Your family has it together. They're supportive and tight." He nods his head. "It's good to see. I was never around a family like that."

She should slip her hand into her purse and pull out the letter. This is it. This is the time she's been waiting for. "Well, my mom and I don't see eye to eye all the time, and my brother is living in a bubble. My sister and I aren't as close as we used to be, ever since she had the baby." Carla felt a mixture of emotions when Sadie told her she was pregnant. She was so happy for her, yet disappointed that she wasn't feeling the same happiness and excitement as her sister. Carla had tried to act happy around her when she was dying inside. Envious that

Sadie had what she was dreaming about. Sadie never experienced the loss of a miscarriage and got pregnant without trying. She didn't understand the pain and the drive of wanting something so bad that it seemed so close yet so far away. When Brinley was born, Sadie's life had changed. She was caught up in day-to-day mom duties. Sadie was too busy to meet for a latte and had no interest in catching a movie. Her life had changed without Carla in it, and it frustrated her and made her slightly jealous. All Carla could think about was this little baby. She adored her niece, but she was a reminder of what she didn't have. The baby looked like her mother and Carla could see herself in the delicate features as well, only adding to the disappointment. Brinley could be her daughter, Carla thought many times. It was hard to accept that she didn't have her as her own. When Carla confronted Sadie about not spending time with her, she said being a mom took up all of her day and she didn't have time to have a shower, let alone meet at a coffee shop. Carla eventually made little effort to see Sadie and avoided calling her to hang out, which had put a distance between them. Sadie was too preoccupied to notice that the two of them had drifted apart.

Carla unzips her purse without distracting Devin into thinking she's going to check her cell phone or something. She feels around for the letter. It must be at the bottom of her purse.

"Family is like that," Devin says. "I've accepted that I come from a broken home. My dad walked out on my mom and me when I was five. I thought he was on a business trip." He grins and looks away. Carla's hand freezes on the letter. She has to let him finish talking. This is the farthest she's gotten with him.

"Sorry," she says. "You must miss your dad." Her fingers grab the envelope and she brings it to the top of her purse.

"Don't be. I don't want to talk to him. He's a jerk. What he did to my mom and me was cowardly. What guy walks out on his family?"

Carla releases her fingers and zips up her purse. Maybe this isn't a great time to give him the envelope.

"You're still angry with him."

"I don't know if I'm angry. I don't understand why anybody would do that to the people he loves."

"Maybe he was confused."

"About what?"

"I don't know. Maybe he was depressed and didn't know how to deal with real life. You hear about people not sure what to do in certain situations because they don't have the knowledge to help them through."

"There's no excuse for what he did."

Carla shrugs. "Maybe he had a problem and needed to get help."

Devin blinks his eyes. "My mom said he needed to get help. She didn't know for what exactly."

"Whatever it was, I'm sure he didn't mean to hurt you," she says, thinking about Keith, hearing in his voice how much he cares for his son. "Even though you haven't spoken to him, he loves you."

Devin swallows hard. "Okay. Enough about that. I didn't mean to talk about my problems, or for you to know."

"It's not a problem. Don't worry. I'll keep it to myself. You know, sometimes we just need to talk." She looks past him. The crowd is thinning out; it's not so populated for once. It feels good to just breathe the fresh air.

"Is that why you do what you do? You like to talk?"

She laughs. "Doesn't feel that way. I love sports and being in the moment of a story unfolding. It's a good fit for me."

"You're good at what you do."

"Thanks."

Devin steps close, and as she brings her chin up, her lips are met by his. Warm, easy, like the stroke of a paintbrush. Her body tingles from head to toe. This time she lets Devin kiss and hold her. She likes how his hand feels on her hip, as though he's keeping her still. For a strong, built guy, he is gentle, which surprises her.

His lips release hers and are a breath away when he asks, "Do you still want to go up on the mountain?"

She is suspended in his embrace. "If you want."

"I'd like to check it out."

"Let's go, then," she says.

Devin pays for admission, and with only a few minutes waiting, they board the Skyride. It's packed, but they are able to stand at the window to view the glorious mountain terrain. The higher they get, the more there is to see, and Carla is pointing out the Pacific Ocean and where the Gulf Islands are. Above Vancouver, it's a sight to see, and Carla watches the expression on Devin's face as he takes in the amazing view.

They get off and decide to look around and do some exploring of the gift shops and even sneak into the theater playing a documentary on bears.

"I didn't know black bears can smell food more than half a mile away."

"Neither did I," Devin says. "Wouldn't want to be camping in these woods."

She laughs, rubbing arms with Devin as they exit the theater. "You don't camp?"

"No. I never have." He moves his head from side to side.

"Never? Really?"

"I had no one to teach me. My uncle invited me once, but I ended up getting a bad cold and stayed home. There was never another opportunity. How 'bout you?"

"We did the tent thing when I was little, but after my brother was born—he's the youngest—my parents bought a trailer. So much better. We traveled halfway across the country. My parents were big on showing us the tourist sites."

Their walk becomes slower as they finish looking at the landscape. They take one last look at the scenery.

"Beautiful day," she says, looking out toward the massive Douglas firs that cluster the trails.

"It is," Devin says, drawing closer. "I'd like to kiss you again." He looks at her with admiration.

"Oh, yeah?" she says with a big smile.

Devin lays his fine lips on hers, tasting and sucking her bottom lip. The kiss is filled with intensity. New emotions are taking hold of her. Her insides melt and she's not sure she can hold herself up much longer. Devin lets go and they stare into each other's eyes. She wants him so bad. It's not like her. She can't let him get to her.

"The Skyride is almost here. We should get in line if we want to catch this one down." How long can Devin stand here and kiss her? "People are watching."

"They recognize you."

She laughs. "I don't think so. Hopefully nobody is taking pictures or videotaping us."

"Too late if they did."

They walk hand in hand to the tram. It takes fifteen minutes to get to the bottom. They both are admiring the beauty of nature as they stare out the window.

"What a ride!" Devin tells her as they make their way to the parking lot.

"It was, wasn't it?" It was even better riding it with Devin. "The last time I went to the top was when my friend Gabby and I hiked the Grind." And before that, she remembers riding the Skyride with Timothy, and that had been far from romantic. He couldn't look down and was getting nauseated. They'd had to sit on a bench when they got to the top so he could relax.

Devin drives out of the parking lot in a hurry.

"Have you seen most of the city?" Carla asks.

"I think so. You'll have to show me where the best restaurants are."

They drive through the city, and Devin turns down a street that leads to her town-house complex. He parks in front of her private gate.

"Thanks for the outing," Carla says.

"My pleasure." He grins.

It's close to dinnertime. He probably wants to be on his way. When will she see him again?

"Thanks again," she says, looking over at him. Is he going to kiss her again? Should she wait to see if he will? He looks so good in just a T-shirt, all muscular and firm.

"Thanks for taking the time." He clears his throat. His eyes skip around the dashboard and at her. Is he nervous? What does he want to say?

She's nervous. She still has the envelope that she should give to him. If she can reach into her purse, hand it to him and tell him the truth, she will have time to get out of his car and into her house without a confrontation. If she gives him the letter, will he want to see her again? That's the question.

"Well, have a good night." She opens the passenger door.

He'd had a chance to kiss her and didn't. Devin is testing her to see if he's attracted to her. It's all in the kiss. He doesn't want her. Can she blame him? She's divorced. A product of failure. He doesn't want her.

He nods. "Good night."

Carla shuts the passenger door. Is this it? Will they see each other again? She walks up to her gate, her head hanging as she turns the key in the lock. She opens the black steel gate.

"Carla. Wait!"

She turns around.

He runs up to her. "I . . . I thought maybe we could . . . do this again sometime?"

Carla nods. "Yes. That would be great." She doesn't want to sound too eager. They stare into each other's eyes. Devin is in a sideways stance; he takes a step forward and then back. He rocks forward, cups Carla's jaw with his hands and kisses her fully on the mouth. They release and kiss again, like once isn't enough.

She stands there helpless, caught in a string of emotions. She's not sure why this is happening, but she loves it and doesn't want him to stop. She lets him kiss her, hungrily, madly, deeply. Devin kicks the gate with his foot without letting go of her mouth until he suggests, "We should go inside."

"Good idea," she whispers, keeping his mouth close to hers. She takes a couple of steps backward until she has to turn around to walk up the two steps to her door. Once inside, she locks the dead bolt and drops her purse to the ground. Devin puts one arm around her waist and the other hand through her hair. She touches his neck and feels the smoothness of his skin. Her mouth opens to his for a pleasurable taste of his tongue.

Devin breaks away, their noses touching, and whispers, "I want you so bad."

Her heart is racing. Her chest is tight like she can't breathe. She's never slept with a guy she didn't love. Devin she likes. A lot.

"I don't sleep with just anybody."

"I hope I'm not just anybody." He kisses her again.

"It depends where I stand with you," she says as she catches a breath.

"I'm falling for you, hard."

She leads him to her bedroom, where he slips her shirt off over her head and throws it on the floor. He unbuttons her jeans, yanking them down, and then, kneeling, tries to pull them off. Once the jeans are left on the floor, he begins to kiss the top of her foot, her leg, the inside of her thighs, making her whole body shiver and feel like pudding. He kisses her deep, exploring her mouth. She tastes the sweetness of his lips.

Devin stops kissing her and takes off his shirt, revealing his fine, sculpted abs, and once his jeans are off, he stands before her in his tight boxers, his thighs chiseled. He's an underwear ad. His obliques are so well formed that Carla follows her eyes down the muscle to his solid package. Before she can even close her mouth, Devin takes her into his arms and begins kissing her with passionate sweeps of his lips. His hand on her back is holding her to his body. She is pressed against his firm chest. The attraction is so real it hurts. With a flick of her bra clasp, it falls to the floor. He runs his hand over her breast and down her stomach. She flinches at his feathery touch. He kisses her neck and proceeds to her cleavage and to the top of one breast. Slowly, he explores her body, taking it in as though not wanting to miss an inch. Her hand runs over his forearm as though she can feel his eagle tattoo.

"Does it mean something?" she asks, capturing a glimpse of his eye before he looks at his arm.

"Strength . . . soaring over great heights . . . got it when I was drafted."

"Ah."

He brings her close to kiss her. As Devin's lips move over her body, she holds his head, her fingernails tangled in his tiny loops of curls. His kisses become more feverish, striking every nerve with tingling sensation. He takes off her lacy thong and places his hand around her backside as he draws her in with his tongue. She throws her head back at the sensation that's running through her body at the speed of light. He lays her on her bed, propping her head up with a pillow and then reaches for his wallet in his jeans and pulls out a condom. She watches him in the dim light. He is the most beautiful man she has ever seen.

"What?" he asks, catching her looking at him as he unwraps the plastic square.

She doesn't say anything. A little tongue-tied at the sight of him and amazed she's in this situation—in bed with Devin Miller—yet it feels right.

"I don't usually sleep with a guy I'm not dating."

"I don't kiss just any girl and want to sleep with her," he answers as he slips on the condom and lies on top of her.

"So this isn't the last I'll see of you?" she asks, surprising herself by the question. She'd expect Devin to sleep with her and that would be it, or they'd have a causal fling until he moved on to the next girl.

He stops before coming inside. "I like you, Carla," he whispers, making goose bumps on her arms. "I want to keep seeing you."

That is enough to put her mind at ease, although she can't believe he'd want to see more of her. She wants the moment and aches for his touch. She wants to feel loved again.

Devin pushes himself inside her and she moans with such pleasure she can't seem to control the energy building between them. Hot, intense, feverish sex. Nothing she was expecting. With each kiss and each thrust, she is electrified by emotion and hunger. She's never wanted someone so bad as she wants Devin. Not just physically but emotionally, she's becoming more attached. Will this craving, this needing him last?

Could they have a relationship? If he really does mean what he says about him falling in love with her, she may fall even harder.

When they're done, sweating, she lays in his arms. She doesn't want to move. She could stay like this for the night.

Her mind is spinning with what-ifs, but all she knows is that she wants more of Devin. More life. More happiness. Being in his arms, there is no better feeling than being wanted.

Chapter 17

After a home game, the locker room is loud. Guys are pumped up and talking about the plays, the hits and the goals. Devin feels good too. He scored his fifth goal since being a Warrior and feels good at belonging to a team that wants him and is proud of him too.

He showers and dresses in a suit with an open collar and no tie. It's late. Some of the guys are going out for a drink. Devin wants to go home and sleep. He's been on the road for only three days but looks forward to coming home and resting. Maybe he'll even unload the last of the boxes that have been taking up space in his living room.

"Are you coming out, Miller?" Jared Landry asks as he walks by him.

"Nah. Not tonight."

"Ah, you've got plans with that chick?" he asks, referring to Brittany. Nobody knows her except Mark Buckley, her being a friend of his wife's. Devin likes to keep things that way.

"No. I think I'll go to bed early. I'm tired," Devin answers, wondering what Carla is up to. Did she watch the game? Does she go to bed early? He wants to know more about her. Wants to hold her, make love to her and tell her he wants to take it one step further, making it a habit of seeing each other on a regular basis.

"See you Wednesday!"

Devin gives him a side smile. The first play-off game. There is reason to celebrate, but not tonight.

He shuffles his feet, heads outside the rink, looking forward to going home. It's starting to feel like home now. Anytime he's lived in a new city, it's taken months to settle in. Living in Vancouver is different.

He has Carla now, and once she knows how much he wants her, they can take it to the next step. He hopes she feels the same way.

Sauntering out the door, Devin is greeted by fans. Thankfully, there are security guards hanging around to make sure he isn't clawed as he tries to leave.

"Devin!"

He keeps walking, signing autographs as he walks.

"Devin! Devin! It's Keith!"

The only Keith that knows him by name is a guy he went to elementary school with and that was a long shot since he grew up in Seattle.

"Devin! It's Keith!"

My dad's name is Keith.

Devin's chest grows heavy, like his lungs are filled with a thick substance. He struggles to take a breath. It can't be.

"Devin!" the voice says again. It's grainy and weak, hearing his name through the crowd.

Devin looks over at the frail, tanned reflection of himself and stops. His heart is sinking so far and so fast. His stomach tightens into a knot.

Dad.

A name he doesn't recall using. It doesn't even feel right on his tongue.

He stares at the man he's been thinking about for twenty-four years. Devin can't move. He can't even say his name.

Keith holds out his flimsy hand. Devin stares at him. So many questions and not enough answers. *How could he walk out and never come back?*

Keith slowly brings his hand down. "You must have a lot of questions."

Devin begins to talk, but nothing comes out. He pauses and looks around himself. There're a lot of people crowding around. It's not a place to have a sensitive conversation.

"I hope you have the answers," Devin says, keeping himself from letting out his emotions.

Keith eyes the people around him and then comes back to Devin. "Can we go somewhere to talk?"

"I don't feel like talking," Devin says, yet burning questions linger in his mind. He wants to punch this man for all the grief he put his mom through. A second punch for not providing for his family and being a man. Thirdly, for walking out and not coming back. There was no excuse for doing what he did.

"I can do all the talking. Please. Give me the time and we won't have to ever talk again, if that's how you really feel. I promise you, you'll want to hear what I have to say."

"It won't make it better." Devin can't take his eyes off this man. He could ask for ID to make sure he really is his biological dad, but there is no doubt he is Keith Miller. He has the same wide forehead, a hairline that outlines his round face. He even has the same crooked bottom tooth that Devin can hide with his full bottom lip.

"I have something to say," Keith says. "It can take a minute or an hour. Depends on how much time you'll give me."

Devin sucks in a breath. "I know where we can go."

Keith follows Devin to the parking lot. "We can't stay here," Devin says. "There are too many people. Someone is always listening."

"I guess that's how it is with this life," Keith says as he hops into Devin's Range Rover.

"Are you here by yourself?"

"Yes."

"You drove from Seattle?" Devin looks over as he starts his truck.

"Uh-huh."

Devin nods as drives away. "Is your car in the parking lot?"

"Yes."

"It should be okay for a while," Devin says, remembering the places Carla took him. "Have you been to Stanley Park?"

"No."

"We can talk there."

Devin tries to remember which road to turn on to. He follows the signs and drives into the park, remembering Carla and how cute she looked with her hair down and her fitted jeans. He can't wait to get his hands on her again. Her sweet-tasting body and quick wit have Devin imagining her naked again, but at his house, in his bed.

"Nice city," Keith says, looking out his window.

"I like it." Devin is watching for a good place to park, where they won't get bugged. It's eleven o'clock at night and surprisingly, the park is busy, with a steady flow of traffic. He pulls into a spot that looks onto the ocean and turns off the engine.

"Good game."

"Thanks."

"Good shot from the blue line. You've scored that kind of goal before, last time against Philadelphia."

"Do you watch every game?"

"Always."

"How did you know I played?"

"I checked in with your mom every now and then."

"You didn't want to talk to me?" Devin's face is sour; even his tongue feels chalky.

"Your mom didn't think it was a good idea."

"Why? Because you weren't planning on coming home?"

Keith nods slowly. "You must wonder why I left." He takes off his seat belt with one hand and lets it slide back to his side.

"Sure. I've always wondered."

"Your mom didn't tell you?"

"She said you were on a business trip." Devin stares straight ahead. "After a month, when I asked her where you were, she told me you weren't coming home." He swallows to moisten his throat. With one glance at Keith, he sees his age and the hardness of whatever it was that controlled him for all those years. "She said you might, but she wasn't sure. I knew you weren't working. Mom didn't have to lie. I don't know why she was protecting you.

"A year later I asked again, and she said she didn't know. Said you needed help." Devin remembers holding the pillow over his head and crying silently so he wouldn't be heard. He asked his mom if his dad was ever coming home and she always said he would when he was feeling better. Devin didn't know his dad was sick. He didn't know what sick meant, or why it meant Devin couldn't help him get better.

"On my sixth birthday I told her you were never coming home and she didn't say anything. I didn't ask again."

"I'm sorry."

Devin looks at him with anger and hurt all mixed up into one. Keith moves his legs, as though trying to unstick them.

"It's years too late," Devin says. "You have no place in my life. You walked out. You chose to leave your wife and child. A cowardly man is what you are. You don't deserve any piece of me."

"You're angry."

"Damn right! Why did you leave? Did you leave Mom for someone else?"

"No."

"Do you still have a problem with drugs and alcohol?"

"No. I've been clean for the past eighteen years."

Devin sucks in a breath. His head is spinning. "And you've made an effort to see me now? You haven't been in my life for twenty-four years when you've been sober all this time? Why? Why did it take you so long?"

"I tried."

"You didn't try!"

"I wrote you letters. It was the only way I could say how I felt, in my own words, and you could read it whenever you wanted. Have you read any of my letters?"

Devin shakes his head. "Nope."

"If you had, you'd know the reasons why I did what I did."

"You mean why you left?"

Keith nods.

"It's not fair." Devin swallows. For years he's envisioned this moment and it's not at all how he pictured the conversation. He thought it would be a fired-up screaming match, with yelling about who was to blame, but now that Devin sees such a fragile man, he doesn't know what to say or how to say it. He tried to erase the image of Keith, even though he was always in the back of his mind. What he looked like, who he was with, if he had any other children. So many questions, and yet the answers don't matter as much now. He doesn't want Keith in his life anyway, so why start something that will only be a memory of today?

"Why did you leave?" Devin asks.

"Your mom kicked me out."

"Don't blame my mom for your demons. It was you who left because you wanted to."

"No, Devin. That's not true." He stares ahead.

Lit-up boats are on the open water. The Lions Gate Bridge is outlined in white lights and traffic is still a steady flow through the park.

"I lost my job," he says, gazing out the window. "I was working as a welder. . . . The company shut down. There was no work. I applied all over the city and even out of town. Nothing," he says with bitterness. "I stayed home for months. Months." He shakes his head. "I tried working at the gas station, but even they weren't hiring. I went all over the city and nothing." He pauses. "I started drinking. Not much, but every day. It was the only way I could pass the time and forget about what a failure I was. I couldn't provide for you or your mom. I was taking prescription drugs to help with my anxiety. I was a train wreck." Keith looks at his son with a gentle stare. "I didn't know what to do. Your mom had had enough. I don't blame her. She kicked me out. Told me to get help. The only help I knew was what was in a bottle."

"But I was your son," Devin says impatiently.

"You *are* my son."

"I'm not," he says. "You left. You left your family. If you wanted to be my dad, you would have stuck around, or at least been in touch. I never heard from you. You can't blame Mom for the damage you did. It's your fault. You made that decision."

"You're right, Devin. But at the time I wasn't thinking clearly. You don't know what it's like to have a family depending on you financially. It's a man's duty to his family." Keith rubs his hands on his jeans. "When I lost my job, I let my family down. I couldn't face you. You're my son." Keith makes eye contact with Devin. There's a pause, as though Keith is taking in the moment. "I wanted you to be proud of me. Look up to me. I knew for years you wouldn't accept me when I let you down."

"You let me down when you didn't come home," Devin says, his eyes burning.

"I know now that I shouldn't have listened to your mom. I should have come back at least on weekends. I know what I did and I'm sorry." He faces his son with heavy eyes. "I never wanted to hurt you. I thought by not being in your life that you wouldn't know about me and judge me for being a failure." He pauses and swallows. "Your mom and I separated, and she sent me divorce papers. I couldn't undo the damage I'd done. I didn't know how to fix it. Fix us. Be a family

again. I needed help and had no one. By that time your mom was done.
I don't blame her. She wanted to move on with her life and provide
for you, something that I couldn't do."

"Did you get a job?"

"A year later. Yeah. Part-time stocking shelves at a grocery store.
It wasn't enough to get you back. I'd lost everything by then. Even
your mom."

"Why didn't you tell her? Why didn't you make an effort to come
back?"

"She didn't want me."

"Why now?" Devin asks. "Why did you want to see me?"

Keith slides his leg over, positioning himself so that he is facing
his son. "I'm proud of you. You made it. What an accomplishment."

Devin grins. He's waited all these years to hear the words.

"I have to hand it to you; not many guys would give it their all after
they got turned down and rejected from playing an NHL game."

Devin's eyes widen. "How did you know about that?"

Keith's lips come together. "I've been in touch with Stan."

"You've been talking to Uncle Stan?" Devin asks, bewildered. He
doesn't speak to his dad's brother very often, and his mom only talks
to him if she runs into him at Rite Aid.

"Over the years he's kept me posted. He wanted us to reunite just
as badly as I did. He helped me turn my life around."

"That's good."

"Tell me, what was it like to play your first NHL game?" Keith
smiles. "I've always wanted to know."

Devin thinks about it, holding the top of the steering wheel with
his left hand. "Nerve-racking. Exciting. . . . I was nervous." He grins.
A memory he can't forget. "It was the time of my life." It was when
he got his eagle tattoo. Strength to fly. To soar above everything to get
what he wanted. This was what he wanted: his career and his father.
The only thing that's missing now is a family of his own.

"I bet. You played a game. They weren't even going to call you up,
but a player was hurt. That night you got into a fight and scored a goal;
after that they kept you on."

Devin watches his dad. "You saw all that?"

Keith grins. "Of course! I've watched you play junior, even came to the rink when you played in Seattle. I was there in the stands."

Devin bobs his head. All this time, his dad was sitting in the stands, where he always wished he was.

"Where are you staying?" Devin asks.

"Sandman Hotel."

"You can stay with me for the night if you want. I don't have a spare bed, but I have a couch."

Keith relaxes back into his seat. "Thanks, but I have my things at the hotel. If you don't mind dropping me off at the Dome, I'll pick up my car."

Devin starts up his truck. "How long are you here for?"

"I go home tomorrow. Back to work."

Devin drives out of the parking lot. "Where do you work?"

"I've been working for the same company for the past twelve years, welding fences, gates. . . ."

Devin concentrates on driving. "Did you ever remarry?"

"No. I've been with Tracy for the past eight years. She's wonderful."

"You guys never married? Being with each other that long?"

"She doesn't want to."

"But you do?"

Keith nods. "Tracy has a daughter from her marriage. We've talked about it. She has her reasons.

"I hope you settle down," Keith tells Devin. "It makes your life complete. Marriage. Kids."

"One day, hopefully."

"Did you get the letter?"

Devin's eyes narrow. "The letter? Yeah, when I moved here; Mom forwarded it to me."

"No, no, not that one. The one from Carla Sinclair?"

Devin's eyebrows furrow. "I didn't get a letter."

"I gave her a letter to give to you."

"Wait a minute!" Devin says, raising a hand to stop his dad from talking further. "How do you know Carla? Why would she give me a letter? What letter?"

"I gave her a letter to give to you. Did you get it?"

"No. What letter? I don't know what you're talking about."

"I wrote a letter to you. I tried getting her to talk to you—"

"About me?"

"I asked her because I knew you would talk to her before you'd talk to me."

Devin stares out the window, whispering, "Why didn't she tell me?"

"I don't know. She was scared."

"You've been communicating with her? For how long?" Devin asks, his mind trying to build a timeline.

"Oh, I don't know. Three weeks. Something like that."

"You and she have been talking behind my back?"

"She was helping me."

"I didn't know she could keep secrets."

"She did it for me."

"I didn't think the person you care about would keep secrets. She didn't tell me you were talking to her."

"I guess there wasn't a good time. I don't know. She didn't want to at first, but after I told her our story—"

"She knows about you and me?" Devin sucks in a breath. His face is warm. He's concentrating on the road. Carla's known about his background all this time and she hasn't even hinted that she knows? He doesn't like that she can keep secrets, especially this. He's tried so hard to keep his private life private, and yet Carla, the best-known sports journalist in the city, knows about his past.

"She had to know. It was the only way I could get her to help me."

"You didn't need her help."

"I guess not."

"Why didn't you just get Uncle Stan to reach me? Why Carla?"

"You wouldn't have taken Stan seriously or wouldn't have reacted to him as quickly as a woman like Carla. She's in the perfect position to get your attention. Come on, a woman like Carla can't be ignored. She's in the public eye too. What more do you want from a woman who understands your lifestyle? You need her. She's good for you."

"Why Carla? Do you know her?" Devin's blood is boiling, thinking about the two knowing each other and Devin left in the dark.

"No. I happened to flip channels and came across her. Happened to tune in one day, and she was talking hockey. It's always a big deal here in Vancouver. I remembered who she was, and when you got traded here, I thought it would be perfect if you knew each other. I called her up and chatted with her. If this wasn't going to work out, then I'd say she wasn't for you, but she was willing to help."

"Yeah, to get a story." He rolls his eyes.

"She didn't, though."

"She tried."

"There's nothing to be ashamed about, Devin. No one's life is perfect and for those who think theirs is, they're bullshitting. Life isn't perfect. It's full of mistakes." Keith talks with his hands. "I wish somebody had told me that when I was married to your mom. It might've saved our marriage."

"You have Tracy now."

"I'm thankful for her."

"It was meant to be." Devin shrugs. "You and Mom might have divorced down the road anyway."

"All I'm saying is, I learned the hard way. It wasn't easy, but the more you fight for what you want, the more you accomplish." Keith shakes his head. "You gotta want it bad, though. Like making the NHL. You're good, no doubt about that, but you didn't give up when you were told there might not be a spot for you on the roster."

Devin takes a deep breath as he turns the corner and heads down the street toward the arena. It's in the middle of the city. There are colorful lights reflecting off the Dome's white cover. Devin stares ahead. His arms are jellylike, his stomach tight. Why didn't he contact his dad years ago? Why didn't he open the damn letters? He can't blame his mom. She's been telling him to open the letters for years, but Devin couldn't bring himself to do it. He was afraid. Afraid of what? Afraid he'd forgive his dad when in his heart he was still angry for his leaving?

"Look, Devin, I want you to know that just because we didn't speak and don't know each other, that doesn't mean I don't love you." Keith swallows and brings his fist to his mouth and clears his throat. "There hasn't been a day that I haven't thought of you. You'll always be my son."

Devin pulls into the parking lot, thankful he can stop his truck before getting all teary-eyed. He can't bear to look at his dad. He holds his forehead, rubs it and releases his hand to the steering wheel, staring out into the open lot, wondering which vehicle is his dad's.

"If you read the letters, you might understand a bit more," Keith says.

"Sorry," Devin says, the last thing he expected to tell his dad. "I should have read the letters."

"It wasn't the right time for you."

Devin shakes his head slightly, looking at the dashboard. "I should have," he repeats, his eyebrows furrowed. "We didn't have to wait this long." Devin looks at his dad, wearing baggy jeans and a loose T-shirt. Was he always a scrawny man? He sure didn't get his build from his dad's side.

"I didn't know what to expect. Thought you only cared about me because of what I do now."

Keith laughs. "No. You're my son. Doesn't matter what you do. It was me who had the problem. If I'd gotten help earlier . . . we would have known each other."

"I'm glad you came. You have my number?" Devin asks.

"No. Your Mom wouldn't give it to me."

"She's protective." He writes down his number and gives it to his dad.

"You have a good mom," Keith says. "I talked to her many times about you. She wouldn't give me your address. Instead I sent the letters to her and she forwarded them to you. I don't know what she thought I'd do with your address," he says with a sideways grin. "Probably thought I'd show up at your door and not want to leave."

"Does Mom know you're clean?"

"Yes. It took her years to believe me. I don't know why." He shrugs. "I guess she didn't trust me."

"Does she know you're here?"

Keith shakes his head.

"She'll be surprised," Devin says.

"Maybe not. She knows I've wanted to see you. The letters weren't getting anywhere, but I couldn't stop writing them. It kept me connected with you and gave me a way to talk to you. Sounds crazy, I know, but at least writing gave me a way to tell you about me and to show you I'm not a bad person, I just made a mistake."

Devin inhales through his nose. It takes a few minutes to get his head wrapped around the conversation.

"I've never left you," Keith says. "I wasn't there for you to see, but I was there. I knew where you were and the highlights of your life."

"You mean every game?"

"No. Christmas concerts . . . graduation. I was there in the crowd."

"You were?"

"I know it's hard to believe, but any chance I got to see your face, I made the effort. I wasn't your father, I know, but I wanted to be a part of your life."

"I'm sorry you weren't."

"So am I. I hope you'll forgive me and we can start again."

Devin tries to smile. So many years have gone by. Where does one start? All he can do is nod his head.

"Thanks for talking to me. I wasn't sure if you were going to ignore me." There is a brief silence. "I'd like to keep in touch with you."

"We can do that."

"Maybe grab dinner or something."

Devin keeps nodding. "Yeah. You've got my number now." There's a pause. "Where's your car?"

Keith points in front of them. "Right there. There's one more thing I need to tell you. I want you to know in case anything happens from now until then." Keith closes his eyes for a second. "My health isn't very good. My doctor tells me I may need a new liver. My odds are slim, but I keep hoping."

Devin's stomach sinks. "Do you need money?"

"No, no; maybe a liver," Keith says with a little chuckle. "Know anybody? Just kidding. My only wish before I died was to see you again. That's all I wanted. I knew you were doing well for yourself. I just needed to see you, and I have. Thank you for not turning your back on me."

"I wouldn't."

"We'll be in touch?"

"Yes. I'll be in San Jose. First round of the play-offs."

"You'll do great," Keith says with a smile. "You'll do well."

There is a pause before he opens his door and gets out. Devin watches his dad walk over to a compact car. The idea of his dad walking away makes him hurt more, and to know he's ill and they may only have a short time together crushes him even more.

Devin jumps out of his truck. "Dad! Wait!" He's not sure what he wants. A hug? One last look? Devin stands in front of Keith and holds out his hand. "Good to see you."

Keith takes his hand and pulls him into a friendly hug that is quick, with a couple of pats on the shoulder. A sign that everything between them is all right.

Chapter 18

Carla is sitting at her desk, typing up a news story, when Pamela wanders in wearing her hair down and a skirt that's cut above the knee. Pamela's on a mission. She sees Timothy at his desk and walks toward him with a bounce in her step.

Carla watches the pair interact. Timothy smiles, showing off his crooked left tooth, a feature she liked about him because when his mouth parted and he was pleased, it showed a genuine smile. She knows he's happy.

"Hi, Carla," Pamela says as she passes.

"Hi, Pamela. You look good today."

Pamela stops. "Thank you. I'm trying a new look," she says, touching her long hair behind her back.

"I like it. Hey, I wanted to talk to you about something."

Pamela steps closer. "Sure. What is it?"

"You seem to be hanging around the newsroom a lot more."

Pamela's eyes wander. "I, uh . . ." She pauses, fiddling with her hands.

"I think there's going to be an opening for a junior reporter, and I'm wondering if you're interested."

Pamela brings her hand to her chest. "Me, report?" She laughs. "No. That's not it at all."

"You should try for it, if you're interested in what goes on in the newsroom. I mean, you're always here; you'd probably do okay. You know what goes on—"

"Carla? I'm seeing Timothy."

"Oh." Carla's face falls.

"We've been seeing each other for a while now. I didn't know if I should tell you, how you would react."

"I'm okay," Carla says, trying to picture the two of them together.

"You are? I didn't want you to hate me—"

"Why would I? Timothy and I are divorced."

Pamela blows out a breath. "I was afraid of what you would think of me."

"I . . . I'm happy for you and Timothy." Carla folds her hands together. "I'm okay with you and Timothy . . . uh, together. . . ." Carla swallows and straightens herself. Pamela's wearing red lipstick for a change, and a fitted, light-knit dress. She is showing off a figure Carla never knew she had.

"You don't have feelings still for Timothy, do you?"

"No. No! Not at all. We're divorced for a reason."

"Yeah, but it doesn't mean you're okay with it."

"I am. Yes! It's been three years now . . . I'm okay."

"Good. Phew. I thought for a minute there you were going to tell me you still loved him and wanted him back."

Carla gushes, "Timothy means a lot to me. I'll always care for him," she says, closing her eyes for a second or two, and then looks at Pamela. "I'm glad he's happy. And you make a good couple."

Pamela smiles. "Thanks. Can we still be friends?"

"Of course!"

Pamela relaxes her shoulders. "Great. Do you have any idea what I can get him for his birthday?"

"Tell him to keep Freddie."

She tilts her head. "Why?"

"Why wouldn't he keep his cat? He loves Freddie."

"It's going to be a full house with my two cats."

"You can't ask him to get rid of Freddie."

"I didn't."

"Then why did Timothy ask me to take him?"

"Oh, I . . . I don't know. . . ."

"Is it because I bought Freddie for him for his birthday one year?"

"Timothy did mention it. . . ."

Carla glares. "He needs to keep his cat."

Pamela sighs.

"Get him a fish bowl for his desk for his birthday. It will give him something to look at when he's stressed."

"That's a good idea!"

"Sure." Carla's cell phone rings. She watches Pamela walk away and grabs for her phone, which is tucked into a pocket of her purse. Her fingers fold over the information from her doctor on in vitro fertilization and adoption. She hasn't given them much thought lately. Her tummy tightens as she thinks of the possibilities. She could be a mom if she wants. Does she still want to? With or without a man? Could she do it on her own? A glimmer of hope rests with her as she says hello.

"Carla." The voice is gruff, and at first she doesn't recognize it. "Can we meet? I need to speak to you."

"I'm at work," she says, fishing for the name of the caller.

"Do you have some time this afternoon?"

"No."

"Not for twenty minutes? I have to see you."

It's Devin, she thinks. Why does he sound upset? Did Keith find him?

"I'm actually finishing up a story, and then I'm heading out to do an interview."

"Then I'll tell you now." He takes in a breath. "My dad came to see me after the game last night." He pauses. "You know Keith?"

"Yes."

"You kept a huge secret from me," he says, his voice escalating. "Why? Why?" he shouts. "Why didn't you tell me?"

"I didn't want to hurt you. Besides, I didn't know how to tell you." She closes her eyes, her fingers pushing on her forehead as she rests her elbow on her desk.

"You couldn't have said, 'Hey, your dad contacted me and wants to speak to you? Here's his number.' It doesn't seem that hard," he mocks.

"Well, it was. I know how you feel about your dad. I didn't want to come between the two of you."

"Not saying anything was better than telling me the truth?"

She falls silent, trying to collect her thoughts.

"The whole time we were together you knew about my dad and you didn't say anything. How could you?"

"I didn't want to come between you and Keith."

"You have."

"I'm sorry," she whispers.

"You wanted to know about my personal life, wanted to know about my dad, my family—" He stops himself and laughs. "But you know what gets me? You knew all along. You wanted me to look like an ass. Well, thank you, Carla. Thanks for making me look like an idiot."

"Never! No. I don't think that at all." Her eyes tear up.

"If you wanted to know about my dad, why didn't you just ask him yourself?"

Carla presses her lips together.

"Or did you? Ha! So you and my dad had a secret of your own. I see."

"It wasn't like that," Carla says, scanning around the newsroom to see if anyone is around listening. She hushes her voice. "It really wasn't like that. I swear!"

"Then tell me, how was it?"

"Did you speak to your dad about what I know?"

"Yeah."

"Then you know I didn't want anything to do with your dad or the situation. At first I didn't know if Keith really was your dad. I didn't believe him, but he persisted and wanted to speak to you. He loves you and wants to see you. I'm sorry I didn't tell you. I was waiting for a good time."

"Anytime would have been a good time."

"No, it wouldn't. That's not true. Had I told you, you probably wouldn't have believed me."

"That was up to me to decide. I don't need you deciding who I speak with."

Carla shakes her head. "That wasn't my intention."

"You wanted to know about my family, my background, but you knew all along. You couldn't keep your nose out of my business, had to get involved. I'm done. I don't want to speak to you again." Devin hangs up.

Carla holds her phone in her hand, dumbfounded. She exhales and rests her head on her hand. She saw this coming, yet she couldn't stop herself. Why didn't she tell Devin from the start that Keith was trying to contact him?

"Carla!" Russ calls out from across the newsroom.

She pops her head up, watching him march toward her.

"Can I see you in my office?"

She stares at him blankly.

"Right now."

Carla follows him out of the newsroom and down a hallway. Russ swings open the door and heads straight to his desk, taking a seat on his swivel chair. He makes an adjustment and leans back, as though testing for comfort.

Carla folds her hands in her lap, straight-faced, waiting for bad news. It has to be, considering she's in the station manager's office with nothing to say and no meeting scheduled between the two of them. She squeezes her fingers together. This is it; her job is over. "I often wonder if you like your job," he begins with squinted eyes. "There are other jobs available at the station that you might be interested in."

"Oh?"

He clicks the end of his pen and taps it on his notepad three times before making eye contact again. "Are you enjoying your position?"

"Yes!"

"I'm going to hire a news reporter. Are you interested in switching titles?"

"I'm a sports reporter." Carla's body twitches. "It's what I do."

"So there's no interest in news?" he asks, hunching over his desk. "I've got a position I need to cover."

"That would confuse our audience. I'm known for sports."

He nods and puts his hand under his chin. "We're restructuring our sports department."

Here goes! I'm fired. I'm really fired. Will I get escorted out the door? Or will I go freely?

"I'd like Ryan to be front and center in sports. He's a young guy with many connections."

"You mean take over my job?"

"Not entirely."

"Then what?"

"I want Ryan to be on location, be at the games and take care of anything extra that needs doing."

Carla sucks in her lips. "You don't want me at the games?"

"I want Ryan to do all the on-location interviews."

Carla exhales. "Ryan might be leaving." She clams up. Maybe she shouldn't have said it, but it's a war now. She wants to keep her job, even if she has to lie a little.

"Leaving for where?"

"I don't know. It's something I heard," Carla says, shrugging it off.

"Why don't you like me at events?"

"It's not that I don't like you there."

"I'm a woman in a man's world? Is that it?"

Russ wipes the smirk off his face with a hand. "I'm not the type to believe rumors. I like to get the facts before I know it's a true story, so I'm going to ask you this: Are you in a relationship with Devin Miller?"

Carla's eyebrows furrow. "No."

He clicks his pen, staring her down like he's waiting to hear the opposite. "Are you sure?"

"Yes, I'm sure." She lets out a huff, as though she's going to laugh. "I know him, and that's as far as it goes. Is this what this is all about? You think because I'm interviewing guys there's a potential for me to be more than friends with them?"

"I'm just saying . . ."

"I'm not. You know my status."

"That's what I'm afraid of," he says.

"Since when is my personal life a concern for others?"

"It is when you're doing favors for his family."

"What are you talking about?" she asks, fiddling with her fingers.

"You're not to abuse your position."

"I know that!"

"Didn't you try to get Devin's father downstairs to see him?" His eyebrows furrow.

"I . . . I . . ."

"You used company recognition for your personal use. Now, I don't know what your relationship to Devin is, but I will tell you, what you did is not acceptable, Carla." He frowns. "It weakens our credentials and takes away the trust we've built." Russ flattens his hands on his desk. "I didn't like what I heard, and if one person saw, others saw you too."

She squeezes her hands together. "Who told you?"

"It doesn't matter."

"It had to be someone from here, someone you talk to."

Who would snitch on her?

Russ shakes his head. "What matters is that if you get away with it once, there will be another time."

"You make it sound like I did something horrible, Russ. I was helping Keith see his son. I didn't hurt our reputation."

"I don't care if the mayor wants to go downstairs. You're not allowed to bring anyone down there. That badge"—he points at her—"is for you only. You don't have a right to escort people out of the goodness of your heart. Got it?"

She nods.

"For the next week, I want Ryan doing the after-hours interviews."

"Wait! That's not—"

"Next time," Russ says, slapping his hand down, "you bring a cameraman with you. Understood? A story like this shouldn't be swept under the rug. It's news! You're a reporter."

Carla purses her lips. "It wasn't supposed to be publicized," she says, hoping for one last chance to justify the situation. "I was only helping."

"It's news! What's the story?"

"Keith hadn't seen Devin in twenty-four years." She looks at her folded hands in her lap. "Keith needed help to get Devin's attention. I wanted to give them a chance to see each other."

"You should have been a news reporter."

"I didn't find the story."

"It would make a great feature for sports, though. Why aren't you following it up? It's your job. Now, think about putting the story together, or are you already doing that?"

She shakes her head. "It's none of my business."

"You're a reporter. Make it your business. It's a story our audience would want to hear."

"You're not suggesting—"

"Why not? Have they met yet?"

"Yes, they have," she says, pouting for the wrong reasons. She won't see Devin again. He's angry she made his business hers.

"Then it shouldn't be hard to get the story."

"I can't. I don't want to get involved."

"You already are."

"Devin doesn't want to speak with me. I knew about his dad before he did. He won't let me interview him."

"Did you ask?"

"Russ? I've been trying to interview him for a long time."

"And you did."

"Yes, but he doesn't want to talk about his personal life. I have to respect that."

He clutches his jaw and tilts his head in a jerking motion. "You're passing up an opportunity."

"For who? This station? Not me. I can't do that. I won't do that."

"Carla, I thought you had a backbone. You're a reporter. It's what you do."

"Even if you did air the story, do you think it would draw a big audience?"

"Yes, I do."

"We're not a celebrity TV channel." Carla tries to keep her voice steady and relaxed, even though she's angry her boss would suggest such a thing.

"You're right. We're news, and the story, from what I hear, is a news story that deserves an audience."

Carla controls her breathing to calm her mind. It's the first time in her career when her job doesn't mean anything to her. She doesn't care about an exclusive story or how many people like her. She doesn't even care about people unfollowing her on Twitter. It's just a job. "What do you know about the story?"

He picks up his pen, sits back in his flex chair and rocks himself while tapping the pen on the palm of his hand.

"That Devin's father walked out on him and his mother at a young age and he hasn't seen him since. You can fill me in on the rest."

"Why is this so important?" she asks without a second thought.

"Because it is to you. Must be a good story."

"Look, I don't know who told you about Devin, but I think it's ridiculous for us to get involved with a player's life when he's asked us not to."

"How about from the dad? Did he say he didn't want to talk to us?"

"No." She has no intention of telling Russ that Keith was the one who'd called her and asked for her help. That would only get him to ask more questions, and who knew what other questions he'd have.

"So, you're not doing it?"

She shakes her head.

"It's your job and you're saying no?"

"That's right. I don't want to put myself in that position."

"Okay. I'll get Ryan to do the story."

Carla's stomach sinks. "Ryan?"

"Yes, Ryan. He'll do it. Give him your contact info."

"I don't have any."

"Sure you do."

"Ryan can get his own contacts." She stands. What's Russ going to do, fire her?

"I want you to," he says, talking with his hand.

She blows out a breath and walks to the door. "Devin won't talk about it."

"Ryan can ask him."

She crosses her arms over her chest. "He can, but Devin won't talk."

"Ryan can try."

She puts her hand on the door.

"Big mistake," Russ says.

She knows it is, but what does she have to lose? Her job? Devin was already the bigger loss.

She pivots and looks at Russ. "Is it?"

"You're not doing your job, Carla. I count on you to turn out original stories, but if you can't do it, then I'll have to find someone who will."

How is she supposed to get Devin to talk?

"I want a story by Friday evening's newscast."

She sucks in a breath. "That's too soon." How is she going to get Devin's forgiveness and get him to want to do the interview in three days? Two, if all she has left is Thursday and Friday. Impossible.

Russ isn't backing down. His strained eyes hold her gaze, waiting for her to commit.

Should she at least try for the interview? Or give her notice now? Then what? Where does she go from here? This is her job. The one Timothy helped her get. He put in a good word for her. She'd moved from Kamloops back to Vancouver to take a junior sports reporter job. It was a risk, seeing as she went from working full-time to being a fill-in. It didn't take long before she started working longer hours and moved into a permanent position. She found out later that it was

Timothy who'd put in a good word for her. Then, when the sports director position came up, it was Timothy who stood behind her. These jobs are scarce, unless you know someone or you work your butt off to prove yourself. It's not every day a job like this comes around, and now that she has it, moving far away to another station isn't so appealing. Besides, she has no chance with Sports National; not now anyway.

"You can do it, Carla. You need to do it."

The fire in his eyes tells her that her job is on the line.

Chapter 19

Devin makes a trip to Children's Hospital to see Jason. He turns off his phone when he enters the boy's room, giving Jason his full attention for the next half hour, and plans to visit with other children across the hall afterward.

Devin walks into the room, escorted by a nurse. "How are you, buddy?" Devin's smile disappears when he realizes that Jason is either in pain or has been medicated and so doesn't have the usual reaction. He's slumped against his pillow, staring across the room. Devin takes a step closer and places his hand on the boy's blue blanket.

"Jason?" Devin whispers, trying to determine whether it's a good time to be visiting.

The boy blinks his eyes and turns his head toward his idol.

"Rough day?" Devin asks.

"Jason had treatment today. He's tired," the nurse says.

"I can come back another time," Devin says, taking a step back.

"No," Jason whispers. "Stay."

"Rest if you're tired," the nurse says. "I'll be back in twenty minutes to check on you."

Devin is lost for words. He stands at the foot of the bed. There's nothing to say that will cheer Jason up. What can he offer? He stands for a moment, rubbing the back of his neck. "Mind if I sit?" He slides a chair closer to the bed. "This is a comfortable chair," Devin says, resting his elbows on his thighs and folding his hands together.

"My mom sits there."

Devin freezes and watches the boy's eyes staring back at him.

Jason gasps. "She sleeps there sometimes."

"I bet she does," Devin says, letting his weight sink into the padded seat. If he had children, he'd be sleeping beside them too. "Where are your mom and dad?"

"My mom went to buy a drink."

"And your dad?"

It takes a couple of seconds for Jason to answer. "He's working."

Devin rubs his hand behind his neck again. How much longer can he stay?

"Does he work a lot?"

Jason shrugs.

"Does your brother visit you a lot?"

"After school."

Devin bounces his head. "Do you have big plans for when you're out of here?"

Jason lays motionless.

"Climb a tree? Go swimming?" Devin stares at the boy, looking for a reaction. "Go for ice cream? Play at the beach?"

Jason's lips part, as though he's about to say something.

"If you weren't here, where would you like to be?"

"At school."

Devin sighs. "School. To see your friends?"

Jason nods.

"I used to like playing baseball. My friends and I would set up a game at recess. I had a friend, Tony Matei; do you know of him?"

Jason's eyes widen. "The baseball player?"

"Yeah."

"You went to school with him?"

"I did," Devin says, relaxing into his chair. "He was great at baseball, even as a kid."

"Wow. Do you still know him?"

Devin nods.

"That's cool."

"It is," Devin admits. "What do you like to do after school?"

"Play."

"Doing what? I'm curious."

"With Cole. He lives next door."

"Do you and Cole bug girls?"

"No," Jason says, his mouth opening enough to show his front teeth.

"Does Cole have a sister?"

"Two."

"Two sisters?" Devin exclaims. "Double bugging there!"

Jason giggles.

"You have, haven't you?"

Jason giggles more.

"Good to see you smile, Jason." A woman holding a to-go cup with a tea bag string hanging from it walks to the other side of the bed. She has long brown hair and is wearing jeans and a bright knit top with large gold hoops.

Devin jumps up. "You must be Jason's mom." He holds out his hand. "Devin Miller."

"Shanna," she says, extending her hand over the bed. "Nice to meet you. Jason has told me all about you."

"Oh, yeah?" Devin asks, putting a hand on his hip.

"He talks highly of you. Thank you for coming to visit. It means a lot to Jason."

Me too.

"You have a remarkable son," Devin says, fishing for words. "He's a fighter."

"Yes, he is." She looks at her son and smiles. "The doctor says you might be out of here soon."

"Can we go to a water park? It will be summer."

Shanna doesn't let go of her smile. "Yes. And maybe we'll go on a vacation."

Devin watches the interaction between the two.

"Can we go to Disneyland?" Jason asks, his smile wide.

"We'll see." She takes a sip of her tea. "Daddy has to see if he can get time off."

"Aw."

"Let's find out when you can come home first, okay? Then we'll plan a trip . . . somewhere. It would be nice to go to Tofino. We can body boogie, or whatever they call it, and look for sand dollars."

Jason pouts. "I guess so."

The nurse walks into the room with her hands in the front pockets of her scrubs. "How're you doing, Jason? Are you hungry? It's lunchtime." She takes out a pen and writes something on a clipboard that's by his bed.

Devin stands. "I have to get going. Take it easy, Jason." He pats the blanket. "I'll see you next week?"

Jason nods.

"Thanks for coming," Shanna says.

"My pleasure." Devin says a last good-bye as he leaves the room. He has one more visit across the hall before he leaves.

Devin leaves the hospital and calls his dad. A female voice answers, and automatically he says, "Sorry, I have the wrong number."

"Is this Devin?"

"Yes."

"I'm Tracy."

"Hi. Is my da—dad there?" Devin asks.

"He's resting. He's scheduled to undergo a liver biopsy."

"Is he okay?"

"I don't know," she says, her voice trailing. "We'll find out soon."

"Should I come see him?"

"If you want to. He's doing okay, though."

Devin thinks about his schedule. "Is it serious?"

"Well, the biopsy will tell us if there's been any liver damage."

Devin is quiet. If he leaves for Seattle now, he can be back for Friday's game. "Would he mind if I came to see him?" He feels like a kid asking for permission.

"He'd like that."

He can hear her smile. "Okay. I'm on my way."

It's been two days since Carla spoke to Russ about doing an interview with Devin. What does she do now? Devin hasn't spoken to her, and to call him and ask for an interview seems ridiculous. She can't stop thinking about him, at work, at home, driving to work, driving home. He's on her mind. Yet she can't pick up the phone and call him. Ultimately, he doesn't want to talk to her. The fear of asking for him and hearing his outrage and disappointment in her makes her want to hide from him. That will come first; then, if she asks him about an interview, he'll probably hang up on her.

She puts on a fake smile and goes to work, avoiding Russ's request.

Her cell phone rings as she types a story. Without looking at the call display, she picks up her phone and answers it, typing one more word before saying hello.

"Care Bear!" her mom says.

"Hi, Mom."

"I have big news."

Carla takes her eyes away from the computer and concentrates on her phone call. She's in need of a break, having been stuck at her desk since she got to the station, working through lunch and into the late afternoon.

Her mom says, "Guess who's pregnant?"

"Jeez, I don't know. It's not me," Carla says, trying to make light of it. Even if she was, it wouldn't be the right time for her.

"Mia."

"What? Mia? Really?" Carla's mouth drops. "Is that why they're getting married?"

"No. They love each other."

Carla rolls her eyes. "Of course they do."

"I wanted to tell you before you heard it from Gavin. I didn't know how you'd handle it."

"I'm fine."

"I wanted to make sure."

"I am, Mom. Honest."

"Okay. Gavin wants to tell you. You didn't hear the news from me."

"Sure," Carla says. "How did you think I'd take it?"

"I don't know. I wanted to prepare you."

"Thanks, Mom, but I'm fine. Babies aren't in my future right now. I need to sort work out, and then relationships. Not that I have one, but still . . ."

"I'm proud of you," she says, warming Carla's heart. "You've worked so hard to get to where you are. I wish I had done more with my life when I was younger. It takes a lot of guts to prove yourself and excel in a male-dominated job."

"I didn't think of it as something I shouldn't have. I thought of it as something I *should* have. It's where I belong. This is me. Everything else should follow, right?"

"Yes, and it will. You'll find a man who loves you, and if there's a baby in your future, you'll make a great mom."

"That's nice, Mom, thank you."

"There are a lot of children out there who need loving homes. You could be that parent."

"Yes."

"If you're not comfortable with babies, there are older children who need homes too."

"Yes, I know," she says, putting her lips together. "I don't want to think about that until the time is right. Is Gavin and Mia's wedding being moved up?"

"We're going to talk about it tonight. You should come over. I'm making spaghetti."

"I'd love to. See you later." The last time she ate spaghetti at her parents' house was with Devin. She remembers sitting beside him, having him rub his arm against hers and telling stories of the two of them, her giving him a hard time when they first met. The interview. Her stomach tightens. She needs to call him and arrange a time to meet with him. Should she ask him over the phone? What happens if he hangs up? Then what? Does she then tell Ryan to take over and lose the opportunity to speak with Devin one more time? She wants to see him again. The moments they shared were remarkable. No man has held her with such strength and passion as Devin did. Those muscular arms felt good around her and his hard, defined abs . . . she felt like she was playing the harp when she ran her hand over them. Her face heats at the thought.

Was it just a one-night fantasy? But his kiss, the way his lips felt on hers, had been incredible. She can still picture the way he smelled and feel his skin against hers. There was more than an attraction; it was a natural hunger for each other. She wants to see him again so badly, but the fear of him not wanting her hurts. She has to call him for her own good.

Carla picks up the phone and dials his number. She rubs her forehead as she leans into her desk, preparing herself for the power of his voice and to hear him out. With every ring, she rubs her head harder, as though the pressure of talking to him is great. Then Devin's recording comes on the line: "Hey, it's me, leave a message. . . ."

"Hi, Devin!" she says, pulling her hair away from her face. "It's Carla . . . I . . . uh . . . need to speak with you . . . it's important. Please call me back." She hangs up and runs her fingers through the ends, feeling the silky strands as they pass through her fingers. She has an hour before the evening news. If Devin doesn't call her back, she'll try again before she's on air.

"Who is he?" Timothy asks, breaking Carla's concentration on Devin's miraculous body and what she'd give for him to forgive her and want her in the same way he had in her bedroom.

"Why do you ask?"

"The last time you smiled this much was when you got this job and married me."

"Very funny."

"So?"

"So, what? I can be happy."

"Not like this. Who's the guy?"

Her cheeks warm. "Nobody." She doesn't have Devin anymore. . . .

"Come on."

How long can she keep Devin a secret? "No one you know personally." She waves him off.

"Whoever it is, I'm happy for you."

"Thank you." She takes a breath. "I'm happy for you too," Carla says, looking him in the eye and discovering a sense of peace. What used to be a desire for affection has turned into reconciliation, a letting go of the past and concentrating on what lies ahead.

Timothy's head arches, as though he doesn't know what she's talking about.

"Pamela. You and her . . ."

"How did you know?"

"It's pretty obvious. She flirts with you. Besides, she never used to be in the newsroom, and now I see her in here all the time." Carla snatches a pen from an old mug on her desk. "Anyway, Pamela told me."

"We're having a good time together," he admits, putting one hand into his front pocket.

Carla nods. "That's great. I'm happy for you." She taps the pen on her desk.

"Thanks."

There's a pause. Looking at each other now makes her feel so distant. She sees him in a different light. Flashbacks of their marriage and what it was like to be in his arms come and go. She is reminded every time she sees Timothy that now they are better working together as friends than as a couple.

"Do you still want me to take Freddie?"

It takes Timothy a moment to answer. His lips part. "I'm going to keep him."

Carla takes a breath. "Good." She's going to regret asking but wonders about Pamela. "Can I ask you something? Does Pamela," she says, lowering her voice so that people can't hear their conversation, "does she listen to you? I mean listen to your dreams and what really matters to you? I don't think I did that enough and I'm sorry."

"It's not your fault. Honestly, Carla, there were other issues. We married at the wrong time. We both had some growing up to do and we rushed into things because our families pushed us."

"My mom," she says and smiles. "Sorry, she's a little bossy."

"Don't let her push you around. Do what's right for you."

"Thanks. That means a lot."

"So, are you going to tell me his name or keep me wondering?"

"I don't want to say."

"It's Devin Miller, isn't it?"

She bites her bottom lip.

"You have a soft spot for the guy who ruffles your feathers. Well, isn't that a surprise."

Her cheeks heat. "It's nothing." She shakes her head. "We're just getting to know each other. Actually, he probably doesn't ever want to talk to me again."

"What happened?"

"His dad contacted me to get in touch with Devin, whom he hadn't spoken to in something like twenty-four years."

Timothy whistles.

"And I didn't tell Devin I was speaking with his dad. I was waiting for the right moment, but every time I tried, I worried he was going to be mad I was going behind his back."

"You were."

"I know." She fidgets with her fingers. "I didn't know what to do. His dad approached me and I thought I could help, but really, I wasn't helping at all. I should have told Devin right away and been done with it. I knew Devin's past and how he felt about his dad. . . . I was scared for him and how he might react."

"You can't control people's feelings," Timothy says. "What you can do is tell him the truth. Tell him what's in your heart. You can't hide from him. He obviously means more to you than you think."

"He doesn't want to talk to me."

"Sure he does. He probably doesn't know why he's mad. Give him time. He'll figure it out."

"Thanks. I've tried calling him, but he's not answering."

Timothy zeroes in on her eyes. "He needs time."

"Russ wants me to interview him for an exclusive for tomorrow's broadcast." She sucks in her lips, blinks her eyes and takes a deep breath. "I can't do it," she whispers. "I don't want to expose him to something he's not willing to do. Where do I draw the line between work and my personal life?"

"You have to make that choice and stick to it. You have to do what you feel right about."

"He said he'd get Ryan to do it if I don't, and it sounded like my job is on the line."

Timothy waves his hand. "If you're not comfortable with it, he can't make you. Are you more upset that he wants Ryan to do it because he doesn't think you will?"

"I don't know why this is so important to Russ. Why does he care?"

"I think he cares because you care about Devin. There's a news story when it matters to someone."

She ponders the thought. "I guess so."

"Well? Russ only wants the story as bad as you want to keep peace with Devin."

"So, what do I do?"

"Talk to Devin. Ask him if he wants to do the story, and if not, blow it off like it's not a big deal. Warn Devin you're not the only one asking."

"I don't want to guilt him into it."

"Trust me: Devin's not going to be guilted in. He'll do what he wants. He's a celebrity in Vancouver now. What he wants people to know about him is up to him. Call him again. Get your answers and then tell Russ what he's waiting to hear, whether it's good or bad news for him. Devin will back you up if he cares."

Carla smiles. The thought of Devin excites her. Her cheeks heat up and must be glowing.

"It's a start."

"I'll see you later," he says, tapping her desk with his hand as he walks past.

Carla picks up the phone and redials Devin's number. No answer. She listens to his voice again and decides to hang up. She gets back to work and is writing a story when she hears her name being called.

"Carla?" Ryan stomps toward her desk. "Russ wants me to talk to Devin. Do you have his number?"

Carla stops typing and looks at him. "I don't have a number for you. You'll have to go through PR." She looks at her screen and begins to type, although she can't concentrate. She types a few words, preparing to delete them later.

He places a hand on her desk. "Russ said you had a number to give me."

"I don't!" she snaps. "I told Russ, Devin doesn't want to talk. I've tried. It's personal, and I don't want to get involved."

"Are you seeing him?"

"Excuse me?"

"Well? Why else wouldn't you interview him? It's a great story for our sports department."

"Yes, it is, if the person wants to talk." Her lips are butted together, holding back words she will regret later.

"I'm going to ask him."

"By all means."

"You still don't want to give me his number?"

"What makes you think I have it?"

"I know you do."

She places her hands in her lap and turns her body to face him. "Did you tell Russ I was trying to get Keith into the basement to meet Devin?"

Ryan shuffles his feet. "No. I . . ."

"Who else was there who knew who Keith was?"

"I didn't know who he was."

"You were there, Ryan. You knew about the situation."

"I don't know what you're talking about."

"You could have figured it out." Her chest tightens. "You saw me there."

"I didn't know what you were up to."

"I'm sure you had an idea."

"I swear!" Ryan says. "I was there to work, not pay attention to what you were doing."

Carla stands so she's at eye level with him.

"You don't like that I have more seniority than you," she says. "Didn't you get the job in Toronto?"

Ryan tightens his lips and shakes his head.

"No? You didn't? But I gave you a good reference."

He nods again.

"So, you're upset you're stuck working with me."

"I'm not stuck. I could have had that job. . . . I turned it down," he says with a flinch of his shoulder.

"Why would you do that? You wanted that job. Your family is there."

"I like it here."

"And not be with your family?"

"I can visit them." Ryan crosses his arms at his chest. "I like it here."

She's not sure if she should believe him. Was Ryan the one who told Russ to get her into trouble? Why didn't he talk to her at the game?

"I gotta get going. I've got to talk to Devin. Russ wants the story. Are you sure you don't have his number?"

Carla purses her lips. Devin already doesn't want to speak with her, and if she gives Ryan his number, that might make him more angry at her. "No, sorry. I can't."

"You don't want me talking to Devin," he says.

"That's not it at all." She shakes her head. "I don't want us hounding him."

Ryan touches his chin as though he's thinking of a plan of attack. Why is he so against her?

"I don't know why you're protecting him."

"I'm not!" she says, keeping her voice firm. Is she protecting him from the media? Why does it matter? It's not like they're friends anymore. Does she care too much about Devin to see him angry? He must be livid at her to not want to speak to her again. The pit of her stomach is tightening. How can she prove to Devin she wasn't planning on hurting him? How can she make him see what she did was because she cares?

"Then what is it?" Ryan asks. "Don't act like you don't care about Devin, 'cause obviously it's come to that."

What can she say?

"I'll talk to Devin and ask him," she says, nervous all over again. He won't be happy to hear from her, so she'll have to be all businesslike and ask him straight-out questions and hopefully get the answers she needs.

"What? You're going to do the interview?"

She nods. "I'll do it."

"Figures."

"You really want to interview him? Why?"

"I just do," he snaps. "Russ asked me."

"Fine. Call media relations and see if he'll talk to you. Hopefully they'll give you a quick turnaround."

"That's easy. They will," he says with a sideways grin. "It's go time!" He whistles and hustles past her.

Carla plunks herself in her chair with her head in her hands. What has she done? As much as she doesn't want to admit it, there's a competition and it's a race to see who can get Devin's attention first, granting the interview. How will she talk to him if he's ignoring her calls?

Chapter 20

Carla dials Devin's number again and waits impatiently for him to answer. She clicks her red nails on her desk as though punching numbers on a calculator. "Come on, Devin," she says through gritted teeth. "Answer."

She lets it ring until she hears his voice mail.

"I know you're ignoring me, Devin, but I need to speak with you. Please. Just hear me out and then we can go our separate ways." She pauses. Her eyes water as she hears herself. Can she let Devin walk away? Forget about what they had and shared? Carla breathes deep and finishes her message. "I need you to call me back as soon as you get this, please. I really need to speak to you. I'll try calling again in half an hour." She hangs up unsatisfied and empty that she hasn't reached a conclusion about the interview she's supposed to be doing with Devin. What happens if Ryan has already reached him and he's told him about their race to talk to him? Will Devin want to talk to her when he finds out?

She busies herself with other assignments and catches herself thinking about Devin for the umpteenth time. She's flipping pages.

"Carla!" Russ yells, marching toward her. "There's a Warriors conference call at the Dome. Jared Landry fractured his wrist this morning in practice."

"Why didn't I get the call?"

"I don't know. Can you be there?"

"Yes. I'm on my way," Carla says, gathering her notebook and throwing it into her purse. She logs off her computer, pushes in her chair and sets out to find a cameraman to bring with her.

* * *

He sits in the driver's seat and checks his phone, remembering he has the ringer turned off. There are two messages and a missed call, all from Carla. He didn't want to talk to her up until now. He needed enough time alone to figure things out after what happened. His dad, for whatever reason, knew he could trust Carla and had had a good feeling about her. How did he know to trust her from the beginning? When was she planning on giving him the letter? The letter. He sighs. There was so much written about his life that he had to reread the handwritten pages three times to understand that Keith was just a guy who loved his family but didn't have the resources to help himself through. If there was something Devin could do for people like his dad, he would. How many families could he save?

Devin drove the two and a half hours to Seattle to be with his dad, every bit of him eager to see him, wanting to be at his bedside. Never in Devin's life had he wanted to show that he was there for Keith, until now. Has he finally let go of the past?

Devin cruises down the I-5, listening to the radio. He's home again, yet for different reasons. It feels a little distant, but perhaps it's because his mom doesn't know he's here and he's visiting a man he doesn't really know. He can't live in the past anymore. It's cost him short-lived relationships and a hardened heart.

He wonders who will be there. He hasn't seen his family in years. He'll meet Tracy, his dad's common-law wife. Thoughts come to mind. Thoughts he hasn't let himself have the pleasure of thinking because it would transpire into lost time with his dad. A surge of adrenaline shoots through his body. Anger. He's still unnerved about his dad's choices made all those years ago. Whenever he felt this way, he released the emotion by running or skating, and that would suffice until the next time he was overcome with questions he didn't have the answers to.

Devin turns off at an exit, reads the scrap of paper with his dad's address on it. He knows this street. He drives farther, and flashbacks of his childhood come to mind: riding his bike down these streets and buying Slurpees at the 7-Eleven.

He turns down the next street. Why is this so familiar? He knows the area. He's lived here. Is it possible Tracy and his dad live in the same neighborhood he grew up in?

Devin moves his hands up and down his steering wheel, taking deep breaths as he makes a right turn. He eases his foot off the gas, approaching the house with the same address he had as a child.

Devin pulls up to the house and stops on the street as he takes a moment to look at the house. The three-bedroom bungalow with a front lawn and gravel driveway brings back childhood memories. The white paint is peeling, and there are blinds in the windows instead of long, swaying curtains. There is a rosebush at the corner of the house, underneath the living-room window. Did his mom plant that? He can't remember.

His bedroom was at the back, facing an unruly garden. His mom never had the time to grow the vegetable garden she wanted, or add the stepping stone path leading to the gazebo she talked about one day of having. Devin was ecstatic the day he bought his mom the house she had dreamed of and never thought she would own. The best feeling he ever had, giving his mom what she wanted and deserved.

A woman with long, dark, tight curly hair opens the front door. She leaves the door half open and skips down the two steps, running across the lawn in jeans. Devin gets out of his truck and saunters toward her. He stops when they meet face-to-face.

"You must be Devin," the woman says, extending her hand.

He nods, grins and shakes her hand.

"I'm Tracy. Thanks for coming. I didn't tell your dad because I wasn't sure if you'd come."

Devin walks up the driveway, kicking rocks and remembering the gravel getting stuck in his bike wheels. "How long have you lived here?"

"As long as your dad and I have been together." She slows down her pace. "Must be strange for you to come back here."

"A little, yes."

"Your dad told me the story of the two of you. I want you to know there are no secrets." She pushes the front door open and kicks off her shoes.

Devin stays at the front door. "Where is he?"

"Lying down on the couch. Come in."

Devin drops his shoulders and hangs his head slightly as he walks inside. From there, he can see his dad on the blue cushioned couch with a pillow behind his head and a quilt laying on top of him. Slowly, Devin makes his way over as Tracy whispers Keith's name.

Keith opens his eyes and stares. "Hi, Devin," he says in a husky voice, as though it takes great effort to draw each breath. "You came to see me?"

"Tracy invited me. How are you feeling?"

"Have a seat," Keith says, raising his hand toward the chair across from him.

Devin sits, leaning forward, his arms on his thighs.

"I'm okay," Keith says. "Sore, to say the least."

"Why did you get the biopsy?"

"To see how bad my liver is. I have some cloudy spots. . . ."

"Cancer?"

"Doesn't look like it. The doctor says I have liver disease. The biopsy will tell us what exactly."

From drinking.

"Will you need a transplant?"

"I don't know."

"You'll tell me?" Devin asks, staring into his dad's dark eyes.

Keith grins. "Yes."

"What kind of liver disease? Did they tell you what it could be?"

"Could be fatty liver disease or—" He pauses.

"Cirrhosis," Tracy says, walking into the room carrying a tray of tea and cookies. She sets them down on the coffee table that has been pushed within arm's reach of Keith.

Devin watches her sit on a chair and pour a cup.

"Would you like some?"

"No, thank you," Devin answers, folding his hands together.

"Can I get you something else to drink? Juice? Water?"

"I'm okay, thanks."

Tracy sets the cup down and stands to adjust Keith's pillow as he tries to sit up. Devin jumps up, willing to help.

"I'm fine," Keith says, slowly sitting up, and Devin sits back down.

Tracy hands Keith a cookie.

"Cirrhosis of the liver?" Devin asks, wanting an explanation.

"He could have it. We're hopeful that whatever he has will be reversed, and we're told it can. He could have a mild disease." She brings her cup to her mouth. "We're not thinking about it."

"I'm in good hands," Keith says, looking at Tracy. "She takes good care of me."

"That's good," Devin says, meaning it. He sees the love between them.

Carla comes to mind and then is forgotten when his dad asks a question.

"Is it strange for you to come back here? To this house?"

"Yeah. You didn't tell me you lived here."

"Your mom put it up for sale and I bought it."

"But wasn't it half yours anyway?" Devin asks, knowing that when a married couple split up, so were their belongings.

"Your mom and I made a deal." He takes a breath. "I always loved this house. I remodeled the kitchen and knocked out a wall to make our bedroom bigger. It's the right size for Tracy and me."

The house still looked the same, only modernized.

"You have a game this week," Keith says.

"Yes."

"How long are you staying?"

"I dunno."

"You can stay here. The second bedroom is our guest room."

"I might go home tonight."

"Is Carla expecting you?"

"Actually, no."

"Are you two together?"

"Apart." Devin takes a breath and exhales as he speaks. "I'm not talking to her."

"Because of me?" Keith's eyes open wide, his forehead wrinkles.

"She kept a secret from me. She doesn't care about me. She wanted a story."

"I'm to blame. I put pressure on her to interview you. I wanted to see you and wasn't sure how I could get you to meet with me."

"She carried your letter around in her purse and didn't tell me she was talking to you. All this time she had that letter but didn't give it to me."

"She wanted to make sure the time was right. There probably wasn't a good time. You hated me."

"I don't hate you."

"You did."

How can Devin deny that? He'd despised the man. Now he's sitting in the very living room he did as a child, looking at the man he'd wondered if he'd ever see again.

"And that's okay. I knew you hated me. That was the hardest part for me about making contact with you. I had to let you see that I made some bad choices, but I'm okay, and thanks to Tracy—" He looks at her and smiles. She smiles back with a twinkle in her eye. "I turned my life around and I can say I'm sorry. If I could turn back time, I would." He pauses to collect his thoughts. "I'm happy to see you. Thank you for driving all this way to see me. Are you visiting your mom while you're here?"

Devin shakes his head. "Probably not. I have to get back for the game."

"What are you going to do about Carla?"

"What do you mean?"

"You need to see her and tell her you're sorry—"

"*I'm* sorry?" Devin laughs. "I'm not sorry!"

"You should be. You don't want to lose her, do you? She means something to you. I know she likes you. Don't turn your back on her. I made that mistake and look how many years it took for me to accept my responsibilities and face the fact that I lost what was most important to me?"

"What am I sorry for? I'm not the one who kept a secret."

"She cares about you. She didn't want to hurt you. Why else wouldn't she have given you the letter right away, as soon as she got it?"

Devin looks down at the beige carpet. He misses Carla. Misses her peach lips on his and the smell of her body lotion. Would she care enough about him to have a serious relationship with him?

"What about the story? She wants to publicize me for a story, and I don't want that."

"That you'll have to ask her about. What I do know is, work aside, she cares about you, and I think that's all that matters. Don't you?"

Devin thinks about what his dad is saying.

"Do whatever it takes to get her back. Even if you have to apologize. You can't let her go."

Devin takes in the only advice he remembers getting from his dad.

"Now I know why Tracy is making a roast beef dinner. She knew you were coming."

"We'd like you to stay," she says.

Devin agrees, deciding to spend the night. He wants to know what it will feel like to stay in the house he has so many memories of.

Chapter 21

Devin wakes up early the next morning. He hadn't slept as well as he thought he would. He could hear Tracy getting up in the middle of the night, getting water and whatever else his dad needed. She was helping him. The bed wasn't as comfortable as his own, and all he could think about was what he would say to Carla and whether she would accept his apology for overreacting.

Devin said his good-byes and drove home from Seattle. He can't shake Carla from his mind, so he takes his dad's advice and decides to stop at the television station to see Carla face-to-face. It's the only way to figure out what their relationship might hold.

According to her message, she has a lot to tell him, but he needs to tell her something first. It's been weighing on his mind for days. Carla means too much to him; he can't let her slip away so easily. He realizes that now. He can't let her go.

Devin parks in visitor parking and walks into Channel Five, forgetting about security and the many locked doors there are to pass through.

He makes his way to the front desk and is met by a woman with dirty blond hair tied up in a clip and long dangly earrings. Every time she jerks her head from side to side, the earrings sway.

"Can I help you?" she asks.

"Yes. I'm looking for Carla—" He pauses, not comfortable with using her last name. "Sinclair." He smiles.

"Is she expecting you?"

"Ah, well, no, but she's been trying to reach me."

"Are you Devin Miller?" she asks.

He folds his hands to his chest and then releases them, placing his fingers on the counter. "Yes, I am."

"I was here that day you sent her the fruit bouquet. She loved it!"

"She did, did she?"

"Absolutely! What a nice idea. Original. Better than flowers, I say."

Devin continues to smile.

"It lasted her two days and she still has the vase on her desk. Of course, there's nothing in it. It's empty."

"Oh."

"Maybe she should put flowers in it," Pamela says, exhaling a breath and clapping her hands together. She stares at Devin. "Carla is out, but she should be back within the hour, I think. If you want, you could leave her a message."

"That's okay. I'll wait."

"Wait?"

He nods.

"She might be a while."

"That's okay." Devin walks over to the leather chairs. He heads to the corner chair.

"Devin? Devin Miller?"

Devin turns around. He doesn't know anyone else working at the station.

"Wow! I didn't expect you to come here," Ryan exclaims, hightailing it toward the defenseman. "I told media relations I needed to speak with you. I didn't expect them to make you rush over here so quickly, but hey," he says, extending his arms, "you must want this interview as much as we do. It says a lot about a player when he opens up about himself. People can relate to you when they know you worked hard through troubled times."

"What are you talking about?" Devin asks, tilting his head, trying to figure out what this guy is saying.

"The interview. I called Keri from PR to ask her if we," Ryan points his finger at Devin and then himself, "could do an interview today. Last minute, I know, but you're off today, so I thought it was the best chance. We're putting together player profiles of the team and want you to start things off. I'll be conducting a ninety-second interview with each player."

"Carla's not doing this?"

"She, uh, no. No. I'm doing it."

"I'm here to see Carla."

"How about we go into this room over here," he says and points to the door across the hall. "We'll be quick. I can ask you a couple of questions and that will be it. Promise."

"Sorry. It's not my thing," Devin says, walking toward the front door.

"We're interviewing all the players."

Devin opens the door and walks outside, ignoring him. He wants to see Carla. Was this why she wanted to see him? Because of an interview? She can forget it. He isn't going to talk about his childhood drama. He's a professional hockey player. He doesn't need to reflect on his past. It's his future he wants to concentrate on, whatever that entails.

He pulls his keys out of his jeans and catches a white Mercedes pulling into the parking lot. He stops and watches to see if it's Carla driving. He can't tell. The car disappears. He has to know if it's her.

He wanders through the parking lot, searching for Carla. His footsteps quicken as he looks around for her car. He's never felt such a need to speak to her. Why can't he let her go? He wants to be with her. He can't seem to shake her out of his mind.

His head perks up when he sees a blond-haired woman bobbing in stride with her footsteps through the parked cars. "Carla!" he shouts, diving into step and jogging toward her. "Carla!"

Her pace slows when she recognizes him. There's an uncertainty about her that makes his heart pound. Will she reject him? Did he hurt her feelings? Will she forgive his actions?

He stops jogging and walks the short distance with determination, focusing on getting to her as quickly as he can. Her eyes are deep blue, sucking him closer with every step. If he could take her into his arms and kiss those taut, peach lips of hers, he would show her how much she means to him.

Carla stops between parked cars, staring at him as though wondering what he's doing there.

With only a few more steps until he reaches her, he says, "I came by to see you. . . ." His words feel stuck in his throat as he stands in front of her, taking in her cautious eyes and the free-flowing hair that covers her shoulders.

She doesn't say anything.

"You . . . you needed to speak to me."

"So you drove here?" Her eyebrows furrow.

"Calling didn't seem like an option."

She pulls her purse strap over her shoulder and keeps her hand there. "Oh, no? You could have called. It would have given you the option of hanging up on me if you didn't like what I had to say."

"Now you're making me feel bad."

"Am I?"

"Yeah. I'm sorry. I know what you did was because you were trying to help."

"I did it because I care," she says, her hand slipping down the purse strap to her hip. "I thought what I was doing would help you and your dad come together."

"Carla!" a voice yells, pausing the conversation. The two of them turn around to see the man running toward them.

"Carla! Devin!" He speed walks. "Wait! Devin! I have the room ready for the interview."

"You're interviewing Devin?" Carla asks.

"I'm not—"

"Yes! Russ wants me to, and Devin's here," he says, talking with his hands. "So why not?"

"What gives you the right to tell me who I'm talking to?" Devin wants to know. "I'm not doing any interview."

"Carla, tell him!"

Devin looks at her.

She tilts her head. "Tell him what?"

"That you're interviewing him."

"I'm not," she says, shaking her head.

"Isn't that why he's here?"

Devin looks at Carla. "Actually, I have something to talk to Carla about."

"Oh." He takes a step back. He smacks his hands together down low. "I see. It has nothing to do with Channel Five?"

"No," Devin tells Ryan. "It's personal."

"Your job is on the line, I thought."

Carla purses her lips and takes a deep breath. "Apparently."

"You're going to get fired if you don't interview me?" Devin asks. "What kind of business is this?"

"It's my job," Carla says.

"Do you want to interview me?" Devin asks, searching those blue eyes of hers for something bigger. Maybe that's what was on her mind. "Is that what you want?"

"Not now," she says.

"What's going to happen about your job?" Devin asks.

"Russ won't like it," Ryan says.

"I don't care," Carla says.

"Do you mean that?" Devin asks. "I don't want you to lose your job. Not over me."

"I won't. And if I do," she says, looking at the pavement and then up at Devin, "it's worth it. I don't want to come between you and your dad." She stops and looks at the man.

"I can do a quick interview," he says. "Or Carla can . . ."

She shakes her head. "I'm not."

"You're going to risk your job?" Ryan begins to walk backward.

"I have nothing to ask him," she says, staring into Devin's eyes.

"All right," the junior reporter says, making distance between them. He turns around and walks away.

"Are you really going to lose your job?" Devin asks.

"I don't know."

"Is that what they told you, you'd lose your job?" Devin stands with his hands on his hips.

"Not in so many words, but yeah."

"Do you want to interview me?"

"You don't want me to," she says, her eyes squinting.

"If it's going to cost you your job, I will."

"You don't want to talk about your personal life and that's what Russ wants me to do. It's none of anybody's business."

"Do you want me to talk to him?"

"No. It's no use."

"It won't change his mind?"

"I don't think so." She shakes her head.

"Interview me."

"But you don't want me to ask—"

"I have nothing to hide. My dad doesn't either."

"But I thought—"

"It's all good between him and me."

She tilts her head.

"I was there, in Seattle, to see him. He's sick," Devin says, swallowing hard.

"Is he okay?"

Her concern relaxes him. He grins. "I think so. I'm going to help him get the care he needs. It's his liver. From all the years of drinking alcohol, there's scar tissue on his liver. We'll know soon what his outcome will be, but I think he's going to be fine."

"That's good." She blinks and her lips comes together. "How do you feel?"

Devin stares blankly at her. *How do I feel?* He hasn't been asked that before by a woman. His heart swells. Looking into her eyes, he answers, "Relieved. I have a dad I didn't know because I didn't want to. I had a drawer full of unopened letters I kept for years. I finally read every one." Devin skims his hand across his forehead. "It was tough. A lot of things I didn't know about him and the struggles he went through. I wish I could have helped him . . . let him know he had me, had a son. I was too ashamed to face what I didn't have that I almost gave up what I did have. I made a poor decision not to know my dad when all I wanted was him. So, thank you for getting involved. Without you, I wouldn't have been in touch with my dad. It's been a long time coming and, to tell you the truth, the weight has lifted."

"I couldn't imagine not knowing my dad or mom, and to live all those years unknowing resonated with me." She looks at the pavement and then up to meet his eyes. "I care about you. Hard for you to believe, I know, but I do." She ends with a lightness in her voice, as though she can't quite believe it herself. "I really do." Her eyes are searching his for reassurance. "I don't care that you play hockey, what I care about is who you are. I didn't think I'd fall for you. . . . I guess I did the first time we met." Her cheeks flush. "As dumb as that may sound."

"I haven't stopped thinking of you since." He looks away to gather his thoughts and then returns to her with desperation. "I need you. I really do." He presses his lips together, watching her eyes gloss over. "I want a life with you. I like you too much to let you go."

She wipes a tear from her eye.

"I'm sorry," he says. "You're the last person I'd want to hurt. I'm sorry if I came across cold and isolated. I never share my feelings with anyone, and you seem to read me like an open book."

She gives him a sideways grin.

"Must be the reporter in you." Devin's smile turns serious. "Will you forgive me?"

She nods.

Devin reaches out his hand and pulls her into his chest. "I want my life to be fulfilling. I want to do something with it."

"But you have!"

"No," he says, shaking his head. "I want meaning . . . I want to do something more than be known for being a hockey player." He rubs her back. "I've been thinking a lot about different things. I want to start a foundation to help men get back on their feet and be with their families. Provide help for them. I don't know . . . do something. There must be something I can do."

"I believe you will. That's an excellent idea." She smiles, pressing her hand firmly on his hip. "I think you'll accomplish anything you set your mind to. That's why you're playing professional hockey."

He smiles at her.

"You're not as cold as you make people believe you are," she says with a wink.

"I've never been much of a talker."

"I don't know why. You have a lot to say."

"Only to you." He holds her tight. "I don't know how that happened."

"I'm glad you feel that way," she says.

"Carla, I feel a lot with you. My life hasn't been the same since I moved to Vancouver. I want you in it." Devin lifts her chin and brings her lips to his. "I want you; I want us. I don't want to live life passing me by and not do anything about it. I want to start right now. You and me, together," he says, firming his hand around her back. "You mean too much to me to let you go."

"Don't ever let me go," she whispers.

"I won't. You're mine." Devin kisses her and holds the back of her head to secure the passion he feels for the woman he's always wanted.

Epilogue

"**M**om! I told you, I don't like to wear dresses."

"Just for tonight. For your dad," Carla pleads with her four-year-old daughter, tying a bow at the back of the satin blue dress. "This is a big night for him. He's going to be so proud when he sees you." Carla spins Lily around. "Aw, sweetie, you look good." She brings a hand to her chest.

"Are we about ready to go?" Devin asks, standing in the bathroom doorway with his six-month-old son resting in his arms. "My dad is meeting us there at four. He was worried he'd be late getting through the border."

"We can go. I was just about to pin Lily's hair back and we can go," Carla says, wearing a blue satin dress that matches her daughter's. She always thought dressing the same was pathetic, but now, having a daughter of her own, with Devin's almond skin tone and her blue eyes, it was hard not to pass up.

Devin takes his free hand and brushes Carla's hair off her shoulders. "You look amazing."

"You look pretty sharp yourself," she says, reaching for Devin's tie and tightening it as she lets his lips brush her forehead. The warmth of his touch eases her mind for the accomplishment of her husband's charity, to help men with substance abuse get the help they need to provide for their families. "I'm proud of you." She smiles, her nose touching his chin. "You'll do great tonight."

"I love you," Devin says, lowering his mouth to hers. He kisses her full on the mouth until they are interrupted by a shriek.

"Mommy! Mommy! I want this too!" Lily says as she tries to open the tube of mascara.

"No! Sorry, honey, that's Mommy's." Carla takes the makeup from her daughter and shoves it back into the fabric bag. "Not tonight."

"When you're twenty!" Devin says, making eyes at his wife.

"Daddy!" she whines. "Pleeease!" She starts to cry.

"Come on! We have to go!" Devin says. "I don't want to be late."

"Let's go, Lily," Carla says, grabbing her daughter's hand. As she follows her husband and baby out of the bathroom, she's in awe of the family she and Devin have created.

She got a second chance at love.

Please turn the page for an exciting sneak peek of

Charlene Groome's next Warriors romance,

PRACTICE MAKES PERFECT,

coming in August 2015!

"You're late!"

"I'm sorry! Sorry!" Meghan fingers a long strand of hair away from her face and wipes her palm on her skirt. "I couldn't find parking." She hopes to get away with it considering she's never parked at the old stadium before. It's home to the Vancouver junior hockey team, but today, the ice was taken out, leaving just a concrete floor where a Warriors fund-raiser is taking place. "And there's a line around the building."

"I noticed the crowd when I drove by on my way to work," Keri, the events director, tells her. "You have a parking pass."

First day as the events coordinator and already Meghan's got a strike against her. She blows out a breath. "It was full."

"Full? Really? The players must be arriving. Hurry, we still have stuff to do." Keri waves her hands around. She's wearing a gray skirt and blazer, reminding Meghan of a stewardess. Her hair shapes her round face, resting at her collarbone, and her makeup is minimal, except for her bright red lips desperately in need of another coat. "Tables need to be set with name cards. They each need a Sharpie pen and water cups, and the stanchions have to be placed properly. Do you have your checklist?"

Meghan reaches into her briefcase and pulls out a paper protected by a plastic cover.

"What happened to your shirt?"

Meghan flicks her hand at her chest as though it will magically come off. "Coffee. I'm having one of those mornings." Well that's strike two. Maybe she should be carrying extra clothes in her car.

"How many cookbooks did you order? I don't think we have enough."

"Five thousand." Meghan's heart starts to race. "Just like we talked about."

"It looks like we may only have half the order. I can't tell."

"What? Only half?" Meghan paces.

"You need to find the rest of the order."

Meghan brings her fingers to her chin. "I double-checked the delivery."

"Unless you know where else they could be." Keri seems to get sidetracked by an employee carrying a water cooler. "Over here!" She scurries over to lead them where she wants the station set up.

Meghan skims over her checklist. Her feet are killing her. She wiggles her toes in her new shoes. She should have worn ones that were broken-in.

"Meghan!"

Meghan sees a girl race toward her. "Where do you want these potted mums?"

"One between every table. There needs to be room for fans getting autographs. We don't want clutter. We also need these name cards at every seat." She hands over a stack of printed cards from the clear bin in front of her and walks with a soft step, trying not to put pressure on her foot. She shouldn't have bought the plain black heels because they were half price. *Cheap shoes.* Her baby toe is throbbing.

"Meghan," another voice calls out. "What should I do with these donuts?"

"Donuts? Who are they for?"

"The players, I guess."

"I don't think the players will eat them. You can put them at the beverage table."

Meghan shuffles her foot as she walks to the perimeter of the arena, where there is a stack of boxes. She takes count of how many there are and clearly a few thousand cookbooks are missing. She stands, staring at the boxes. What went wrong? Did she mess up the order? It was a lot of work getting each player to submit his favorite family recipe in time to have the books designed and printed.

Meghan kicks off her heels and runs to where she left her briefcase. She takes out her phone and scrolls for the confirmation e-mail. As she looks through her messages, there are men trailing through the arena.

Casually dressed men wearing jeans and T-shirts and some in button-down shirts. Meghan's stomach flutters. The team is here and she doesn't have enough books. She can't call off the event. There's a line of people outside of the arena who have been waiting for hours to come in and if she doesn't have an adequate number of cookbooks to give away, she will most likely be demoted. How could this happen?

"When do we open the doors?" Deanna, a blond-haired girl with hot pink tips, asks.

"Fifteen, twenty minutes. I have to figure something out, Deanna."

"Dana."

"Dana, sorry. Can you please make sure the players are in the right seats and tell me if there are any players missing?" Meghan catches two girls standing around talking and turns to them. "Can I get both of you to offer each player a beverage? There are donuts, too, if they want any."

The girls snicker.

One of them asks, "Where are your shoes?"

"I . . . um . . . have to put them on. My feet were sore." Meghan excuses herself and rereads her e-mail. Yep, five thousand cookbooks were delivered. *Whew, it wasn't me. Then where is the order?*

Meghan takes a quick look at the players taking seats. Her stomach tightens. It will be a nightmare if the rest of the books don't show up in the next few minutes. She has to track down the rest of the order. Meghan makes a quick call to the office. Nobody is answering, so she goes back to recount the boxes to make sure there wasn't a mistake. She slips on her heels and hurries through the building to find the rest of the order.

"Meghan," a voice calls out across the room, pinning her attention like a deer in headlights. She is stunned at hearing her name paged again, when her boss, Keri, is standing in arm's reach.

Meghan's heart beats faster and she sweeps her bangs away from her eyes. "Yes?"

"You asked me to check off which players are present and it looks like Alex Price and Jared Landry are still missing." Dana holds up the guest list to her face. "Everyone else is here, sitting down and ready to go."

"I'm sure they're on their way."

"Alex will be here. Jared may or may not show." Keri digs through her clear bin. "Where did my pack of Sharpies go?"

"He has to show!"

"It's the chance we take. Have you seen the pack of Sharpies?"

"They're already on each place setting like you asked."

"Awesome! Thanks." Keri closes the lid. "We have to get these players something to drink. They can't just sit down with nothing!"

"Done!" Meghan turns to Dana. "Do you want to put these cookbooks at the entrance with the rest of them? How does the line look to get in?"

"It's wrapped around the building. Some people have been here since early morning."

"I heard. Just to buy a cookbook." Meghan shakes her head. "Insane." At least some people will appreciate the effort she's put into this.

"Yeah, but they get to meet the players. Well worth it. I hope Alex Price shows up. Is he on your list?"

"I think so."

Dana exhausts a sigh and throws her head back. "Ah, what I would give to have him for a boyfriend."

Meghan chuckles. "One that doesn't last."

Dana arches an eyebrow.

"It's true! I've heard the rumors." Meghan gave a sideways grin. "I'm sure you have too."

"A girl can dream, right?" Dana sprints across the room to the line of tables with seated Warriors.

Meghan's phone vibrates on her hip. She looks at the number. A text from Stu: I HAVE TO CANCEL TONIGHT. SORRY.

She blows out a breath. Right. Probably playing Xbox with his cousin again. She needs to break up with him. Tonight. The relationship is going nowhere and it's boring. Stu's boring. All he wants to do is go for motorbike rides or to the movies. There's nothing new. It's the same as their first date five months ago. Does he even care about her? She's wondered about this for weeks now. It only came to light when her friend Brie asked if she and Stu wanted to join her and her boyfriend, Mike, on a day trip to Mayne Island. Stu was the only one that said he didn't feel like walking over on a ferry. Meghan loves the outdoors and exploring nature. She was bummed she couldn't get Stu to budge. At first she thought maybe he wasn't feeling well, then Meghan found out he was driving his dad to the airport. Like he couldn't have gotten his sister to do it. She still lives at home.

"They're opening the doors," someone yells.

"The books." Meghan turns to Keri. "I don't know where the rest of the order is. I checked the order and five thousand are supposed to be here."

"How many are here?"

"Thirty-five hundred."

"They have to be here. Did you check the loading zone? Maybe they were left there."

"Good idea." She snaps her fingers. "I'll check."

"No, get someone else to look. We have to make sure the players have what they need."

"Dana made sure they have everything." Meghan trusts an employee she doesn't know.

"The crowd will be coming through any moment. Alex is here, but I guess Jared isn't showing up." She walks toward the tables one last time.

"I gotta get those books to the front of the line." Meghan gets two employees' attention and has them open the rest of the boxes.

Meghan escapes down the hallway to see if she can find the rest of the order. She makes another call, this time to Eddie, one of the coordinators who's at the office, working on another assignment.

"Eddie, it's Meghan. Listen, we seem to be missing a couple thousand cookbooks. Have you noticed a stack of boxes in the boardroom? Storage room? Someone's office?"

"I haven't noticed, but I can look around for you."

"Would you do that? Thanks." Meghan talks with her head down, walking fast to the nearest room, except she doesn't know exactly what she's expecting. There aren't offices, more like a narrow hallway and the referee's changing room. She stops, lowers her cell phone to her side and scratches the back of her head. Where else can she look? Are there any other rooms? It's such an old arena and she doesn't know her way around. *The change rooms!* Of course! They have to be empty, so why not store the boxes there? It was like an ah-ha moment. She attaches her phone to her side and leans into the bright blue door with an unlocked latch. She opens it a crack and peers in to get a better view. She doesn't see anybody, so she opens it wider until she's sure the room is empty. It smells of sweat and wet rubber, except the floor is dry. She looks around at the empty room and nothing catches her eye, so she leaves to make it down the hall to the next door. It's a locked room.

"You won't find anything in there," a security man tells her. "It's the janitor's closet." He chuckles to himself. "Can I help you find something?" He glances at her lanyard hanging from her neck.

"I'm missing some boxes that were delivered here. They haven't arrived for the signing yet, and I'm wondering if they're stored in the wrong place."

"Haven't seen any." He walks away.

Some help he is.

Meghan walks across the hall to the next door. The word *home* is painted across the wall in yellow paint. Amazingly, the door is unlocked for being the home team's locker room, so she is doubtful she will find anything that belongs to her in there, but there are only so many places to store boxes. Meghan leans her shoulder into the door, takes a peek and begins to take a step inside.

"I wouldn't go in there if I were you." A male chuckles.

As she turns around, a guy's walking past her. He is wearing jeans and a polo shirt. Meghan doesn't recognize him. His deep-set blue eyes and the curl of his upper lip stun her like she's seeing something breathtaking for the first time.

"I'm looking f-for something." She rests her weight on the door.

He stops, makes eye contact with her, which makes her breathe just a little bit harder and stare just a little bit longer. She gulps.

"I haven't heard of a dressing room being used for anything else. I wouldn't go in unless you have to." He pauses, butts his lips together as though he's thinking about something and takes a step closer. "I've heard about people like you."

"Like me?" Her voice raises with concern.

"Yeah. Sneaking in to the dressing room to get a selfie and post it on social media."

"What?"

"Oh, yeah. I saw one posted once. There was a girl in Brampton, where I'm from, and she snuck into a dressing room. I don't know how she did it, but she managed to get a shot of herself in a player's cubby."

"Never heard of it."

"So if you want a picture . . ." He turns around. His feathery blond hair falls softly to his neck, the typical hockey cut as it's called. "Go ahead. I won't tell. Do it quick."

She raises an eyebrow. *Who does he think he is?*

"Does it look like I'm about to take a selfie?" She holds up her lanyard with a swipe in the air and puts it down. Is he trying to be funny?

"I guess not. . . . I didn't notice. . . . Sorry." He rubs his thumbnail across his forehead.

"I'm just checking whether something was left here." She opens the door all the way to take a look. Nothing. She closes her eyes, bites her bottom lip and turns on her sore foot to leave. These shoes are going into the garbage can when this event is over, even if she has to drive home barefoot.

He chuckles. "You might want to check upstairs for the lost and found."

She shakes her head as he saunters down the hall toward the arena. *Who is this guy?*

"Excuse me."

Automatically Meghan steps to the side to let a man pulling a flatbed dolly with stacks of boxes on it through.

"Wait!" she shouts. "Are those cookbooks?"

The man slows. "I heard they were books." He shrugs.

"Okay, great! Do you know where you're going?" Meghan tries to walk with him but is falling behind. The dolly takes up most of the hallway.

They get to the arena where thousands of people are waiting in line for their chance to have a cookbook signed or have something autographed by their favorite player. People have come dressed in Warriors attire. She scans the tables. Every player is there. She notes that Jared Landry's place is occupied. From where she's standing, she can't tell who is who.

"Where do you want them?" the deliveryman asks.

"Follow me." She walks away from the crowd to a place near the front of the line. Security is letting people through. People only get a few seconds with each player, but it looks like the event is running smoothly and Meghan can breathe easily now that there are more cookbooks to give away.

The man unstacks the boxes and puts them with the rest. Meghan calls some employees over to help open the boxes and get them ready for the public. She's happy she made the decision to keep the limit to one item signed per player, whether it's the cookbook, a hockey card or a jersey. She couldn't expect the players to sign everything. That would be asking for too much and she wants to be on everyone's good side, especially when there will be many more team events. Meghan helps out at the front of the line and then strolls the arena to make sure the event is running the way it was planned. So far, so good. People are smiling, laughing and having a great time meeting their icons and the players seem to be enjoying themselves. Meghan walks around the facility, making sure everyone is doing their job and the players have what they need.

By the afternoon, the crowd thins and Meghan instructs security to lock the entrance and to warn people the event is coming to a close. She has to take these heels off. Her blister is getting bigger and she might even have another on the top of her foot.

There are still around hundred people trying to get through to have something signed.

"Good job today," Keri says. "I'm heading back to the office to finish up on a few things. See you tomorrow."

"Yes, see you tomorrow." After Keri leaves, she kicks off her heels and hides them under a table with her briefcase. Instant relief. She sighs and throws her head back as she wiggles her toes.

"Exhausted?" Dana makes a pile of the crushed boxes.

"I'm okay. It's my feet. They're killing me."

"You look like you could use a nap."

"It will be an early night for me, that's for sure." Meghan takes out her cell phone to check the time. "It's three already!" Meghan touches her stomach. She missed lunch. Early dinner, early bedtime. "We can start cleaning up. The event is over. You can tell the players to wrap it up. I'm going to start clearing off the tables."

"Did you need me to sign any extra books?" a guy asks.

Him again!

"They're for charity, right?"

This guy really is stuck on himself.

"I think we're okay. Thanks." She continues to collect the Sharpies.

"Do you need a hand?"

"No, I'm fine, thanks." She ignores him as he clears off his place setting and hands her his name card. Jared Landry. It had to be him. She takes the card.

"I thought this went until four."

"I sent out the updated notice. It ended at three." Meghan throws his card in the tote and places it down with the others on a nearby table, where Dana adds the other name cards to it.

"That was you? You sent the e-mail?" Jared picks up a potted mum. She stares at him. Is he for real?

"You're Meghan." He extends his hand while holding the plant at his side. "Jared Landry."

"Meghan O'Riley." She places her hand in his with a firm shake and releases it, going back to clearing the table of garbage and used Solo cups.

"Are you taking that?" Dana points to the plant.

Jared flinches and hands it over. "No."

"I can take it." Dana leaves with the plant.

"Sorry if I offended you back there. I didn't know who you were."

"And that makes a difference?"

"It does. We kinda work together. Don't want to damage our relationship."

Meghan snickers. "Damage our relationship?" What relationship? This guy is too much.

"Let me help you." He reaches for another plant.

"No, I'm okay. Really. Thanks. I'm fine." She tries hard to grin, even though she wants him to leave and not bother her again. She starts clearing the tables.

"The least I can do is give you a hand." He puts the plant down as Dana comes for it and takes it away.

She raises an eyebrow. "Don't worry about it. Thanks. I've got it. I'm sure you have things to do."

Jared scratches his temple, looks around and starts to stack the empty Solo cups that line the tables before tossing them into the garbage.

"Are you always this helpful?"

"I don't mind helping out."

"You don't have to feel guilty for accusing me of being some random woman checking out locker rooms."

"I didn't know who you were."

This guy's not letting up. Why is he still here?

"That makes a difference? Is that what you like to do, spy on people?" She stares into his eyes. She swallows, waiting for an answer, but he, too, is gazing at her as though unsure what to say.

"I was walking by. I wanted to make sure you weren't lost."

She bursts out laughing. "Okay."

"Seriously."

"It was nice meeting you." She turns on her toes. *There is no way this Jared guy is going to think he's God's gift to women, the way he cocks his head and smiles at me. No way will I fall into that trap of forgiveness. What does he want?*

"Are you having a bad day?"

She looks at him inquisitively. "No, I'm not."

His eyes skim her outfit and he stares at her bare feet.

"I was wearing new shoes."

"You spilled something." He points to his chest, mirroring her reflection.

Her shoulders sink. "Thanks for pointing it out. I spilled my coffee on the way to work. Will you be at the next event?"

He nods.

"Good. Well, I'm sure you have things to do. I've got this." She pulls off a white tablecloth.

"I tried calling you on my way here and I got pulled over—"

"You tried calling me? Why?"

"To tell you I was coming. I was running late . . . and then I got pulled over for holding my cell phone."

"Don't tell me, you got off."

"Yeah." His top lip tightens into a grin.

Typical.

"It was close. I got a warning."

Meghan ties the Sharpies together with a rubber band. "It happens, right?" She throws them into the bin. *Probably happens all the time.*

"It's never happened before."

Yeah, right. Is he reading my mind? I hope not because I'm thinking his biceps are incredible and his chest is probably just as tightly chiseled.

"I better go. Looks like you're done here. He backs away. "Get your boyfriend to look after you tonight and give you a foot massage."

Her cheeks feel suddenly warm. As if Stu would even think of doing such a thing.

Boyfriend. Breakup. I gotta leave so I can get in touch with Stu and tell him we're through.

Jared saunters across the concrete floor without a care in the world. He probably has a nice girlfriend and a nice life.

www.ingramcontent.com/pod-product-compliance
Lightning Source LLC
Chambersburg PA
CBHW020755250626
47155CB00003B/1086